Before he c... tween them and reached up to hold his head between her hands.

Startled, he drew his breath in sharply.

Maybe he thought she was going to smack him. Furthest thing from her mind. Jane closed her mouth over his surprised lips, kissing him for all she was worth.

Sometimes, you had to grab the bull by his horns. Or, in this case, the gentleman by his ears.

Books by Dawn Calvert

HERO WORSHIP

HIS AND HERS

Published by Zebra Books

HIS AND HERS

DAWN CALVERT

FROM THE LIBRARY OF
DAWN
READ & RETURN IT

ZEBRA BOOKS

Kensington Publishing Corp.

www.kensingtonbooks.com

ZEBRA BOOKS are published by

Kensington Publishing Corp.
850 Third Avenue
New York, NY 10022

Copyright © 2008 by Dawn Calvert

All rights reserved. No part of this book may be reproduced in any form or by any means without the prior written consent of the Publisher, excepting brief quotes used in reviews.

If you purchased this book without a cover you should be aware that this book is stolen property. It was reported as "unsold and destroyed" to the Publisher and neither the Author nor the Publisher has received any payment for this "stripped book."

All Kensington titles, imprints, and distributed lines are available at special quantity discounts for bulk purchases for sales promotion, premiums, fund-raising, educational, or institutional use.

Special book excerpts or customized printings can also be created to fit specific needs. For details, write or phone the office of the Kensington Special Sales Manager: Attn. Special Sales Department. Kensington Publishing Corp., 850 Third Avenue, New York, NY 10022. Phone: 1-800-221-2647.

Zebra and the Z logo Reg. U.S. Pat. & TM Off.

ISBN-13: 978-0-8217-8060-2
ISBN-10: 0-8217-8060-3

First Printing: January 2008
10 9 8 7 6 5 4 3 2 1

Printed in the United States of America

For my mom

Prologue

His hand rested on the small of her back with an ease that belied the sense of astonishment and delight that pulsed through him. Just when he thought he had lost her, they were reunited for a future that held such promise he could scarcely believe it.

She turned, her eyes looking up into his. And then she smiled, with a heart-stopping intensity that weakened his knees. He straightened and smiled back, following as she began to lead them out of the coffee shop and into the pages of their new life.

Right before the door, he stopped, raising his free hand and opening it to glance down at the small stone in the center of his palm. Who would have believed such an innocent object could change everything?

She would. *He* would.

He glanced around the nearly empty shop, at the small square tables with two chairs neatly pulled into each, at the barista and at the green-aproned employee at the register, happily bantering with a customer about the coffee of the day.

Who would be the one to find it? Use it? It must be left up to the fates to decide. The man spied a corner of a windowsill, where the stone could safely rest. Until called into action. He pulled a piece of paper from his pocket and placed it carefully beneath the stone, with a silent wish that both would be found by the person who needed them most.

It would happen. He had no doubt.

After all, he could be considered living proof.

Chapter 1

Jane Ellingson, Woman Wonder with a shredded cape flapping in the virtual breeze, watched as the barista poured a bag of beans into the espresso machine. You knew your life was up to no good when you could seriously relate to beans being chewed up and spit out in a high-pitched whine.

Some days you're the machine, some days you're the bean.

Jane buried her head in her hands, pressing her fists to her ears to dim the sounds of conversation, chairs scraping across the wooden floor and bursts of steam. The voice of a cheerful employee sailed above the din. Normally, she loved Starbucks, craved Starbucks. Not today. She stared at the cup in front of her, holding a White Chocolate Mocha Frappuccino with a shot of peppermint, no whip. Hadn't even yet lifted it to her lips. Maybe wouldn't at all, given the stomach crawling over itself in agony and the headache pressing at the edges of her temple.

Unbelievable. One pretty great life, destroyed in a matter of days. Twenty-six years to get to this point and less than a week to chuck it all down the drain.

She didn't want to think about it. Unfortunately, all

she could *do* was think about it. Run it over and over in her mind. The face of her boss, Senator Alice Tate's chief assistant, open-mouthed in disbelief as he stared at his screen. Jane had included a paragraph on the senator's stint in alcohol rehab in a news release on the bill that would assist struggling apple growers. The same news release Jane had so efficiently distributed to the media list. It was her job, after all. She did it so well she'd been given the "Woman Wonder" nickname after only a few months on the job. But this time, it turned out she had a challenge with the cut and paste functions.

"You knew," Chase had said, between lips pulled so tight, they had turned white, "that was something we were working on *in case* of a news leak." He had clutched his thick brown hair so hard, Jane was sure he was going to pull it out in clumps. "We weren't intending to *announce* it."

And she could only stammer, "I—I—"

Because she had no comeback. No excuse. She'd been in a hurry to get home, and have time to change for her date with Byron. He of the brilliant, white-toothed smile and deep blue eyes. He, who it seemed, she'd waited all her life to meet.

The news release had been a last-minute task, like most in the senator's office. A hasty, pull-this-bit-from-this draft and this-from-that one. She hadn't proofread, for the first time in as long as she could remember, or she would have seen what she'd accidentally included.

A politician who championed tough legislation on drunk driving could not have it hit the press that she struggled with her own alcohol issues. Especially if an enterprising member of the press dug deep enough to find what else was there.

Jane rubbed one pink manicured finger hard into her

forehead, as though physical pain could help obliterate the memory.

Byron, when he'd arrived at her apartment, found her shattered from her day and the realization she could be out of a job. She'd sunk into his familiar arms, heard him murmur in her ear and somehow believed everything would be all right. If only she had him around permanently, she'd thought, to soothe her every night, instead of seeing him just a couple of times a week.

They could have a life, the two of them. In a house with a white picket fence in the suburbs. Maybe kids, eventually, on a swing set in the backyard, under the watchful eye of Mother of the Year candidate Jane and a protective, but playful, collie named Shep. Or Bob. Something. One of those names people gave to dogs.

Jane, the kids and the dog would wait patiently for a smiling Byron to come home from his job at the investment firm. Where he would have skyrocketed through the ranks fast enough to be able to afford that house in the suburbs and all the Pottery Barn furniture that would go inside it. She knew just what colors she'd paint the walls.

The picture had its appeal. Didn't matter that Jane didn't have much experience with kids. Or dogs. Or even like the suburbs, when you compared that sort of life to the excitement of the city.

What mattered was that it was a *life*. One she'd been sure she'd grow used to. Even *like*. Better yet . . . love.

In a burst of spontaneity that at the time had seemed so romantic, she'd whispered the idea in Byron's ear. "Let's get married." And felt his entire body freeze.

"What?" he'd choked.

That had been her chance. She could have, just that fast, turned it into a joke. But instead, she'd repeated the words, with a desperation even she heard in her voice.

He'd ruffled her hair, a little more firmly than usual,

and broken from their embrace to bolt for the bottle of wine he'd brought, banging the cupboards open and shut in a search for glasses. She'd stood in the middle of her Persian lookalike rug, surrounded by generic off-white walls, feeling more alone than she ever had. With her boyfriend no more than six feet away, turning a visible shade of pale beneath the tan he'd acquired on a sales-reward trip to Mexico. Tiny arrows of hurt stabbed at Jane's heart until it felt like a sieve, raining tears she couldn't shed.

They'd put on music and drunk wine. Lots of wine. Just as her eyelids had begun to flutter between open and shut, she'd seen Byron, shoes in hand, tiptoe from the couch to the door. And, she'd been sure, out of her life.

She highly suspected that, once terrified, boyfriends rarely returned to the scene of the terrification.

Just because she'd asked him to marry her. How . . . *sixties* of him. She'd be offended, angry, glad to be rid of him. If only she didn't love him. How sixties of her.

As if it wasn't enough for her to delete her *own* chance at ever-after happiness, the very next day, she'd had to try and wreck Holly's, too. Holly, who'd been her loyal friend since the ninth grade. Jane stifled a groan as she relived spilling an entire glass of red wine down the back of Holly's wedding dress as it hung on display for the bridesmaids to admire.

It had been an accident. An *accident*. One minute Jane was talking to redheaded Brianna Brisbee about the groomsmen they'd be matched with and the next, wine was spreading like blood in a horror film.

Holly wasn't speaking to Jane at the moment. Wouldn't let her FedEx a replacement or find a dry cleaner who worked stain miracles. Nothing. *"Just stay away from me,"* her friend had said. The wedding was in two days.

Stay away. What did that mean when you were supposed to be a bridesmaid?

Jane pressed the small of her back into the stuffing of the coffee shop chair, letting her head rest against the top, and stared up at the ceiling. It wasn't the first time she'd screwed things up in her life, but it could be the first time the screwups had all converged at once.

Maybe she could write a book. A memoir. Call it, *Jane: A Life in Chaos.* Only one problem with that. If you're going to have chaos, you pretty much have to pull it out with a happy ending or no one will buy the book.

Hmmm. All things considered, she'd put her chances of a happy ending at about fifty million to one.

Her finger brushed against something on the windowsill. Something that made a clinking sound on the aluminum. Jane let her head flop to that side and looked down to see a small stone, with a piece of paper tucked under it. She pulled both upward for a better look. The paper appeared old and fragile and the stone unnaturally heavy for its size.

The sport of wishing. A guide for those so disposed.

So disposed. Hah! Was she ever. A strangled laugh made its way out of her throat. Like she hadn't done enough wishing in her life, for all the good it had ever done.

"You okay?" Jane's head whipped upward to see a freckled face crinkling in concern. "Something wrong with your drink? We can make you a new one."

More frappuccino can take care of a lot. But not this. Jane shook her head.

"What's that?" The green-aproned woman pointed to the paper and the stone in Jane's hand.

As if she knew. "Nothing." Jane grabbed for her purse, hurriedly tucking both into it. "Just a—doesn't matter."

She pushed herself up. "And my drink is fine. I'm taking it with me." She stood, waiting for the woman to move aside. "Nothing wrong. Nothing at all."

Thank God she could still lie. Sort of.

She left the place, pushing so hard against the door that it banged into a metal chair outside and she found herself apologizing. To a chair.

Then she walked the seven blocks home, past mild-mannered houses with neatly trimmed lawns, past the Italian restaurant that had started cooking for the day, sending its spicy aromas into the air, past the row of storefronts that offered everything from fresh bagels to stationery, and two more coffee shops.

Her shoes beat out a steady rhythm on the sidewalk, where she carefully avoided cracks, in order not to break her mother's back. Her mother. Who had moved to Florida last year and even now was soaking up the sun, oblivious to her only daughter's most recent debacles. The response would be kind but baffled. Why did this sort of thing always happen to Jane, her mother would wonder aloud, and not to Troy?

Jane's older brother Troy led a predictable, organized life, working as a tax attorney in Seattle. Things didn't happen to Troy that he hadn't first "penciled out" and made a conscious decision on. The siblings couldn't be more different.

She glanced to her left before stepping into the street. A car slowed and came to a stop, the driver waving her across. After raising her hand, Jane crossed the street to her apartment building, recently converted from an old elementary school into highly desirable units with hardwood floors and lots of windows. Her apartment had been a seventh-grade classroom, once upon a time. MARY LOVES JIMMY was still scratched into the old wood in a corner of her bedroom closet, apparently missed by the remodeling crew. She loved the place. Hoped she would be able to keep paying the rent on it, now that she was likely not employed.

Home, on a Thursday. When she should have been at the office, preparing press releases and on-the-road-in-the-home-state schedules and answering the phone with a brisk, "Senator Tate's office, Jane Ellingson speaking." The day off had been her boss's idea and not a bad one since the senator had a reputation for tantrums. At least Jane would get paid for this day, if not for any that followed.

She turned her key in the lock and stepped inside her apartment, taking off her jacket and laying it on a chair. She avoided looking at the couch, where she'd been curled up, half-asleep, when Byron made his escape. And she stayed away from the bedroom, where her dress for Holly's wedding hung on the front of the closet, practically shouting the fact that *it,* if not the bride's gown, remained stain-free.

If only . . . she could turn the clock back. Make it all go away. Start over again.

Wish all you want. Won't make it—

Hold on. The sport of wishing. She'd almost forgotten what she'd tucked in her purse. The crazy thing from the windowsill. Somebody's idea of a joke.

She reached into her purse to pull it out, dropped into an overstuffed chair and lifted her legs up and onto the ottoman. Absently, she rubbed the stone between her fingers. It felt smooth, except for one rough spot. Then she looked at the paper, which listed instructions for wishing. Who knew you needed a manual? She'd been doing it all of her life, without any directions. Could be part of the problem.

Head to one side, she reflected on how much easier life would be if *it* came with instructions. Graduate from high school, the checklist would say, *without* riding in the car of Amber Wycliff, who, it turned out, earned money to buy her designer purses by selling drugs on the side, and *without* downing spiked punch at prom and accidentally knocking down one date and one chaperone, who ended up with a broken nose and a minor concussion, respectively. In the official photo with its background of fake clouds, Jamie Wheeler's puffy red nose had matched the corsage she'd been so proud to pin on him, stabbing herself with the pin only once. But at least he'd been willing to have a photo taken. To remember the night.

Like either of them, or old Mrs. Delbert, could forget it.

Moving on. Graduate from college *without* . . . Oh, forget it. Life didn't come with a checklist. Back to the instructions. She placed the stone in the palm of her right hand, just as the paper said. Next, it told her, form a wish.

No. Problem. What-so-ever.

She began to rub the stone in a circular motion, repeating the words *a posse ad esse* over and over. The part of her that thought it a silly thing to do was quickly replaced by the part disposed to wishing. *Really* disposed.

Next, it said, she should wait for the stone to heat, and then voice the wish aloud. It was, actually, getting warm. The wish bubbled on the edge of her tongue, frantic to make itself known. "Please," she said, in a voice surprisingly strong, "take me away from here. Let me start all over. Someplace where no one knows me." Wouldn't it be great to wipe out all the mistakes of the past and start from scratch? No one ever got a chance like that. They had to carry baggage around until it had them hunched over and leaning to one side. She repeated the Latin words again, in case they hadn't been heard the first time by . . . whoever. *"A posse ad esse."*

Might be good to know what the words meant but, on the other hand, when playing with something that probably came out of a cereal box, it didn't matter. They had a certain lyrical quality, she thought while fighting disappointment that nothing had happened. And never would happen. Because she was stuck with this life she had created, the one that resembled a stock car race, where she crashed and burned at every turn. Not because she barreled into other cars, but just because she was *there*, riding around the track. Unlike Troy, her steady, practical brother, who stuck to the back roads—one lane, no traffic, no roadblocks.

She should try it his way, sometime.

Her hand dropped to one side, fingers barely holding on to the stone. Just how low had she sunk, thinking this cereal prize could actually—

A loud boom on her right jarred the thought from her mind. Then a rushing, deafening sound of air, whirling and spinning all around her, and her body knocked straight out of the chair and into darkness, where she tumbled head over heels. Slivers of light appeared in vivid shades of red, green, white, until her eyes squeezed shut in self-defense. Panic shot through every inch of her, rendering her limbs useless.

Don't play with matches, her mother had told her. Not . . . Don't play with wishing instructions. Oh, God. Really. This was. Bad. She tried to move an arm. It remained glued to her side. The thing couldn't have taken her seriously. No one started again. *Ever.*

She tried a new wish. *Okay. I didn't mean it. Please stop—*

And it did. The rushing noise disappeared, replaced by a steady clip-clopping sound and a movement that jerked her back and forth until she put a hand down on each side to keep her balance, petrified to open her eyes. She felt smooth, supple leather beneath her fingers and heard a horse whinny.

A horse? Not only the sound, but the *smell* of a horse and . . . leather. The feel of clothing. Lots of it, weighing her down and cinching her in tight. More clothing than she'd had on a minute ago, that much was for sure.

Jane pried open one eye and then the other. Snapped them shut and opened them again. She was in some sort of moving carriage. The seat squeaked beneath her as she looked down at the clothing that felt soft, and unfamiliar against her skin. *Blue silk,* covering her from neck to ankles. The skirts were voluminous, with rows of fabric edged in lace. She was wearing some sort of long jacket over the dress. The jacket had tight upper sleeves that were bell shaped at the end, with more lace. Lots of it. What the—? She'd been wearing her favorite jeans, the ones that fit perfectly, with a pink tank top under her white gauze shirt. And flip-flops. Not an explosion of silk.

She put a hand up to touch her hair and realized that a hat sat firmly on top, with long ribbons tied in a bow under her chin. How bizarre. Had she wished herself right into a theatre piece?

As the carriage slowed to a stop, Jane's chin lifted and her shoulders drew up straight and back . . . all by themselves, as though someone was pulling invisible strings while she sat back, an interested observer. Weird. *Really* weird. And the door. It was opening, inches from where she sat. She watched, fascinated, as a gloved hand reached inside.

"Miss Ellingson," said a man in perfect, cultured British tones. "Welcome to Afton House. This is indeed a delight."

A delight. Not a shock, a surprise or a bolt from Heaven. A *delight.*

He knew her name. But she didn't have any idea who he was or why he would be standing outside her horse-drawn carriage dressed like someone straight out of the nineteenth century. She opened her mouth to ask, but other words came tripping across her tongue. In a lilting British accent. "Thank you, Mr. Dempsey," she said, extending her gloved hand to take his. One foot moved forward, toward the carriage step, as her other hand grasped her skirts.

No. Oh, no. Something that required this much coordination was sure to end in disaster. Damn. And he had a great-looking suit on, too. Too bad it was going to end up covered in mud or something worse after she'd—

Descended. With a grace as alien to her as the funny half boots on her feet, she ended up standing on the ground after nothing more than a few delicate steps. Standing, actually, straight up. No dry cleaner's dream roll in the mud for either one of them.

Now *that* was a delight.

Her body. Had to have been possessed. That was it. By someone with coordination. Social graces. And a British accent?

Wait. What was that? She heard herself speaking again.

"I should like for you to meet my aunt, Mr. Dempsey." She nodded toward the carriage. "Mrs. Hathaway."

A plump woman, whose eyes blinked so rapidly, it must have been difficult for her to see, emerged, murmuring pleasantries.

Interesting. Her aunt. Even though both her mother and father had been only children.

"Mrs. Hathaway. Welcome," Mr. Dempsey said with a broad smile.

"And my sister," she heard herself continue. "Miss Anne Ellingson." One hand extended toward the carriage.

A fresh-faced girl, her cheeks rosy and her eyes sparkling, prepared to alight. She looked about fifteen or sixteen. Her *sister?* And how was it Jane knew the names of these people—and they knew hers?

Nothing made sense here, least of all the carriage with the sour-faced driver and the let's-just-call-it-what-it-is *mansion* they stood before. Yet, she could not feel her face contorting in the way it usually did when confused and this Mr. Dempsey wasn't giving any indication he could *see* she was confused. Instead, he turned in one grand motion, crooked both arms and offered them to her and her aunt.

They took them as though it were the most natural thing in the world and began walking toward the house, shoes crunching on the dirt, the teenaged Anne following closely behind. Jane's skirts swayed elegantly as she moved, with the confident step of someone other than herself.

This was some . . . dream?

She could feel Mr. Dempsey's warm arm beneath her gloves and his jacket. As he began speaking, she heard a giggle and tossed a look that seemed like a frown in the direction of her "sister," who quickly pulled her face straight. Wow. That seemed a little harsh to do. Nothing wrong with a giggle. Jane tried to follow with an apologetic smile, to no avail.

Hello? Person inside here, not being allowed to do what she wanted to with her body?

Meanwhile, Mr. Dempsey, whoever the hell he was, had begun talking again. "My father, alas, has taken to his bed. He is once again ailing. But he insisted that nothing should deter your visit, which we have anxiously awaited these many days."

They had awaited her visit. Anxiously, even. Very nice. To be wanted. Not something a lot of people seemed to be doing when it came to her, at least not lately.

"Of course," Jane murmured, with perfect diction. "But I do so hope your father will recover his health soon."

Mr. Dempsey turned toward her, rewarding the con-

cern with a perfect smile. He was good-looking, in a chiseled, *GQ* sort of way, with dark blond hair and green eyes.
He stood even with Jane's five foot seven inch height and
walked with a confident stride, something she herself had
never managed to do. Until . . . now. Weird.

"Here we are," said Mr. Dempsey, ushering them
through the door to the massive house, where a servant
gave a deep bow.

"I confess I have also been eager for a visit to Afton
House," Jane said, with a tip of her head.

Their eyes locked. Jane tried to look away but couldn't.
Her head remained firmly in place, as though someone
else held it between two hands.

And she could swear, ninety percent for sure, that she
saw an actual twinkle in his eye. It was there and then
gone. A twinkle. But you only read about something like
that in books. She'd never actually seen one in real life.

A pause. And whatever had been holding her upright
seemed to loosen its grip, allowing her to breathe freely
for what seemed the first time in several minutes. Except
that breathing freely seemed to be a relative term since
something hard and unyielding on the inside of the
dress seemed to be working at cross-purposes with any
movement she might try to make.

"Ah," said Mr. Dempsey, a furrow appearing between
his perfect brows. "She has decided to retire. I shall take
my leave." A courtly half-bow. "Until tomorrow, then."

"Who's retiring? And who are you?" Jane blurted.

He turned to her in surprise. "James Dempsey," he answered, in a tone that clearly said that should explain
everything.

She shook her head. "Why are you dressed that way?
Better yet, why am *I* dressed this way?"

He regarded her gravely for what felt like an eternity
before saying, "You, Miss Ellingson, are the heroine of

the book *Afton House*. And I am the hero of the tale. At
your disposal." With a dip of his chin, he made it clear
he awaited her joyous approval. Or possibly screams of
delight, if she had any waiting to leap forward.

Jane looked at James, then at Anne and back again.
"Book," she repeated.

"Book." As though this should all be so obvious. A
vague sort of suspicion began to creep through her, beginning at her feet and moving upward until it came barreling out of her mouth. "And exactly who is the *she?*"

"Our author. Miss Mary Bellingham."

"Author."

"We shall resume in the morning. Surely you have no
expectation she will write at every hour," James replied.
He made Jane sound demanding.

"No. Of course not." Did she?

"She is well tired today. It is such when one is under-
taking the beginning of the story."

"The beginning." She felt dim-witted, repeating every-
thing, but she had to get this straight. "And you're saying
I'm supposed to be *in* the story? Me. Jane Ellingson.
Actual person."

He exhaled while his eyes did a slight but unmistakable roll. "You, Jane Ellingson, are more than *in* the
story. You are, in fact, the second most important character in the story." He gave a sweeping gesture and another gallant bow. "After me, you understand."

Chapter 2

Jane blinked at James. "Second most important character," she repeated.

He rose from his deep bow to flash a killer smile. As if that were the only answer necessary.

Anne turned to the waiting servant and chirped, "If I may be shown to my rooms?"

The servant dropped a hasty and deferential curtsy, murmuring something unintelligible as she led the girl away. "Good-bye, Sister," Anne said.

Sister. Right, that was . . . her? Jane lifted a hand in uncertain response. Then she turned back to James, who seemed to have bits of amusement playing around the corners of his mouth. She'd had about all she could take of people writing her off. Wait . . . *writing* . . . her . . . She shook her head. "Living, breathing *people* do not end up in the pages of a book," she said. "Fiction is just that. *Fiction.* Something an author makes up." There. He'd understand now.

One of his shoes beat out a tip-tap against the floor. "And how are we to believe an author is able to portray her characters if not for the fact that she pours her heart into their creation? They do, or, rather . . . *We* do exist, Miss Ellingson, in a world entirely of her making."

"Her—making. Mary Bellingham."

"The very one."

"But I *already* exist." This shouldn't be so hard. Who had to argue their existence? "Mary Bellingham, whoever she is, didn't"—she bit back stronger words before adding—"make me up."

He stilled his foot, pondering it for a moment before sweeping his gaze upward and saying, "As you wish." His green eyes held hers, making it clear he indulged her with a heroic level of patience.

Irritation stabbed at her. As you wish, he'd said. As though *she* were the one losing touch with reality here—

Wait a minute. Oh, no. *Wish.* She *had.* In fact, she'd asked to be taken away to a place where she could start over. Somebody had heard that wish. But the somebody hadn't figured out that "away" meant a pulsating city or an island in the Caribbean, and not the pages of a book?

"Your manner of speaking is most unusual." His forehead puckered.

"American," she answered, while her gaze scanned the hall, looking for something, anything, to hold on to. Had she really wished herself into this place, with its elegant, polished hallway and gold fixtures? It looked real, smelled real. She took a few steps to her right, laying her hand on a table. It *felt* real, cool and smooth beneath her fingertips.

"American," James repeated, sounding unconvinced.

"Yes, we—aren't British." Mary Bellingham could chime in anytime now, supplying sparkling dialogue. Jane stifled a small snort, earning a frown from James.

Again, she let her gaze take in her surroundings. On the other hand, "playing" here, for however long the wish, or dream, whatever it was, lasted, might not be all that bad. Could the table be . . . ? Felt like marble.

He motioned toward another servant, who had glided in unnoticed by Jane. "The girl will show you to your rooms," James said. "I pray that you will rest comfortably. We are certain to have a tiring day tomorrow. I believe we are to begin at dinner."

There was . . . what? Some sort of a schedule of events issued to the hero? Jane wrapped her arms hard around her waist, which felt a whole lot smaller than usual, and fanned her face with a gloved hand. She stopped, bringing her hand closer. Gloves. Of pale yellow. Who wore gloves? Then she caught sight of James's expectant face. "And so, you and I will be at the dinner," she stumbled. "Together. You're the—um . . . hero?" Just to be clear.

"Indeed." He flashed a quick grin.

She wobbled a smile in his direction. Her hero. Too bad more men weren't actually *assigned* to that role. James Dempsey, hero. At your service. She wondered if he had a white steed, by any chance, and the ability to scoop up damsels in distress, unstress and kiss them passionately until—

Wooo. Yes. Something to think about. She fanned her face harder, ruffling the hair on her forehead. She'd never tried damseling, but it could be fun. This time her smile had more substance to it. "Well. Until the morrow, then." Hah. She could be as British as the next person, especially when it was all make-believe, due to disappear any minute now.

"Until the morrow." James bestowed yet another courtly bow upon her.

Jane tried to suck in a deep breath, stopping short when something pinched at her sides. Whatever was making her waist smaller had her breathing at half-capacity.

James waited.

And he was waiting for . . . ? Oh. "Thank you, kind sir." *Yes.* She'd get the hang of this. A teenage love of all things Brontë was sure to pay off.

James gave the slightest nod and Jane followed the servant, a mere slip of a teenager, through a winding hallway and up an impressive staircase, their footsteps tap-tap-tapping in synch. They passed finely appointed furniture that looked both expensive and uncomfortable. Candles flickered in sconces on walls dominated by paintings the size of one whole wall in her apartment and high ceilings gave an impression of spacious grandeur. Looked a lot like a home she'd seen profiled on the History Channel once.

Her thoughts raced at lightning speed. A book. A story in the process of being written. Her, in it. As the heroine.

An author, Mary Bellingham, credited with "inventing her." Jane's parents might have some trouble with that idea, since they mostly claimed that honor. And now she, Jane, was supposed to embrace the idea that someone else would decide what would happen to her, would script her life, would—

Wait just a minute. Someone *else* scripting her life. Controlling what she did, what she said. Might not be an entirely bad idea. Someone who didn't have Jane's decision-making record could do a better job of it. They absolutely couldn't do any *worse.*

She supposed she could hang around for a while, see what happened, if she could learn a thing or two. She still had the stone, didn't she? Her hand darted to her pockets, searching. Yes. She rubbed it between her fingers, just to be sure. There was the rough spot she remembered.

Okay, then. She could do it. Probably. Maybe. It was an insane idea and no one would ever believe her, but sometimes you had to let go of what made sense and take a chance. She clutched the banister hard for support.

When they reached the top of the stairs, the servant led

the way down a long hall. "What's your name?" Jane asked, hurrying to keep up. This skirt, with what had to be yards and yards of fabric, wasn't the easiest to manage. It seemed to have a life of its own. She wouldn't be at all surprised to see it take off running ahead of her.

The servant turned to look over her shoulder. "Sarah, miss."

"Nice to meet you, Sarah."

The girl shot her a confused look. "Yes, miss."

"Do you know much about . . . uh . . . this story? About Mr. Dempsey?"

"I could not say, miss." Sarah's voice was barely audible.

"Oh. Sure," Jane said quickly. "I understand." She didn't. "Where is my sister staying?" She'd always wanted a sister. They could be best friends, share each other's secrets, trade clothes . . . She hoped, really hoped, the unseen Mary Bellingham would write it that way. Something like a giggle began in the small of her stomach and rose quickly. She passed a hand over her mouth.

"Miss Anne Ellingson is next to you, miss." They came to a stop in front of a broad wooden door. Gravely, Sarah pointed to the one just beyond and then opened the door of the room apparently assigned to Jane.

It swung open as if in slow motion. Inside she saw a four-poster bed and a dark wooden dressing table with a mirror and hairbrushes on its top. She hesitated and then walked inside the room for a closer look. A night-gown was laid out on the bed. White, high-necked and long-sleeved, with lace around the edges, it was the great-grandmother version of the camisole and panties she normally slept in. Victoria could keep any number of secrets in that thing.

Sarah followed her, reaching up to tug at the jacket Jane wore.

"Oh." Jane turned back and took a step away, looking at her. "You can go now."

"But, miss—"

"Really. I'm good. Go ahead." To prove the point, she removed her hat, which turned out to be some sort of unbearably sweet close-fitting cap kind of thing, and set it on the bed.

The servant clasped her hands in front of her. "Good?" she repeated, as if Jane were speaking a foreign language, instead of perfectly acceptable English.

"I can handle this myself," Jane said, by way of clarification. She hoped it was true.

Sarah walked back toward the door, where she lingered for a moment, looking uncertain. Then she seemed to make a decision and bobbed another curtsy. "Miss." She went out the door, closing it behind her.

Jane surveyed the room. Gold curtains hung from ceiling to floor, set off by wallpaper striped with red and gold. Armchairs and another small table, with books and a vase of fresh flowers, were against the other wall. The room was formal, elegant. Feminine, without being fluffy. She liked it. Not Pottery Barn but nice. Very nice.

A servant at her disposal, a handsome man as her "hero," a sister she'd never before had, someone else writing her life . . . There could definitely be worse things.

As bizarre as the whole scenario sounded, wouldn't it be something if it was true? If she really *was* living in the midst of a novel, with the blank pages of her life yet to be filled in and most important, a happy ending in her future?

She'd wished for a place to start all over again. Sure, she wouldn't have dreamed of anything like this, but didn't people say that truth was stranger than fiction? Wait. In this case, would it be fiction stranger than . . . Never mind.

A new beginning. It might just be weird enough to work.

* * *

It couldn't be bedtime. Not yet. Jane had no sense of the time of day and there wasn't a clock to be found anywhere in the room, but she knew, just *knew*, she was not ready to sleep. Her mind raced, asking questions she couldn't answer.

Back and forth she paced until she was sure she'd begun to wear a path in the rug. A character in a novel. The heroine. She should be screaming, laughing, *something*, but instead she felt almost guilty at her sense of anticipation.

Already, Mary Bellingham had given Jane a grace she'd never before known. Out of the carriage without falling flat on her face and taking James with her? Would never happen in real life. And right after that, Jane had said exactly the right thing, with manners and decorum. She'd opened her mouth and out the words came. As though she knew what she was doing.

It felt good. Strange, yes. Psychotic, probably, because who actually spent a life in the pages of a novel, waiting for someone to write what happened to them. But still, she had to award points for the sheer release of it all; the freedom of having another person set her on the right path and even help her walk it.

Jane crossed the floor to the door of her room, palms pressing against her silk skirts. Her legs had to be under there, though it might take a huge effort to find them. At least they were moving her from one spot to another.

She opened the door as quietly as she could and closed it behind her, stopping at Anne's door to press her ear against the wood. If the teenager was awake, they could find cocoa to drink and talk over the day, the hero, whatever. Even giggle. For all of her years growing up, Jane had longed to do that. It wasn't much fun having a brother who read textbooks practically from kindergarten, wore a tie in the first grade and never once got into any trouble. He was a rock, her brother, while Jane was the pebble that skipped along the water until it inevitably sank with a thud. And that was pretty much the problem.

Jane had raised her hand to knock when she heard the unmistakable sound of snoring coming from the other side. So much for cocoa and a late-night talk. Anne had checked out for the night.

Her hand fell back to her skirts and her gaze roamed up and down the hallway. Suddenly, more than anything, she felt a need to get outside, to breathe air that didn't smell of candles, polished wood and heavy upholstery. To feel the cool air on her face and stare up at the sky.

She hoped there *was* an outside. A sky to stare at.

From somewhere beneath her skirts, her legs found the impetus to move and she retraced her earlier steps until she reached the stairs. She rushed down them, looking to the left, the right and straight ahead to make sure no one was around to see her fleeing the scene.

Fleeing. The *scene*. A sense of irony knocked at the edges of Jane's consciousness until she brushed it away.

Halfway down, her foot slipped on the smooth surface of the stair and she half-fell, half-slid the rest of the way, with first one hand and then both clinging to the banister. Ow. That thing cinching her waist in didn't exactly bend. *At all.* It was probably bulletproof, as well. Still she'd managed to land with the only casualty a ripped seam in the arm of her dress. Turned out the fabric wasn't quite as flexible as her favorite tank top.

When at last she reached the door to the outside, she rushed through it, barely taking enough time to close it behind her, and inhaled the air in small gulps. The enormity of the situation began to sink in as she looked around her in the evening dusk, at the stately house, the dirt walkway and road, and the conspicuous absence of concrete, power poles or cell towers. All the normal trappings of life she'd taken for granted until now. *No Internet.* How did these people communicate?

With one fervent wish, she'd transported herself back in time, at least one hundred and fifty years or so. Where women were suppressed, treasured, stifled, revered. And in many ways, at the mercy of their . . . heroes.

One more wish, if anyone was listening. Mary Bellingham, if this was truly the adventure Jane was to have, *please* color outside the Victorian lines.

Jane walked, and then walked some more, until she found herself following her nose away from the house and into a large garden, fragrant with the scent of flowers in the dusky evening air.

Head down, she watched her skirts move of their own accord as she strolled the well-defined rows of the garden path, the leaves of low-hanging tree branches brushing against her hair. She reached up to touch one, rubbing it absently between her fingers. She could leave this place. Well, she was pretty sure she could, anyway. Forget that. She *definitely* could leave, whenever she wanted to.

All she had to do was break out the stone and make another wish. But what would she return to? A mess with her job, with her boyfriend, with her friend. All things she had to fix and she had no idea how.

Here, she didn't have to think about any of that. Definitely a plus.

A solid, dark object materialized in front of her, causing her heart to leap straight into her throat. "Oh!" she screeched, slapping a hand across her mouth. Stepping back, she looked upward, to see that the object was a man. A tall, broad-shouldered man, outlined against the sky, with a hat pulled low over his eyes.

He removed it now, with an exaggerated sweep of his arm and a curt nod. "Madam."

"You scared me."

A long, silent moment passed before he answered, which only served to speed up her heartbeat. When he did answer, it was with a voice that rumbled so deeply, the tall green stalks on either side of Jane seemed to shrink. She had to will herself to hold her shoulders straight and not do the same.

"My intent, I assure you," he said, "was not to frighten."

"Could have fooled me." Her heart continued to pound. "So if you weren't trying to scare the life out of me, what were you doing?"

"I simply sought to inquire what you might be doing in the garden at this hour."

He could inquire all he wanted to. It was the explanation that might take a couple of hours. She took a shallow breath and exhaled, wishing she could get a better look at him. "I could ask you the same thing."

"Indeed you could," he acknowledged. "And we could engage in clever banter until the night turned black, in want of an answer."

Jane gave a small, choked laugh and peered up at him, able to make out strong features, including what looked to be amazing cheekbones, and a lot of very dark hair. "Then we agree that neither one of us has to account for why we're here." She kept her voice light.

He regarded her for another long moment before jamming his hat back on his head and saying, "It would seem to be so."

"Good, because I would hate to feel as though I couldn't take a walk in the garden without explaining myself." As if she could explain *anything* happening around here, but there had to be some perks that came with being the heroine. Maybe one of them would be an "air of mystery." *Yes.* She'd like to try being mysterious, for once. Usually, she was all too easy to figure out. Hope linked arms with anticipation to take a tentative step forward.

Now he smiled, exposing white, even teeth in the growing darkness. "Defending one's actions does grow tiresome."

Jane opened her mouth and then shut it again, not sure if he was talking about her, or him . . . or *her.* She could have used Mary Bellingham's help, since the perfect comeback escaped her in the worst way. So much for mystery.

"Shall I accompany you to the house?" he asked. "It may be further than you realize."

Not a bad idea. This storyline didn't seem to come with any sort of roadmap of Victorian England and Jane's internal GPS had been missing since birth. "Yes. That would be . . . If you want to."

He fell into step with her, adjusting his longer stride. She wondered if he dominated a room as soon as he entered, causing all to look at him even though he hadn't uttered a sound.

"Who are you?" she asked, squinting up at him.

"I am called Curran."

"Curran," she repeated, letting the name roll around her tongue. It had an edge to it that seemed to suit him. "Do you live around here?"

"I do."

"I'm staying here. As a guest."

"I am aware of that."

"It looks like an incredible house, even though I haven't had much of a chance to look around yet." She gave herself a virtual pat on the back. Without even trying, she'd made herself sound like a normal guest in this very not-normal situation.

"But you went first to the gardens. A place that attracts those in need of solace."

It would be helpful to have a rule book to follow. "It's a logical place to go," she said. "You were there."

He didn't reply to that. Instead, they fell silent, the only sounds their muffled steps on the path and her skirts swishing.

"You will see more of the estate as the days pass," he said after a moment.

The idea of days passing sent a sharp pang of discomfort through her middle. She decided to switch the topic. "My name is Jane."

"Yes," he agreed.

Had there been a character-introduction party she hadn't been invited to? "You seem to know me, but I don't know anything about you." They had reached the house and were passing through the light that spilled from a front window. Jane stopped, peering closer at the man, but the shadows crossed his face in a way that didn't allow a good look.

He also stopped, looking down at her. "It can be such, I am given to believe, at the beginning of a tale. The author's intentions shall no doubt become clearer as the story progresses."

"I'm not the most patient person." An understatement.

His mouth turned up. "Perhaps our author will discover that to be true. And use it to good advantage."

"Would be the first time anyone has," Jane sighed.

She could have sworn she heard the beginning of a chuckle from him, but if so, he checked it by clearing his throat and squaring his shoulders. "As we have arrived, Miss Ellingson, I shall see you inside and then retire."

At the door, she hesitated, then turned to him and stuck out her hand. "Thank you."

In one smooth motion, he took her hand in his own, turning the palm down and bending to touch her glove with his lips.

A gesture that should never have disappeared from society, Jane reflected as a little thrill ran up her spine. If Byron had done that . . . even once . . . When Curran released her hand, she let it hover in the air for a few seconds before she pulled it back and took a few seconds to recover her breath. "Well," she breathed. "Thanks . . . for that." She bobbed what she hoped would pass for a curtsy, just because it seemed like the thing to do under the circumstances, and with another quick glance at him, she walked through the door. Wow. Now that was courtly. She'd felt his mouth, even through her glove.

He followed, closing the door behind him.

Jane whirled in surprise. "Aren't you—?" She broke off the words. "You live here?"

Another bow, this time deep and prolonged. "Allow me to introduce myself. Curran Dempsey."

"Dempsey." She tipped her head. "So you're related to James, somehow?"

"As fate would have it, James and I are brothers." His hair shone in the candlelight, as black as James's hair was blond. Thick, dark brows framed eyes such intense pools of darkness, they seemed capable of hiding anything their owner might choose.

"James. The *hero*," Jane said, more to herself than to him. She had to keep all of the details straight.

"Not as long as I draw a breath," said Curran Dempsey.

Chapter 3

One minute Jane was sleeping in a great-grandmother nightgown, fighting to keep it from strangling her, and the next she found herself sitting with perfect posture before an elaborately laid dining table, surrounded by a symphony of crimson.

Apparently, a character in a book never knew what was coming next.

Deep red ruled the room from the wallpaper to the huge, heavy curtains, accented by the dark wood of the fireplace and the candle flame dancing in sconces on the walls. Large dishes in the center of the table sent heavy aromas of beef and fish wafting through the stifling air. Jane checked with her stomach. Even if she had been hungry, the smells alone would have been enough to quell the urge to eat.

As she struggled to orient herself to the strange scene, she felt her chin glide to the left and heard her voice say, "Do tell me more of your travels, Mr. Dempsey. I cannot hear enough on the subject."

James, clearly in command at the head of the table, rewarded her interest with a broad smile. "You must one day travel to London, Miss Ellingson. I suspect you would find the fine homes and company there to your liking."

Her gaze dropped to stare at her plate, which contained an alarming assortment of food, all of it boiled beyond repair. "London is so very large," she murmured. "It is a frightening thought."

So this is how it's done, Jane thought. Must be chapter one in damseling. Helpless female. Check. Did this stuff really work? And was it okay that she felt so desperate to find something that would?

She felt a hand brush hers. Lightly, barely touching her skin. Warmth began to creep into her cheeks, even though she didn't feel at all embarrassed.

"Though it may seem frighteningly large, London is a hospitable place, filled with various amusements. With the proper escort . . ."

Now Jane looked up at him, her voice coming out in a whisper. "Oh, yes, sir. With the proper escort . . ." She was dying to look down at her dress, which she could tell exposed more than the suffocating silk one she'd worn yesterday. But her chin remained turned toward James. If she wasn't mistaken, her bottom lip had even begun a slight tremble.

A trembling lip. Didn't seem like a particularly seductive move. But then, on second thought, who was Jane to question anything?

James's hand hovered above hers. She looked at it at the same time he did. Would it come down on hers? Or not? Words played on his lips. Jane's fingers withdrew, then inched back.

Both James and Jane froze in place.

A second or two later, Jane's shoulders sank as the invisible grip on her posture relaxed.

"She is at a pause," announced James.

"She?" echoed Jane. She lifted her chin up and to

the side, stretching as she lifted one shoulder and then the other.

"Miss Mary Bellingham."

Of course. That made as much sense as her sitting at a Victorian dinner table in a . . . Wow. Now that she had a chance to look down and see it, her dress was stunning. Made of a pale yellow silk, yards and yards of it overwhelming the chair in which she sat. Off her shoulders and cut low, with a bodice cut tight to her body and large, graceful sleeves. She fingered the fabric wistfully, wishing she ever had a *real* occasion to wear something like this. Made her feel feminine, pretty. *Desirable.*

She straightened her shoulders of her own accord, looking around the room. A slip of a woman perched on a tall chair at the end of the table, her brown hair severely swept to the side and up, in loops flat against the sides of her head. Next to her an elderly couple—

Jane's back stiffened and her chin rose again, but this time, in the blink of an eye, she found herself sitting on the other side of the table, still next to James. An entire body, *hers* in fact, picked up and moved. Just like that. Did George Lucas know about this?

"I trust you are finding the accommodations to your liking, Miss Ellingson?" James asked.

"Indeed, sir," she heard herself reply. "They are most suitable."

"My sister has done an admirable job under trying circumstances," he said, casting his gaze toward the pale young woman, who seemed to shrivel into her chair. Jane's gaze followed his, to give the woman what felt like a sympathetic smile.

"It is not easy, to be sure," Jane said. "How fortunate you are to have your sister."

James seemed to ponder this before replying. "My mother had been ill for many years," he said. "Leaving the household in disarray. My sister Violet has devoted her attentions to what must be done, but I fear she greatly prefers the solitary occupations of needlework and painting to the rigors of ordering a household." His observation ended with a sigh.

"I find great pleasure in a well-run household," Jane replied. "My mother has schooled me well in the art." What? The great cleaning-fluid incident of 1998 might say something different. If Jane remembered correctly, her mother had instructed her to *never again* come up with her own concoction for cleaning the oven, for as long as they both should live. Which might not be long, her mother had pointed out, if Jane didn't stop coming up with cleaning concoctions.

But this was Book Jane, not Real Jane. The one who knew what to say and do and wouldn't dream of having oven incidents.

"An art indeed," James said.

"It is not a simple task, to be sure, yet Violet makes such thoughtfulness and care appear quite without effort," Jane said sweetly, directing her gaze at James's pale sister. "I am greatly admiring."

Violet, who had apparently heard, acknowledged the praise with a dip of her chin and the shadow of a smile.

Then Jane turned back and continued to gaze at James, with what had to be an expression of muted adoration, given the way she could feel her features arranged.

It was nice, basking in James's pleased smile. Maybe life was simpler in a time when women had a clearly defined role, a purpose to serve. When proposing to a boyfriend would be unthinkable, so there'd be no chance of it happening. When there wasn't the risk of a cut and paste accident because, hello, computers hadn't even been invented. When, okay, there could still be a problem with spilling a glass of wine, but on the other hand, a servant would be right there, making sure it didn't happen, so . . .

Being protected, indulged, cared for. Damseled to distraction.

Definitely less risk, if you happened to be one Jane Ellingson, living in the mid-nineteenth century.

She glanced down, taking a bite of something undetermined from her plate and letting it linger on her tongue for identification. Meat. She'd always heard English cooking lacked a certain something. This lacked a lot, but the guests seemed to be enjoying it. Conversation bubbled around her in a steady rhythm, punctuated by spots of constrained, tinkling laughter from the women. Like wind chimes above a breeze.

When at last she was allowed to turn to her right, she saw that Violet had her lips pulled in so tightly, they'd all but disappeared. Her eyes flitted between the guests on either side of her: a man with a flushed face and white hair and an elderly woman whose hair had been curled within an inch of its life. With pudgy fingers, the man lifted a bottle of wine, pouring more for himself as well as for the two women.

Jane's sister sat next to the elderly woman, toying with the food on her plate. Catching Jane's eye, she blinked and sat up straighter.

Mrs. Hathaway occupied the chair directly across from Jane, on the other side of James. She trilled with delight at something the man to Jane's left was saying. "My dear Mr. Stonewalter," she bubbled, "what a delightful sense of humor you have."

A glance at Mr. Stonewalter revealed a sixtyish gentleman with thinning hair and deep laugh lines around his eyes. "It makes an appearance on occasion," he replied.

"On more than one occasion," Jane said kindly. "Do not be so modest, Mr. Stonewalter. I find your twists of phrase most amusing. It has been entirely too long since I have had the pleasure of your company." She smiled.

Not too much. Or too little. She'd smiled just right, gauging from the approving reaction of the others. And the words came out so effortlessly. Jane thought about the time she'd gone to a comedy club with Byron and snorted right in the middle of a gut-wrenching laugh. She'd been laughing so hard, she'd actually been afraid she'd pee her pants, so all things considered, the snort wasn't that bad.

But Byron had thought it was. He'd looked at her, startled out of his own laughter. She'd snorted in public. And snorted loud.

Your twists of phrase. Most amusing. Check.

"Oh, now you are attempting to turn my head, Miss Ellingson," Mr. Stonewalter said. "A younger man would do well to claim you for himself before I am reduced to playing the fool at my age."

Laughter all around.

Stonewalter aimed a meaningful look at James. "A gentleman could hardly find a gentler, more well-bred wife."

Jane felt a blush creep into her cheeks. "You are too kind, sir." *Please, please don't have James bolt from the room like Byron. I don't even know him, but I know I couldn't take that right now.*

"Kindness is an admirable trait," James said, as though he didn't know Stonewalter's comment had taken direct aim at him. "One far too often forgotten these days, it would seem."

"Jane's mother, my dear brother's wife, insists upon it," said Mrs. Hathaway. "A kinder household never will you see."

"And you have demonstrated kindness in abundance, sir," Jane said to James, apparently having recovered herself. "In inviting my aunt, sister and me for a visit, despite the trying circumstances your father, and indeed your family, endures."

James sat back in his chair, hands resting across the silver brocade of his vest. "My father wishes the halls of Afton House to once again ring with the sound of cheerful voices," he answered quietly. "I suspect he believes such gaiety will serve to answer those who contend he is in his last days."

The guests murmured their agreement.

A sudden click of the door and a low, threatening voice cut through the pleasantries. "Last days which you, my dear brother," rumbled the voice of Curran, sarcasm dripping from the edges, "would choose to hasten, if at all possible."

A small cry lodged in Jane's throat as her hand flew to her mouth. In one simultaneous motion, her head, and those of the others at the table, turned toward the doorway, through which James's brother, his expression ominously dark, was about to enter. His stance screamed challenge.

Despite the tension his arrival caused and the shock she had apparently expressed, Jane felt a thrill of appreciation run through her. Curran had a certain Heathcliff air going for him. Or at least Timothy Dalton, young edition. His presence seemed to fill the entire room.

"I had known you to be away on business," James replied, his fingers drumming a beat on the table. He sighed. "Instead, I find you have returned, no doubt intent on laboring under the same delusions you harbored before leaving." He gave a shake of his head, the motion clearly dismissive.

Violet piped up. "I believe—" she said in a high-pitched treble and then stopped, looking in distress from one brother to the other.

"Perhaps you are suggesting the ladies retire to the drawing room, Violet?" Jane offered.

Relief flooded the other woman's face before she managed to regain control. "Yes," she murmured. "I believe that would be best."

"Ah. Right you are, Violet," James said, smiling benevolently. He cast his gaze upon Jane, who was preparing to rise with the others. "Please do not allow this interruption to trouble you, my dear," he added in a low voice meant only for her ears. "It is best to simply disregard Curran's unfortunate fits of temper. He is harmless enough."

Harmless wasn't a term Jane would use to describe Curran Dempsey and she'd known him for all of . . . an hour or so? But she found herself giving James a quiet smile. "Sir, please do not give it another thought. I assure you, I shall not." At that, she rose, chin high.

Curran stepped away from the door and Jane followed the lead of the other women, sweeping from the room in a swish of silk skirts. Without stumbling once. And without giving Curran a single look.

Which was a shame, really. Because she would have liked to.

Curran Dempsey turned from a brief glance toward the departing women to his brother, who remained seated at the table. A pity. Curran would have preferred to allow his gaze to linger on the heroine of this novel, who a short time earlier had revealed herself to be something other than the beautiful, obedient woman Mary Bellingham portrayed.

Beautiful, indeed, but more bold of spirit and tongue than obedient. Intriguing.

"You are not welcome here," said his brother. "Must we go over this yet again?"

Curran crossed the room until he stood before James. "It is my home." Mary gave his words a surly twist.

"Perhaps," James replied. "But only so long as my father does live. You have caused this family much grief, Curran, and I shall not permit it to continue."

"You are not our father by half, nor shall you ever be," Curran would have shot back, had he been permitted. Instead, he heard himself say, "I am the oldest son and thereby entitled to the rights of—" He slammed his palm on the table, causing the dishes to jump and rattle.

A pause. Curran waited. James cleared his throat, waiting as well.

Mary's pen again took over and again he heard himself say, "I am the oldest son and thereby entitled to the rights of—" This time, a lift in his voice implied a weak resolve.

James rose, slamming both of his palms on the table. Glasses overturned, leaving a stream of liquid on the cloth. "You, sir, have no legitimate rights." He narrowed his eyes in contempt. "Once my father is no longer here to protect you, I shall ensure your return to the city of your birth, where you will take up your *rights* to the very meanest of existences, as repayment for causing this family nothing but distress these many years."

The two men glared at each other for a long moment before the invisible hand again lifted. James bent his neck one way and then the other, stretching and relieving his shoulders. Then he left the room.

Curran stayed, staring at the spot in the table that had borne the blow of James's hands. If Mary Bellingham could write a villain no better than this, the tale would be cursed from its opening pages. A small ball of fury formed inside, creating a heat that spread throughout his body. She knew him not. Wrote him not.

It was all for James.

* * *

Halls paneled in dark wood and lit by gaslights were not only dark and smelly, Jane discovered, but also drafty. No wonder she'd heard servants sneeze several times. Let alone the fact that they didn't seem to mind sneezing on each other and into food. In a time before antibiotics. *Eeew.* She shivered.

Mary Bellingham had retired for the night, according to James, which gave Jane a chance to do some exploring on her own. Might be her only chance to roam through a nineteenth-century estate unescorted, even if every fixture and bowing servant lived only in someone else's imagination.

She removed her shoes before tiptoeing down the hallway. The house itself was huge, filled with rooms both large and small. Each time she peeked behind another door, she found elaborate furnishings, curtains and artwork. The Dempseys, it seemed, had done pretty well for themselves. Or at least their ancestors had.

But most of the rooms had a hollow, empty feel. As though they, with their elegant and largely untouched furniture, had grown old. Waiting for life to happen. For laughter. For love, which seemed conspicuously absent in this place.

That had to be what James sought in this story. Why Jane was here, auditioning. *Now appearing, in the role of heroine,* she heard an imaginary voice boom, *Jane Christine Ellingson.* In acknowledgment, she paused long enough in her stocking feet to drop a deep curtsy to her fictional audience. Ha. She'd always wanted to go for a starring role.

"Miss?"

Jane's gaze shot up to see Sarah, dressed in a dark gray dress with a white apron and cap, staring at her, puzzled. When had she arrived? Jane lifted her chin. "I'll be in the garden," she said in her best imitation of an aristocrat, sweeping by the girl, who immediately gave a deferential dip. This lady-of-the-manor thing became easier by the second.

Then she turned back. "But . . . um, thank you. You do a great job."

Who was she kidding? An aristocrat, she wasn't.

Before she went through the door, she jammed the shoes, black and in the style of slippers, back on her feet. Not the best for walking across grass and stone, but they'd have to do.

It looked to be early afternoon, which she now realized could change at any minute. She could find herself at breakfast if the author awoke and began writing. Time seemed to be a random detail, subject to the author's whim. This had to be the best example of "live in the moment" Jane had ever heard of.

She made her way through the house and outside, grateful she saw no one she was obligated to talk with or pretend not to see. As she marched in the direction of the garden, she closed her eyes and drank in the scent of grass, mixed with that of trees and flowers. Moisture hung in the air, clinging in tiny droplets to her face. She opened her eyes, reveling in the familiar promise of rain. Now that she was outside the dark, narrow corridors of Afton House, she had a sudden urge to turn a cartwheel, something she hadn't attempted since the third grade, when she'd accidentally taken out two hopscotchers on the way down.

She decided against it. A dress with mammoth skirts and tight upper sleeves would have to lower the chances for success by a good . . . Well, the chances for success weren't good to begin with. Never mind. Who needed cartwheels.

A broad expanse of lawn stretched before her, bordered by willow trees and flowerbeds brimming with color. Jane walked alongside them, stopping to smell here and there, both the bitter and the sweet, and in all, a stinging freshness. Birds twittered above her, offering up their songs and conversations.

She didn't have to worry about answering phones that rang nonstop with constituents disagreeing on the senator's latest stand. Dumping toner on herself from a malfunctioning copy machine. Agonizing over which pair of jeans made her look the skinniest for a date with Byron and then analyzing his every single word to figure out what he really meant. If he really loved her.

No. Here in this expanse of English countryside, no one expected anything from her. She could relax. Just *be*. If she made a mistake, Mary Bellingham could fix it, with the stroke of a pen.

An inviting path bordered the garden, winding and disappearing from sight. She decided to take it, trailing her hand along the flowers, until gradually, she became aware of someone approaching from the other side.

It was Curran Dempsey, dressed in black, with a white shirt and ascot, holding the reins of a large horse as he walked. She retreated with a step back and to the side, watching as he moved with an easy, determined stride, powerful legs moving in rhythm. Mary sure knew how to write a man who would raise the interest of a woman. Well, this man, anyway.

And, okay, this woman. Even though her interest was purely appreciation of a very fine male body. Byron . . . might come back.

Curran spotted her, pulling his horse to a halt. "Miss Ellingson."

She sucked in an appreciative breath. "Mr. Dempsey."

"Out for a stroll?"

"I needed the fresh air."

"I see." He paused. "May I accompany you?"

She almost responded that it was a free country, but stopped herself in time. It actually . . . wasn't. "If you would like."

He busied himself with the horse for a moment and then stepped through a break in the flowers to fall into step beside her, reversing his previous course. She didn't know whether to be flattered or concerned.

Jane was the first to speak. "You must be needing solace." She raised an eyebrow to let him know the reference to their previous conversation was a good-natured one.

"As much of the family does not find occasion to stroll through the gardens, I find it an excellent place to linger."

"Ah." She nodded. "Your family. I take it there isn't much love lost between you, James and Violet."

"Much less than little."

This was a man who measured his words, Jane decided. She kicked a small rock, watching it skitter across the path. "Quite the appearance you made at dinner."

"My brother is arrogant."

She flipped him a quick smile. "And you're not?"

The muscles of his jaw tightened and his eyes narrowed as he looked down at her. "There is a distinct line between arrogance and purpose. Which do you suppose drives James?"

She stopped, looking up at him. In the way he held his head, tilted to the side, and his hands, clasped behind his back, she saw a man who had asked a simple question. One that he knew the answer to. In his dark, nearly black eyes, she saw something else. Questioning. Drawing her in.

Jane was the last one with any answers. She took a step away from him. "I wouldn't know. I'm not writing this thing. Only Mary would know that."

His features relaxed and he took her arm, urging her

forward on their walk. "It was not my intent to alarm you, Miss Ellingson."

"Jane."

"As you wish. Jane. Perhaps you could tell me what has you seeking the solace of the gardens? I know it is not because you wish to avoid my family."

Her next words spilled out almost before she realized it. "I'm not really—you know, a *heroine*." She sucked in a breath as deep as her corset would allow. There. She'd admitted it. All these people who assumed she could actually lead a story would soon know the truth. Might as well get everything out in the open. Send her back to Seattle, find another heroine.

"I don't understand."

Well, neither did she. Of all people, she was confessing who she really was to the *villain* of the story? "It's all a big mistake. I made a wish, with a stone. Ended up, apparently, in the pages of a novel because my name is the same as the heroine's. Or, something like that happened, anyway. But I'm not really her. The heroine, I mean. And I'm pretty sure I'm not supposed to be here." Almost a shame. Could be worse places than this.

"Your name is Jane Ellingson, is it not?"

She pulled her mouth tight, letting her head bob to one side and then the other in grudging acknowledgment. "It is."

"And you are here. Standing before me, that is."

"Yes. Well, sort of. If you buy in to the idea that I'm only here because Mary Bellingham is writing me . . ."

He pulled to a stop, staring down. "Do your feet not touch this ground? Is your voice not heard clearly in this fresh air you sought?"

"Yes. And *yes*. But it's all a mistake. I'm a *real person*." A small sense of something she could identify only as dread began to build deep within her.

"As am I." He reached out then and took her hand, clasping it between both of his. The touch of his skin on hers sent a shiver running up her spine. His hands were warm, strong. And his hold on her firm.

She felt inexplicably flustered. "I'm sure you're very— You'll have a great life and all, but I have a—a different one."

He said nothing, but continued to hold her hand and gaze intently into her eyes. She was all too aware of those muscular legs, standing only inches from her voluminous skirts. With her free hand, she began to fumble in her pocket, searching for the stone that would explain everything. "I have it. Here. I'll show you," she said. "It's right—"

Except that it wasn't.

Desperation stole over her with alarming speed until she shook off his hands to tear through her pocket with both hands, searching, turning it inside out.

"Have you lost something?" he asked.

Not something.

Everything.

Chapter 4

"I've lost it." As soon as she uttered the words, their meaning sunk in with a weight that caused Jane to stumble and lose her balance.

Curran grabbed her arms, holding on.

"I'm stuck here."

"Stuck?" he repeated.

"Without that stone . . ." She couldn't even think about it. Sure, she'd wished herself here. Wished herself out of her life. But that didn't mean—No. It couldn't. This wasn't forever. She wasn't cut out to be a heroine. Of anything. Hadn't she just admitted as much?

Heroines were adventurous. Confident. *Coordinated.*

"Listen to me." She mustered enough strength to shake off Curran's hands and grab *his* arms. "We need to retrace my steps. You have to help me find it."

He didn't seem to be onboard with that. And he also didn't seem to like her grabbing him. With one quick jerk of his arms, she wasn't holding on to him anymore. And then his hands were on her arms again, holding her in their firm grasp. "You are a woman of some passion," he countered, "but not forthcoming."

Not a compliment. But was that a spark of interest in those intensely focused eyes?

Her breath came sharp and furious, even as her heart pounded. "Never mind. I'll do it myself."

"I shall know what has distressed you so."

"I—It . . ." She pressed a hand to her heart, determined to keep it inside her chest, despite its threat to hammer itself all the way out and onto the lawn.

"Jane." His voice softened. "Tell me."

Her panic began to edge away. "I am looking for a stone," she said, struggling to keep her voice even, "about this big." She made a circle with her forefinger and thumb.

"A stone."

"Yes." She began to regain at least some of her bearings, fueled by the necessity of finding her ticket back home. No time to stand around. He either needed to help or get out of her way.

"And what distinguishes this stone from the hundreds of others to be found in this garden?"

Good question. And she hated that he had asked it, mostly because she had no answer. Pressing a finger to her head, she thought. Hard. "It's flat. And it has a rough spot on one side. My finger hits it about . . . here." She indicated a spot within the circle.

"Should allow for immediate identification," he murmured.

"I didn't say it would be easy."

"Agreed." He raked a hand through his hair. "But I gather this stone is of some importance."

Thank God. He could say whatever he liked, as long as he got that. She unclenched her teeth long enough to answer. "Yes."

He regarded her gravely. "Then search we shall." A bow and a sweep of his hand. "Please. Lead on."

* * *

A good half hour later, they still hadn't found anything, despite a tedious search through blades of grass and clumps of dirt. Jane flexed her stained fingers and began running them through her hair, only to be stopped by a bouquet of curls.

Curls. Just last week, she'd had her hair professionally straightened to get rid of the curls that had plagued her since childhood. "I can't believe it," she declared, throwing a clod of dirt down so hard, it broke apart and spattered clodlets all over her dress. Not that she'd be sorry to dirty it. Every time she bent toward the ground, the skirt did its level best to conceal every inch. She was about ready to hike up the fabric and loop it over her arm, pretty sure there were layers of undergarments to protect her modesty.

Including the corset, which cut her in half and pinched like hell whenever she tried to move any part of her upper body. To search the ground, she had to just about lie prostrate on it. Comfy, butt-hugging jeans wouldn't be invented for another century. No one should have to wait that long. "Keep looking."

"I gave no indication that I would do anything to the contrary."

She met his gaze. "That's right. You didn't." Clearing her throat, she added, "Thank you." He was quite possibly less villainous than he might like to pretend. How many men would search patiently through the grass for an object she couldn't even adequately describe?

He bent his head and picked up a rock to show her.

"No. That's not it." She shook her head. How could she have been so careless as to lose the stone? She reached down to brush aside the stalk of a flower, peering closely at the grass underneath. Without warning, Curran's hand shot before her, brushing against her skin. At his touch, goose bumps rippled up her arms and down again.

"Here."

"Uh—" She blinked, looking up at him.

"Is this the stone you seek?"

"Oh!" Her eyes darted down to see the rock he held.

"I cannot be certain, but there seems to be a rough spot. Somewhere . . ." His thumb circled the stone. "There."

Okay. That circling motion had her stomach performing a double backflip. And why exactly? Thumbs weren't sensual. It just didn't work that way. They didn't look strong and inviting. Promising. Like they could do things to a woman that would have her practically—

"Jane?"

"It . . . uh . . . No. That's not it."

His black eyes burned straight through her. "Then we continue."

"Yes." She lowered her hands, brushing them back and forth on her dress, trying desperately to regain her composure. "We continue." It would be a whole lot easier to focus *without* him here, though.

An endless patch of grass awaited, a testament to how far she'd walked without realizing it. It took all of her concentration not to cast sidelong glances in his direction, checking out that thumb again, and in the end, she couldn't manage it.

Because of a man's thumb.

His gaze met hers. She forced hers back to the grass. She'd just leaned down again when a by-now familiar feeling came over her. The words "Please, not now," didn't make it past her lips before she found herself seated in the drawing room, chin high, head and shoulders perfectly straight. Hands folded demurely in her lap, she seemed to be listening intently as her younger sister played a miniature piano.

Just her luck. Jane *would* get a writer with insomnia.

James was seated in the next chair, also listening as Anne labored through the song. "Has your sister played the pianoforte for long?" he whispered.

"Oh, no, sir," Jane answered with a smile. "But she does desire to play well."

"Perhaps we shall be hearing you play?"

Now that would be interesting. Jane had tried the trumpet, French horn and clarinet before driving her junior-high band teacher to drink so heavily, he'd been fired by the school board. Well, maybe it hadn't *all* been her fault, but her lack of musical talent, combined with sheer determination not to let it stop her from wearing the cute red and white all-city band uniform, certainly hadn't helped.

"I am certain there are others much more accomplished," she heard herself say. "Your sister, perhaps?"

James's gaze became playful as he dropped his voice even further. "While my sister was blessed with a good heart, she was not blessed with a talent for music and can, in fact, only barely tolerate listening to it."

Violet's expression did appear pained. As Jane watched, the other woman laid a finger to the side of her head, her knuckle turning white from the pressure.

Enough was, apparently, enough. Jane rose and made her way to the pianoforte. Her sister stopped playing and looked up, fingers poised over the keys. "Anne, my dear sister," Jane said. "You have played so well for so long, I fear we can impose upon you no longer."

The girl made no attempt to hide her relief, dropping her hands to her lap with a plop.

"How fortunate we are to have heard you play, Anne," James added. "We are most appreciative."

Ever the generous hero.

"Thank you, sir," the girl murmured.

He turned his attention to Jane. "Though Anne must

surely have tired, I confess I have not yet heard enough. Perhaps you would play, Jane?"

"Oh, yes, please do." From another table, Mrs. Hathaway clapped her hands. "Our Jane is such a pleasure to hear," she said, lifting her voice in a not-so-subtle endorsement directed at James.

Violet was conspicuously silent on the subject, though she mustered a brave smile.

"Aunt, you flatter me. Surely someone else——?"

"Nonsense, Jane. Go on, then." The older woman clapped her hands. "Mr. Dempsey, now you shall see."

With a graceful arrangement of her skirts, Jane sat before the pianoforte. "I must confess that Anne has progressed more quickly than I had at the same age," she said with a gentle nod at her sister.

Anne ducked her chin. Whether in pleasure or embarrassment, Jane couldn't tell.

Her fingers moved of their own accord over the keys and the sounds she produced were light and pretty. Where had Mary been while Jane was in junior high? She could have been playing that trumpet in a red and white uniform, no problem.

Before long, James moved to stand beside her, turning the pages of her music. Without looking, she could feel him smiling down at the top of her head.

The author intended for them to marry. Jane knew it without a doubt. It was her fate, her destiny, in a time when women had few other choices. Of course, there could be worse things. James was handsome, pleasant. And money wouldn't be an issue, for once in her life.

But no TV here. She'd have to give up watching *Grey's Anatomy*, which could be a problem. No makeup, which meant the trick she'd just learned for making her green eyes really pop would be wasted. No jeans or sneakers.

No sweats. Only dresses that seemed to take half a day to get into properly.

Servants, though. Which meant no more housecleaning. Jane hated housecleaning with a passion. And there would be horses. She'd always wanted one. A grand, huge English home that was, yes, drafty and smelled of damp, but someday people would go through it on tours and imagine what it was like to live back when there was no TV, no cell, no . . . Hold on. *Someday?* Her inner voice screeched and rose to the top of the high ceiling, banging on the beams in a panic. *Someday?* If she went along with this, she would die before she was *born?*

Her fingers faltered over a note and stilled.

"Jane?" James asked from somewhere above her head. "Are you quite all right?"

"Yes, of course," she heard herself say to the keys. "My apologies, sir." For once, her chin wasn't held high.

No one in the room seemed to know what to do, least of all Jane. That stumble over the music. She could have sworn—Could it be? Had she broken through the author's control and caused something else to happen? The thought caused her heart to skip a beat. She needed the author in control. *Somebody* had to be.

A small cough from the other side of the room. A nervous tap of a shoe against the floor. They all waited.

And then Jane's head rose. Her fingers began playing music again, this time with what seemed a determined perfection. At the conclusion of the piece, she let her hands drop back into her lap.

"Brava," James said with enthusiasm. "You do this humble house honor, Miss Ellingson."

"It is I who am honored, kind sir. What an exquisite instrument."

This was a big moment. Jane could feel it in the way her body tensed as she met James Dempsey's gaze of adoration, in the smile that stretched across her face, in the shy dip of her chin.

He took her hand, gently brushing it with his lips. As he bent before her, she noticed the part in his hair and wondered if he would go bald early in life. The amount of skin showing through seemed odd for someone with a full head of blond hair, but maybe he was a conscientious hair parter who wanted to make absolutely sure it stayed in place.

Oh. He had finished the kiss of her hand, drawing his head back up to lock his eyes on hers. They both froze for a few seconds and then Jane's perfect posture sagged once again.

James straightened. "She has released her pen."

Anne bolted from the room, no doubt glad to be done with adult company. The others left one by one, talking amongst themselves, their voices rising and falling. Jane would be next. She smiled brightly at James, who looked at her with a question in his eyes.

James. Her future . . . husband. "Yes?" she asked.

"Forgive me, but—" He shook his head.

"Go ahead." It took a conscious effort to keep from drumming her fingernails on the pianoforte. She had a search to conduct. A desperately important one.

"I am not certain that scene unfolded as our author would wish."

She blinked. His observation sounded ominous. "Why do you say that?"

"You stumbled over simple music."

Simple to *whom*? "It was a mistake."

"A mistake of inattention. Which does not assist our author." Clasping his hands behind his back, he paced back and forth, heels clicking. "Perhaps you need to put forth more of an effort."

Effort. As though it wasn't enough to travel a couple of

hundred years, give a decade or two, land within the pages of a story in progress *and* go along with it all. Her mouth opened and closed as she tried to take in his words. "She's the one writing what I say, what I do." Unless . . . Jane had more to do with things than she thought.

The winning smile spread across his face again and he lifted his chin in a way that said he knew it was one of his best features. "You are quite right, of course. And we are destined to be, are we not?"

Destined? Well, maybe. If you counted a fateful melt-down at Starbucks that produced a stone, a wish, a . . . She stepped away from him, letting her index finger trail along the pianoforte in the way she envisioned a sophisticated heroine might. "Our destiny is not our own." *Talk* about your 1940s movies. She tried to turn her voice husky, but ended up coughing, both hands spread on the musical instrument. So much for sophistication.

James let that one slide. "Indeed it is." In one swift motion he was by her side, taking her hand and again landing a courtly kiss on the back of her hand. "And we will help her to write more moments neither of us shall ever forget."

Unforgettable moments. Something to look forward to. She did a quick mental check. Not a lot of them in her life, so far. So it took effort. She could dig deep to find some. As long as Mary made sure she didn't do anything like . . . well, anything she had ever done in her life. "Yes. Never forget," she whispered.

With a broad wink, James strode across the room, every bit the relaxed and confident hero.

Leaving his heroine, a woman of no small insecurities, to reflect on the fact that he had referred to *more* unforgettable moments. The problem was, if she and James had already had any, she'd pretty much forgotten them.

That couldn't be good.

Chapter 5

Solace. Curran Dempsey had been right about it on two counts. One, Jane needed it, desperately, and two, the massive garden of Afton House offered just the place to find it.

She slowed her steps, letting her fingertips brush against stalks heavy with blossoms. The scent was an intoxicating mix of earth, sky and the sweet fragrance of flowers in full bloom. Color spilled from one row to another.

There could be worse places to be than an English garden at the height of its glory.

She tread lightly on the dirt path, skirts whispering against her ankles. She could almost hear the music that should be playing in the background. Violins. Or flutes. Something peaceful to counter the panic building from the place deep inside her where reason lived, where she knew she could not possibly be living in a world of someone else's imagination.

Or could she? That flower, the one that had just brushed against her skirt, was red. Vivid red. And the dirt was brown. She dug a toe into it until she hit rock-hard earth, then kicked it. Hard. There you go. If it wasn't real, it wouldn't hurt.

On the other hand, if it *was* real, then she was . . . This kind of thing could make someone crazy. Or, in her case, *more* crazy? This was—Not helping *anyone*.

Her gaze shot up, landing on manicured shrubs, on the sliver of sunlight shining down on the path ahead, shining on . . . a bulk of green dress, topped by pale skin and gray hair. Mrs. Hathaway, lying in wait, her hands folded across her middle.

Jane stopped, trying to reverse her steps. Too late.

"Oh, Jaaa-aane," the woman called, striding toward her. "A moment, if you please."

"I was just—" She motioned in the direction of the house.

"It is a matter of most importance," her "aunt" interrupted.

Hard to plead another pressing responsibility when everyone knew they were all only waiting for Mary to pick up her pen again. Jane smoothed her skirts with both hands. "Yes?"

The older woman walked quickly toward her, taking her arm to draw her to one side of the path. "My dear," she said, lowering her voice, "Mr. Dempsey is at once handsome and in possession of a good disposition, is he not?" Her face crinkled in pleasure.

"Handsome, yes. I'm not so sure about the disposition." The way she'd seen him scowl at James . . . Those dark brows, drawn together over eyes that flashed fire . . .

Mrs. Hathaway drew back. "He is so kind to his unfortunate sister. And at dinner, was he not entirely deferential to you?"

What? "Oh, *that* Mr. Dempsey."

A look of horror spread across Mrs. Hathaway's face. "*That* Mr. Dempsey? Surely you do not refer to the other, to the—the—"

"Brother," Jane finished helpfully. "Curran Dempsey."

Something flickered in the other woman's eyes long enough to give Jane a hint of more than a passing auntly interest. "He is not to be trusted, that one."

A villain who can't be trusted. Imagine that. Jane cleared her throat and agreed, "Of course not." She took a step away, hoping the woman would get the hint.

Instead, Mrs. Hathaway stepped forward to close the gap. "Any woman would be fortunate to find herself the object of Mr. James Dempsey's affection." Her hand closed on Jane's arm.

"I—suppose so." He seemed nice enough. "Isn't that the plan? I'm here because I'm supposed to marry James?" She, or whoever the *real* heroine was.

"And would he not be a splendid husband?"

"I don't really—"

"But he cannot ask you without first writing your father. Has he done so?" hissed Mrs. Hathaway, fingers tightening their grip.

"I wouldn't know." Jane drew her arm up, hoping to wrest it away without a fight. No luck.

"Well, then." The other woman nodded sagely. "Our author shall make it happen. Of that I have no doubt." Her eyes narrowed as she peered into Jane's face. "Perhaps, my dear, a little more . . . effort from you would help the situation."

The *second* person to accuse her of not putting out enough *effort*? "I am doing my best," she assured Mrs. Hathaway. Geez, even when you have coordination, manners, grace, all the right things to say . . . Everyone's a critic.

The hold on her arm released and the other woman gave her a pat, smoothing her sleeve. "Indeed you must be," she said. "For anyone would be utterly grateful to have the attentions of such a man." She winked and added with a whisper, "Not to mention the fortune." A titter behind a pudgy hand.

Grateful. Well, she could probably work up to that. She was at least grateful to be out of Seattle. Here, where no one knew what a failure she was. And thanks to Mary Bellingham, they'd never have to find out.

Jane tipped her head, watching Mrs. Hathaway's skirts swish with purpose as she walked away. Other than looking out for her niece, what interest did the woman have in the whole marriage situation? Something seemed the slightest bit suspicious here.

"Hello!"

The girlish voice startled Jane into tumbling backward on the grass, fabric tangling around her legs. She looked up to see a rosy-cheeked Anne grinning down at her.

Jane extended her hand to be helped up. "Hello."

Anne took it and pulled, but at the last minute, Jane stumbled, pulling both of them back down onto the grass. "Oh!" Anne said as her bottom hit the ground. She gave Jane a surprised look.

"Sorry," Jane apologized. "I tend to do things like that." Damn. Even here. She only got relief from her klutziness when Mary Bellingham took the reins. Or pen. Whatever.

Anne relaxed visibly at that, allowing herself to laugh. Jane joined her. It felt good.

The girl's laugh subsided. "You have been here in the gardens for some time. What is it you are doing?"

If I only knew. Jane opened her mouth to reply and then realized Anne was looking pointedly at her soiled skirts and hands. "I . . ." She pulled her lips in tight and shook her head. "Lost something out here. Something I need to find."

"I myself frequently lose things." The girl nodded agreeably. "May I help?"

Jane didn't answer for a minute, instead fingering her skirts. She could use all the help she could get, but how many people could she trust with knowledge of the stone, her one and only ticket home? "That's . . . um . . . very nice of you," she said, stalling for time. Then she looked Anne straight in the eyes, changing the subject. "How old are you?"

"Fifteen."

An early teen who would, in the twenty-first century, be hanging out at the mall, counting the days until she could get a driver's license and flirting with clueless boys. But in this time period, she was likely already on the marriage market. She decided to go straight to the point. "Are you here for a husband?"

Anne made a face. "I have proclaimed myself quite unready for such things." Her chin bobbed in defiance. "You, dear sister, are the one in need of a husband."

In *need* of one? Not exactly. All she needed was a clean start, a roadmap for managing a calm, regular life. Jane rubbed a stalk of grass between her fingers. "How did announcing yourself not ready to get married go over?" she asked.

The girl shot her a quizzical look. "Our father, as well you know, is not of the same opinion."

"But you're too young. You have forever to get married. After you figure out who you are." Not that Jane had that quite figured out yet at the age of twenty-six, but that wasn't the point. And when had she started sounding like her mother?

"That is not what you said to him directly before we left for this place."

A half-smile toward her sister. "Well, maybe it's what I think now."

"Truly?"

Her tentative smile turned into a full grin. "Truly."

"Miss Bellingham may not make it so."

Ah, yes. The pen-wielder. "Does she have someone in mind for you, do you think?"

She made another face, this time the one of a petulant ten-year-old. "I can only hope she does not. I would far better concern myself with"—she stopped, tipping her face to the sky—"other pursuits." A mischievous grin spread across her face.

An enraged cry broke through the quiet. "Anne Gertrude Ellingson!"

Anne scrambled to her feet. "That will be Aunt Hathaway."

"Answer me at once!" The voice drew closer.

"What's going on?" asked Jane.

An unmistakable gleam appeared in her sister's eyes, along with another giggle, barely contained this time. "A question best left unasked." And then she took off running, in the opposite direction from the voice.

Jane watched the teenaged figure grow smaller, feet flying beneath her long skirts, until she disappeared around the side of a building. Slowly, Jane climbed to her feet, awaiting the arrival of her aunt, whose face had turned alarming shades of red.

"That girl!" she huffed. "Where is she?"

"Not here."

Mrs. Hathaway's eyes all but disappeared in her furious face. "It is beyond belief. This time, she has gone too far. Really she has." She pulled in great gulps of air, dropping her head and pressing her hands to her knees in a very unladylike stance for the 1800s.

This time? "What did she do?"

"She has put salt. *Salt* in the puddings." The horror of the deed was etched on the woman's forehead.

Jane drew her brows together, trying to understand. "That doesn't sound too bad—"

Mrs. Hathaway's palms rose heavenward. "How can you say such a thing? When our hosts find out, as they are very likely doing even now as we speak, whatever will they think of us?" One hand closed into a fist. "I must find that Anne. I myself told my brother, your father, that she should not be allowed to accompany us here, but he insisted."

"He was hoping she would find a husband, even though she's way too young."

Mrs. Hathaway drew herself up straight and made a *humph* sound. "There is entirely too much questioning of your parents' wisdom that goes on in that household, I always say. Too much entirely." She put a handkerchief to her nose and gave a loud sniff.

So *she* could question her brother, but Jane, his own daughter, strange as *that* sounded, could not. "Do you have children, Mrs. Hathaway?"

"You well know that your uncle and I were never so blessed." Her attention turned back to the situation at hand. "Although at this very moment, I find myself quite glad of it."

Now hold on. Accidents happen and this one might not even have been Anne's. A familiar feeling of injustice tightened in Jane's stomach. "How do you know Anne was anywhere near the kitchen? Maybe the cook picked up the wrong ingredient."

"Such insolence," her aunt bristled, dragging the last word into many syllables. "Anne was making herself a decided nuisance in the kitchen, babbling on to Cook as though she had been brought up with neither manners nor sense." Her eyes darted in one direction and then the next. "Now that we have stood here conversing to no good result, she is likely far from my reach. I shall remove myself to the house, with the hope that our hosts will be so kind as to overlook an indiscretion by a very silly girl." She turned with a flounce. "With no ill effects cast upon her older sister."

Jane remembered the mischievous gleam in her sister's eye. Anne had known exactly why Mrs. Hathaway was calling for her. So much for the unjustly accused. "As you said, Mr. Dempsey is a gentleman," Jane called after her. "A gentleman wouldn't hold something like this against a fifteen-year-old girl."

No response. Jane watched the bouncing cap grow smaller, not sure she believed what she'd just said. Red wine on a wedding dress was bad, really bad, but it was an accident. Salt in the pudding was sabotage.

Big difference.

Jane had been at her search for only another few minutes when she felt the stiffening of her spine and lift of her chin that signaled Mary Bellingham was about to take the storyline for another spin. She'd barely had time to wonder where her feet would land next when she found out.

She stood outside the entrance to Afton House on what looked to be a warm afternoon, with a gentle breeze tickling her hair and an open parasol in her hand, shading her from the sun. Beside her, James Dempsey smiled and offered his arm. "Miss Ellingson, I am so pleased you agreed to accompany me on a stroll around the gardens. It is little enough time we have had to talk."

"Your gardens look to be very pleasant, sir," she heard herself say. She took his arm, laying only the tips of her fingers on his coat. "And the sun makes its appearance so infrequently, I find my spirits are quite raised by the sight."

He gave a small chuckle. "I would claim to have arranged for its presence today, but fear you would not believe me."

"Indeed not." There was good-natured reproof in her tone.

They walked several feet in silence, Jane hoping Mary would let her drop her gaze to the ground to continue the search for the stone. She didn't. Apparently, Jane was to keep her chin up in this scene, with frequent adoring glances in James's direction. So instead, she drank in the smell of sun-drenched flowers, grass and . . . *eew* . . . something else. Horses. And what horses left behind.

"Are you enjoying your stay, Miss Ellingson?"

Could this author not write anything else? Afton House was not a hotel, taking a guest survey. A compliment on her dress, which, by the way, was a beautiful shade of mint green, would be a great conversation-starter, or maybe he could ask her a question about her interests. She hoped she was allowed to have some. "I am very much enjoying it," she said. "My family was most pleased by the invitation to visit Afton House."

"Pity your father could not come. And your mother."

"Yes. But my father's business occupies most of his time and my mother's health is so fragile, the doctor would not allow her to make the journey."

"But your aunt, Mrs. Hathaway, has come and your sister, who is an enchanting child."

Really? The salt incident was forgiven? Or maybe Mary Bellingham didn't know anything about it . . .

"And you, Miss Ellingson. You are here." He stopped and turned to her, gazing into her eyes. This was the part where, she was sure, she was supposed to fall madly in love with him or *at least* in serious like.

She dropped her hand from his arm. Waiting.

He reached down and lifted it to his lips, landing a soft kiss on her glove. "Miss Ellingson. Or, may I call you Jane?" His smile had a certain cockiness to it, an understanding that he would not be denied, that no one could turn him down for anything.

"Of course, Mr. Dempsey," she murmured. Mr. Dempsey? Did the first name thing only go one way?

"And you must call me James," he pronounced. "I will have it no other way."

"Then I shall call you . . . James." At this rate, it would take them three years to get to the first kiss. Wait. Was that—? *Mary! Pay attention and get that piece of bread out of his teeth.*

He turned and began to walk again, tucking her hand firmly into the crook of his arm. Must be what happened in this culture when you moved to calling each other by first names.

"My mother had these flowers planted," he said with a sweep of his hand. "They were her favorites. In the first days of her illness, before she became confined to her bed, I used to take her strolling by them once a day. 'Please, James,' she would say to me. 'So that I may breathe their scent. So that it may be the last thing I think of before sleep overtakes me.'"

Sleep in the every-night sense or the forever sense? The thought of James walking his dying mother by her flowers didn't do a lot for Jane, romantically speaking. She supposed it might be intended to make her appreciate his compassionate side, but really, he took his mother for a walk once a day? It wasn't a lot to ask, since he didn't seem to occupy his day with a whole lot else.

But instead, she said, "It was very kind of you, sir. If I had planted these beautiful flowers, I should also long to be near them. And to walk by them guided by a strong and willing arm." She felt the heat rise in her cheeks.

"Why, Miss Elling—No. Jane." There was a teasing note to his tone. "You blush. Fearing that you have made too bold a remark. When, in fact, you honor me with your observation."

"It is good of you, sir." She glided on, the heat fading from her cheeks. If it took years to get to the first kiss, when would Mary let them sleep together? Would she have to tell James how "kind" he was as he undressed her? Because if her character blushed at being bold enough to mention his strong arm, things weren't looking good in the area of unbridled passion.

After a few more moments of silence, he said, "It was good of Mr. Hathaway to suggest an introduction to your family. He and my father have known each other some time now."

"My uncle is a gentleman with many business acquaintances, in London and beyond."

"Now Jane, do not trifle with me. He has not arranged for other introductions, has he? If so, you must confess it at once."

Her head turned to him in a flash. "No, sir!" Then she breathed a sigh of relief when she saw the repeat performance of a twinkle in his eye. He really did have nice eyes, with sort of a we're-both-in-on-this-joke way of looking at her. "You tease me." Her chin lifted.

He stopped, placing both of his hands on her arms and turning her to him. "Jane."

She felt her intake of breath. This was it. The moment when James would kiss her. When she would feel what it was like to be someone a man coveted, wanted for his own. To be doing things the right way, for once. To have the prospect of a happily-ever-after life dangling straight in front of her. For the taking.

To deserve it. For once.

"James," she answered, in a whisper so faint, the name barely escaped her lips.

He was holding her hands now, pressing them hard

with his own. What, exactly, was the thing with gloves? Her hands couldn't be trusted in the outdoor air on their own?

She let her breath escape, gazing intently at James. She hoped, really hoped, that Mary had done something about the bread in his teeth, but he didn't have his mouth open so that she could see. Here she was, waiting for her happily-ever-after in a dress frothing with lace, of the kind that a nineteenth-century Cinderella might wear. All she needed now was the coach and the four white horses. Wait. Were there four, or six? *Anyway*. She had the coach. And the horses. If only they were white. That would be so great for riding off into the distance, clip-clopping along in a romantic fairy tale.

Leaving behind everything in her life that hadn't worked right. For this, a guarantee at a problem-free life, where no one would know her as the one who had spilled copy machine toner all over herself the day of her first, and only, date with Kevin the dentist. Anyone who has ever put natural finish makeup over the semipermanent black smudges of toner would sympathize with the oddly tinged hue that had scared Kevin into making up a patient's emergency. It was as though she'd put eyeliner everywhere *but* her eyes.

Only she would do something like that. But now life seemed so simple. All she had to do was let someone else write her lines, her actions. No one, *ever*, would consciously have the toner debacle happen.

Back to James. There went his hand, up to her face, gently caressing it with his knuckles. He had nice hands. Slender, aristocratic fingers. He probably folded his clothes right away when he took them off. No heaps of pants, shirt and socks for James.

Any time now, she should feel . . . something. But while she was waiting to feel it, why exactly did this guy get to make a move on her out in the open when, according to her calculations, they'd met only a couple of days ago and this was Victorian England?

"I realize that I take liberty here, Jane," he breathed.

His breath smelled like lamb. Must have had it for lunch.

"Yet," he continued, "I confess that I feel a certain—"

A familiar voice cut through James's words. "Enjoying an afternoon stroll?"

She jumped without moving an inch, the sudden whirlpool in her stomach having nothing at all to do with Mary's pen.

Curran.

Chapter 6

James abruptly dropped his hand and Jane whirled toward Curran, her face flaming. He stood with his head to one side, one eyebrow raised in question. "Well?"

"What we choose to do with an afternoon is of no concern to you," said James. He refused to move or look at Curran, instead staring at a point in the distance.

Jane's knees sagged with relief at the sight of Curran. She had no idea why, since she really only wanted to smack the sarcasm right off his face. Not that she actually would, but she could think about doing it. That look on his face made her feel as though she were doing something wrong instead of patiently delivering the lines Mary Bellingham wrote for her. The woman was *writing* here, scratching that pen into paper until her fingers curled into a ball. Jane respected that. *Really* she did. "Please forgive me," she murmured. "I must return to—"

"Stay here, Jane," James instructed. "This coward has nothing to do with you or me."

"Coward, is it?" Curran asked, upper lip curling into a sneer.

"You heard me, sir."

"We will see about that," Curran thundered. "You and

I shall—" The last word choked off abruptly, hanging in the air among the three of them. He tried again, this time brandishing a fist. "Shall—" The fist raised, above his head. Then it dropped to his side.

James blinked.

Jane stared.

A bird twittered in the distance as Jane felt the invisible hand release its grip. Her shoulders dropped.

"Blast it all," muttered Curran.

"What's going on?" Jane ventured.

James raised a finger, signaling for silence.

A moment later, Jane's chin and shoulders lifted.

"We shall see about that," Curran again thundered, fist in the air.

It stayed in the air, while James, Jane and Curran himself looked at it. Another pause. Curran had an extremely masculine fist, Jane observed. Strong, thickish fingers that looked as though they'd pack one hell of a punch.

"We shall see about that," Curran shouted. This time, no fist. Instead, he took a step toward James. "You would be wise to watch yourself," he growled, "at every hour of the day and night. For I, sir, will not rest. And neither shall you."

"Gentlemen, please," Jane heard herself plead. Please what? Stop behaving like dogs circling each other?

They ignored her. "I should sooner hand over my entire estate," James said, fingers sweeping grandly to one side, "than to honor your ridiculous threats with reply." He turned to her. "Jane. Come. The gardens smell of something foul."

Jane, come? What was she, a dog? A pause and then the hold on her released.

James and Curran glared at each other for a moment and moved apart, Curran raking his hand through his hair. Jane's eyes darted to James, who had drawn his brows together. Whether in concentration or distress, she couldn't tell.

Curran's palms shot upward. He clenched his fists and turned on his heel. "I would warn him of a plan? To be *watching*?" Curran demanded of no one in particular as he strode away, boots tearing into the dirt. "I am no such fool." More muttered words were lost on the breeze as Jane gave up her impulse to follow him and turned back to James.

He repeated the sweeping gesture with his hand. Once. Twice. Watching his hand with what appeared to be bewilderment. At last, he looked up. "Effort, Jane," he said with a shake of his head. "It is all I ask of you."

Her jaw dropped. Then she recovered herself enough to say, "She writes everything I—We—"

"And we must assist her. Don't you understand?" His hands closed on her arms. "She struggles so."

She struggles? Has *she* been dropped into the plot of a book, almost two centuries in the past? No. Didn't think so.

James chucked her gently under the chin. "It does not come as easily to her as to her brother."

Her brother. She and Mary might have something in common. *Everything* came easily to Jane's brother. He had written the textbook on hogging all the really good genes before the younger sister came along. It was the only explanation for one superperfect child and one . . . well, Jane. From the same parents. "Tell me about Mary. What is she like?" she asked James.

"Come." He motioned with one hand and began walking in the direction of the house.

Come? She had just mustered a scathing, or at least very warm, response to being treated like a family pet when he began talking. "Miss Bellingham is the youngest of one son and four daughters. Her brother, Thomas

Bellingham, is a respected author who has enjoyed much success. Her three sisters have all married, with"— he paused, looking at a point in the distance—"some success. Mary, however, is quite plain of feature. A serious creature. Unusually timid."

Jane absorbed this picture, in the context of the mid-1800s. Mary probably spent a lot of time alone. "So she began to write."

He nodded. "There was speculation, for a time, that she might be a suitable vicar's wife," he remarked. "But the vicar discovered, to his dismay, that she did not possess a truly pious disposition."

"Really?" Jane liked her better already.

"Her parents were exceedingly disappointed. And, of course, concerned for her soul."

"Oh. Well. Of course." A pang of sympathy went through her. In the twenty-first century, with her less than pious disposition, Mary could have been producing reality shows, running for office, graduating from law school and setting up practice. In this century, she was a lonely spinster who could write only about the love she would likely never experience.

James tucked her hand into the crook of his arm. He glanced to one side, then the other, and dropped his voice. "There *was* another suitor, some years ago."

Jane dropped her own voice. "Gossip. That works." She pressed closer to him. "So what's the story?"

His expression turned uncomfortable and he let loose of her hand. "I do not engage in idle chatter."

"No. I—Right." She shook her head. "But it isn't idle if it's something helpful to know." Her words began to run together. "And it *would* be helpful. The more I know about her life, the better. I'm her heroine. The one she put here for a happy ending—"

"Which can only be accomplished with a suitable hero," he interjected, brightening.

"Uh . . . Yes." She gave a slow nod. "A romance would be a little pointless with only one person." Although she wasn't so sure James didn't think it was possible.

"Miss Bellingham does not author *romance*," he said with some disdain.

He'd crossed a line with that one. If Jane knew one thing, it was that the world would be a pretty bad place without romance, or at least the *hope* of it. The stack of romance novels next to Jane's bed attested to it. She stopped, putting her hands on either side of her corseted waist. "Exactly what do you think you're the hero of, James, if not a romance?" She was going to have to go out on a limb here and hope Mary wasn't writing a horror story.

He blinked, looking confused. "A work of fiction, of course."

"A work of fiction where the romance between—well, *us*—is the central part of the story, as I understand it."

"Yes. Well." He shifted from one foot to the other. "The struggle to claim a birthright is a compelling story, one that our author seeks to tell."

An action hero, that's what he longed to be. She was sure of it. "Do you see guns being fired here, James? Things blowing up?"

His expression turned hopeful. "The story is yet unfolding—"

"I don't *think* so. I think Mary Bellingham has something to prove. To the vicar, her parents, her brother. Whoever else is on her list. And she's going to prove it with a romantic story."

"Enough," announced James. "I shall not discuss the innermost details of Miss Bellingham's life any longer. She would not wish it to be so."

If James had the author's ear, Jane suspected he bent

it some lobbying for guns and action scenes. "How is it you know all about her?"

Now he looked at her as though she were a child who needed the most basic explanation. "I am," he said with a bow and a patient but relatively cheerful sigh, "the hero."

The house was huge and dark. A cavernous place with long, narrow hallways. Not the most welcoming of places, but Jane couldn't sit quietly in her room and wait for creative inspiration to strike Mary.

She still hadn't found the wishing stone, though she'd retraced what she thought was her every step. If she had enough time to think about that, she might succumb to a panic so intense that Mary would throw her straight out of the heroine role and into one playing a scullery maid. Or worse.

Her feet carried her along the long halls even before she'd given them permission. Her eyes watched for signs, for clues that the walls were made of paper or smoke, ready to blow away at a moment's notice. Her new life, her very existence was contained in the pages of a book. She felt like Alice in Wonderland. Or Marty McFly.

Something wasn't right. Or, it was more right than it ever had been. One thing for sure: everything was upside down.

She turned into a hall that led to another wing, her funny little boots making the only sound. Paintings lined the walls of this one, with elaborately framed depictions of men and women in formal poses. She stopped before one, her attention caught by the heart-shaped face and fragile mouth of a young woman in a sweeping white gown. Jane looked closer. The eyes that gazed back at her were gentle, tentative. As though their owner longed to be anywhere but sitting for this portrait. The hand that rested on a chair had the pinky finger extended out, stretching toward escape.

Had *she* ever roamed these halls? Wait. Had she actually ever lived or did she also exist only in Mary Bellingham's imagination? Jane pressed two fingers to her forehead and resumed walking.

"Out!" cried a voice from a room nearby.

Jane halted midstep. A door to her left opened and a woman emerged, carrying a tray. From behind her, a silver dish sailed through the air, hitting the wall with a clang. The woman didn't glance toward Jane as she hurried along in a click, click of shoes along the floor and disappeared around a corner.

A few seconds later, a quavering male voice added, "And do not return until I send for you."

By the time Jane reached the open door, she was walking on the balls of her feet, keeping her shoes silent. A quick intake of breath and she darted past the door, only to slip and have her feet come down so hard that she had to slam her hand against the wall to keep from sprawling across the floor.

At least she'd *tried* to pass by unnoticed.

"Who's there?" the voice demanded.

Two choices. She could run like hell down the hallway and hope that Mary took up her pen again very soon, or she could answer . . . and *then* run like hell down the hallway.

"Reveal yourself!" A coughing fit followed the command.

Jane took a cautious step backward, aiming her gaze to the left to see inside the room. A gray-haired man lay against snowy-white linens, nearly engulfed by an enormous bed. As she watched, more coughs wracked his body.

She raised her voice to ask, "Are you all right? Do you need a drink of water?"

Impatiently, he motioned toward a table with a pitcher

and a glass. After a brief hesitation, Jane made her way across the room. She handed him the glass and waited while he drank in noisy slurps, gripping the glass until his knuckles whitened.

When he had finished, he focused a faded blue gaze on her. "Well?" he asked.

"I—um . . . Hello?" She took the glass.

He heaved a wheezy, impatient sigh, laying veined hands on the covers. "Your manner of speech. Decidedly . . ."

"American."

"*Humph.*" He didn't look pleased. "Introduce yourself."

"I'm Jane Ellingson."

His chin dropped and, beginning at her toes, he looked her up and then down again. "Ah, yes. You have been presented to James."

Presented? As though she was Thanksgiving dinner? She could practically feel her backside turning a golden brown. "I've met him."

As his head sank back against the pillows, Jane regretted her cool tone. He looked bad, with deep shadows around his eyes and his skin deathly pale. Sympathy rippled through her. "How do you know James?"

He struggled to sit higher in the bed. "I am Benton Dempsey. James is my son."

The dying father. Wonder what it would be like to have an author decide you had to die to carry out a plotline. Now she really did feel sorry for him. "Can I do anything for you?"

A shake of his head. "I have had quite enough assistance for one day, thank you. That woman shall kill me yet, I swear it."

Jane followed the direction of his gaze, toward the broad wooden door. "Is she the one taking care of you?"

"If you choose to look upon it such." His exhale was labored. "It would be far more truthful to say she seeks to put me in my grave."

Jane chewed on her bottom lip, not sure how to answer.

"You believe she would have little to do to make it so." Another coughing fit. When he had finished, he looked up at her for confirmation.

Instead, she decided to change the subject. "This room is furnished beautifully," she said politely. With heavy brocade curtains and large pieces of dark, intricately carved furniture, it had a distinctly masculine air. The four-poster bed dominated most of the room and despite his obvious illness, Benton Dempsey gave the impression of holding court in it.

"Such things matter little when one is never again to leave the room." A smile flitted across his features. "It is perhaps fitting punishment, after all." He gestured with one hand. "Sit."

He didn't leave room for argument and, besides, it was hard to turn away from a provocative statement like that one. Jane dragged a chair to the bed and sat with a rustle of silk skirts, folding her hands in her lap. "Fitting punishment for what?"

His eyes fluttered shut. "The reckless indiscretions of youth." She watched as his mouth relaxed into what seemed to be a familiar hard line, then nearly jumped when his eyes opened and he added, "How do you find my son James? Is there a match to be made?"

How did she find him? Did it matter? She was hoping Mary knew best in this case. "James." She hesitated. "He's—I'm sure he's everything I should be looking for."

"That he is," Mr. Dempsey agreed. "Breeding will out."

"Breeding," she repeated.

"My wife, Lydia, came from a fine family. The Worthingtons. London born and bred. She was, however, frail for the demands of a country life." He shook his head, which brought on another coughing fit. When he had finished, he wiped his mouth with a small white towel and said, "Lydia was a most delicate creature."

"Was?" Jane ventured.

"She died some months ago." His mouth quivered.

"I'm sorry."

"I have instructed James that he is to take a wife with a sturdy constitution. One who will bear him many children."

Many children? A), Jane was not a womb machine to be offered up for marriage based on her ability to churn out children, *especially* in a time before birth control had been invented. B), she was pretty sure the bearing of children wasn't the subject of any normal conversation in Victorian England, let alone between two virtual strangers. And C)—

"How is your constitution?" Mr. Dempsey inquired.

"My *constitution* is just fine. But I'm not a horse. And I'm not up for auction to the highest bidder." She glared at him.

He did his best to glare back and then, to her surprise, broke out in wheezy laughter. "A horse," he chortled before going into another fit of coughing.

This time, it lasted long enough that she gave him a few careful thumps on the back and then raised the glass of water to his lips. "It's not that funny."

At last, the coughing stilled and he lay back against the pillows, the corners of his mouth turning up in an attempt at a smile. "You remind me of someone," he said.

"Hopefully someone you like."

The smile disappeared. "You would do well to mind that impudent tongue."

A tongue that either tied itself up in knots or ran off on its own and got her into trouble, *that* she had. But *impudent?* A new one. "This person I remind you of . . . Did she have an impudent tongue?"

He looked at her for a long moment. "It was long ago." His expression turned wistful until he realized the lapse and settled the creases of his mouth back into the hard line.

Jane dropped down to the chair, folding the yards of fabric under her. She looked at one wall, at the other and then behind her, fidgeting with her hands. Benton Dempsey didn't move. "Tell me about Curran," she asked.

"Kindly divulge why you wish to know."

She lifted a shoulder. "I'm curious. And you don't have much else to do."

A short, wheezy cough that could have hidden a chuckle. "You have not the slightest inclination to temper your words."

"One of my best qualities," she answered. But only a few seconds passed before she acknowledged, "Although some people think it's a fault."

"I venture to say your parents have quite despaired of you. How am I to trust you will make a suitable wife for my son James?"

Question of the day. She decided to ignore it. "We were talking about Curran?"

"Curran."

"Yes."

"Very well. Since you hold me captive in my own bedchamber."

"You called me in. I was walking down the hall. And I can *keep* walking down the hall."

Though his brow furrowed, Dempsey's expression didn't quite reach a frown this time. He looked away. "Curran has the Devil in him." His slight grunt didn't make it sound like an entirely bad thing.

"That part must have come from you."

He chortled. "Far from the truth, I fear. Though it would have served him well to have more of his father in him."

"It came from his mother?"

He was silent so long, Jane wasn't sure he'd heard her question.

At last he said, "She was filled with fire. With hair as black as the night and eyes to match."

Jane leaned forward in her chair, encouraging him to continue. After a few minutes he said, "Curran is possessed of the same foolish determination that drove her. And it drives him still. I have done my best to temper him, to entreat him to understand—"

"Understand what?" Jane prodded.

"That he has no claim. I am a generous man and brought him here to live when his mother died." Benton Dempsey's words gained momentum, like a train picking up speed. "Yet that has no bearing on the claim of his brother as the rightful heir to the estate. No claim whatsoever."

"Who is the oldest?"

His eyes narrowed. "Curran had reached one year at James's birth."

"What about Violet?"

Now he turned to look at Jane. "A spinster. Yet her brother will allow her to spend her days here."

"And will he also allow Curran to stay?"

The man's forehead creased. A deep, menacing V formed in his skin. "That is for James to determine," he barked.

"Because one was born to your wife and the other was not."

A fit of coughing consumed him. "Miss Ellingson," he said when it had gone, wiping his mouth again, "you may take your leave."

"You loved her," Jane pressed. "Curran's mother."

"I have fulfilled my vow to his mother, to allow her son to be raised at Afton House, despite the entirely justified objections of my wife." He slapped a shaky hand on the covers. "I owed it not to anyone, yet I gave that promise and suffered the consequences." With a heavy sigh, he added, "Curran must now seek his own fortunes."

"He's your son." The injustice shouldn't matter to her, but it did.

"Is it your custom, Miss Ellingson, to engage in such intimate conversation with all men you meet upon their deathbeds?"

"You don't look that close to Heaven to me. I can only hope I'm doing so well when I'm on *my* deathbed."

A grudging nod signaled his acceptance of the observation.

"So we've established that you love all your children."

"I have tired, Miss Ellingson. I implore you to take your leave."

"Not so fast." She was on a roll. "So why can't you tell them the estate needs to be split equally between James, Violet and Curran?"

"You know little of which you speak."

"But you *don't* speak. Not to them, anyway. About what needs to be done."

One hand flew upward. "Out!"

Probably a good idea. She might not duck as well as the maid. When she reached the door, she turned back to the figure on the bed. "I enjoyed meeting you."

A bony finger aimed straight at her. "You shall ensure you bring only honor to this family."

And then that tongue that seemed to get her into trouble at the worst of times tripped all over itself to say, "You're out of luck on that one. If I could ensure I'd bring only honor to *any* family, I wouldn't have wished myself here in the first place."

Chapter 7

When the author's hand next took over, Jane found herself sitting in the parlor with a china cup in her hand, lifting it to her mouth. In the next moment, she tasted strong tea.

"Oh, my dear Jane, all of the arrangements that have gone into planning for our visit," twittered Mrs. Hathaway. "I hear there is to be another lovely dinner party this evening. It is all so very exciting."

Jane lowered her cup. "Indeed," she murmured. "Violet must be quite near exhaustion, yet not a word of complaint crosses her lips. She is a devoted sister."

Her aunt looked to her left and her right, though there was no one else in the room, and leaned forward. "She is fortunate her brother will allow her to remain here," she said in a loud whisper.

"I am quite certain Mr. Dempsey would have it no other way." Jane watched herself set the cup down and fold her hands in her lap. Demurely. Sweetly. "He depends upon her."

"When he takes a wife, he will depend upon *her*," her aunt said with a firm nod. "Leaving the sister quite at odds. Were Mr. Dempsey to wed anyone with a selfish nature, Violet would find herself in a most precarious situation." She shook her head and then brightened. "But that is not likely, Jane, as we well know he is likely to write your father for permission any day now."

"Aunt Hathaway, I should not wish to presume such a thing. I do not know Mr. Dempsey's intentions." A big part of Jane inwardly sighed at the statement, wishing she'd taken this approach with Byron. If she had, he never would have tiptoed out of the apartment, shoes in hand, scared to death by her sudden proposal of marriage. *So,* she told herself, *pay attention. Mary Bellingham might know something here. I should not wish to presume such a thing. Repeat three times slowly.*

"Oh, Jane, you are a silly creature. The gentleman is devoted to you already," Mrs. Hathaway pronounced. "And I shall think nothing else, as . . . there is nothing else to think."

Aunt Hathaway brought a whole new meaning to the phrase "nothing else to think."

The door opened. Both women turned toward it to see James stride in with a flourish of his hand. "Good afternoon," he declared.

"Mr. Dempsey!" cried Mrs. Hathaway, as though he were a long-lost relative, instead of someone she'd just seen.

Jane felt a gentle smile curve at her lips.

"Mrs. Hathaway." He gave a bow and turned. "Jane." He said her name with a confidence that implied he expected a warm reception. It *was* his house. And he *was* her hero. She just wished she felt . . . well, *something.*

"I must attend to—That is, Miss Dempsey—" Mrs. Hathaway fluttered her hands as she rose from her chair. "I have only just been saying that I must find the child. So I shall take my leave of you now, Jane."

"Yes, Aunt." Hands folded in her lap, Jane shifted her gaze from the departing Mrs. Hathaway to James, who stood waiting, a smile on his face. The picture of nineteenth-century gentlemanliness. Everything a heroine could wish for.

She opened her mouth. Nothing came out.

James opened his mouth. Nothing.

He took a step toward her, mouth still open. Then a step back. And forward again.

Both of them froze. And then Jane felt the sense of release that signaled the writer had loosened her hold on them. She let her shoulders sag and her chin drop, looking up at James through her lashes.

He raked a hand through his blond hair. With a grimace, he paced back and forth before pulling to an abrupt stop in front of her. "You must surely know the cause of her distress."

Jane waited for clarity to arrive. When it failed to, she asked, "What?"

"She holds the pen in her trembling hand, without the strength to put it to paper. Because she does not feel from you what she must." He clasped his hands together in a plea. "A conviction that comes from here." He tapped his chest in the vicinity of his heart. "Effort, Jane. It is but little that she asks."

If she had to hear the E word again, she might just show people what she'd had for breakfast, all over this beautiful Victorian rug. Whatever, that is, she'd actually *had* for breakfast.

Scene after scene, she'd said the lines as written. Wearing a dress with skirts that could easily fit five children and probably a smallish adult under it. Sitting patiently. While *he* talked about her effort. Or lack of it.

She *wished* she could say something. Defend herself. But she couldn't. If she opened her mouth, let her own brain take over and insert a sentence here, it was sure to be the wrong one.

His hands shot into the air, imploring the heavens. Or at least, Mary Bellingham. "How am I to turn this situation to good? The burden most assuredly rests with me to do so." His gaze landed on her. Pointedly.

"I—can't do more."

"Perhaps . . ." He rubbed a finger along his chin, then shook his head. "No."

"No?"

"Yes, it is the very thing."

"What is the very thing?" Pretty soon she would need a guidebook.

"I must kiss you."

Jane was not one to dispute a hero's actions or intentions, given her own track record, but the romance part seemed to be seriously missing here. She struggled with how to respond, finally landing on, "Why?"

"Once we have kissed, your heart will most assuredly be engaged." Relief crossed his face. "Any hesitation will be gone."

She pondered that for a minute, wishing she had one tiny speck of that kind of self-confidence. He did set a certain level of expectation, though, and he'd better be able to live up to it. "But Mary isn't writing now and she did try to write a kiss earlier. Shouldn't we . . . you know, let her?"

"It must be done," he announced.

Nothing like ending up on someone's To-Do list. Jane rose. "I'm ready." She'd actually quite like to experience this kiss now, given the buildup.

His brow furrowed.

Okay. Back to demure. "I mean," she said, walking to him in a swish-swish of skirts, "please, sir. Kiss me." Her heartbeat skipped ahead, hoping James would land a knee-crumpling kiss on her that would send her right off a cliff in ecstasy, able to plunge into Mary's lines with a conviction that would infuse the story with fire and passion.

And no inappropriate lines or accidents that involved red wine or body parts.

His face softened. "Yes," he said, voice lowering as he gazed into her eyes. "You must leave it to me now, Jane, as I have had experience in these matters."

And she hadn't? Rolling around in bed with Byron until both of them glistened with sweat and the sheets had disengaged to wrap themselves around their two exhausted and spent bodies didn't count? Oh. She was Book Jane. Twenty-six and never been kissed. *Got it.*

She lifted her chin and whispered, "Yes, James."

He laid a hand on each side of her face, leaning in until his mouth hovered less than an inch from hers.

She closed her eyes and waited. For her future. For that cliff, for the parasail that would take her off its edge and into—

"Jane!"

The high-pitched female cry pierced the stillness of the room. Jane and James broke apart, James's hands slapping his sides and Jane's wrapping around her rib cage.

"Anne," she said at the sight of the girl.

"Oh!" Anne muffled her giggles. "Dear Sister, please forgive me. I knew only that you were in the parlor. Not that"—she looked at James, mirth dancing in her eyes, though her expression remained innocent—"Mr. Dempsey was here as well."

Behind Anne, Mrs. Hathaway burst into the room, clearly irritated. "There you are, you annoying creature," she said as though she had been searching for Anne instead of hiding behind the parlor door. "You must come with me at once."

"Aunt Hathaway, I seek my sister's advice on a matter of utmost importance." Anne's eyes were round with innocence.

"Nonsense, child. Can you not see that she and Mr. Dempsey are having a *conversation*?"

Once again, James's palms turned upward in a plea.

"Come, Anne." Mrs. Hathaway hustled the girl from the room, fingers clamped on her arm.

"Aunt! You need not pinch so!"

"Hush," the older woman hissed. Then she turned back toward James and Jane. "Pay us no heed," she squeaked over her shoulder.

James turned back to her, his embarrassment both boyish and appealing. "Well, Jane."

She waited. He made no move toward her. *What would Book Jane do?* "Um, sir . . ." she stammered.

"While I suppose we might make another attempt, it does appear as though the time is not ideal. Perhaps it is for the best that we allow Miss Bellingham to take charge of the matter."

She could think of all kinds of things to say, most of them involving the fact that her lips and emotions were not a "matter" to be dealt with, but if she said them, she could be sure only that her hero would be riding fast on his fiery steed in the other direction. Not worth the chance. So she remained silent.

Then he appeared to find his resolve. "We shall await Miss Bellingham's pen. When next we gather, she shall determine what is to be done." He flashed her an apologetic smile, accompanied by a wink.

So, Jane thought, her big moment. Never happened. Story of her life.

Wake up, Mary.

When it appeared clear Mary wouldn't be waking up right away, Jane left the parlor to wander through the main floor of the house and then outdoors. She found herself walking through the gardens yet again, craving the sense of peace and isolation they offered. If nothing else, she could retrace her steps for the fiftieth time, looking for the stone that represented her escape clause.

Not that she could imagine herself using it right away. What kind of a life did she have to go back to? Holly, her former friend, still wouldn't be speaking to her. The bride might even have to resort to a backup wedding dress. All because of Jane's inability to hold a glass upright.

The various organizations that had so enthusiastically supported Senator Alice Tate were probably blanketing the airwaves by now with calls for her immediate resignation. The rehab center director would be on TV, citing privacy laws and refusing to offer information, which would leave everything open to the reporters for speculation. There was a lot to speculate on.

And Byron. He'd be figuring out how not to call her. Ever again. *Marriage.* She had been an idiot to jump ahead like that. He would have come to it on his own. Eventually.

If only life were like a CD. Delete what was on it and burn a new one.

Nothing remotely like this would ever happen to her brother Troy. He led an orderly, organized life. No huge faux pas. No surprises. Thank God the family had Troy to make them proud. He'd be marrying his fiancée, Susan soon and they'd live happily in the suburbs with an obedient dog and 2.2 kids. If anyone could figure out how to have a .2 kid, it would be Troy, who'd scored A's in math all through school.

Things would also be a lot easier if she didn't actually *like* her brother and not just because he was family. He'd never held himself up as a pinnacle of correct living. He couldn't *help* doing things right. Any more than Jane could help messing them up.

She scanned the grass and dirt, searching once again for the stone. How could she ever have lost it? It seemed incomprehensible. Unless, of course, you considered that it was Jane. Tears stung her eyes. Too bad the stone hadn't been able to carry her back to the womb, letting her start again from scratch. At this late stage, her life might be considered beyond repair.

Gradually, she became aware of someone else beside her. As she glanced up, Curran said, "It appears the search for the elusive stone continues." His expression softened when he saw the moisture in her eyes.

Embarrassed, she brushed it away with the back of her hand. Then she straightened, meeting his eyes. His steady, dark gaze had a way of causing her stomach to fold over itself in anticipation. She pressed a hand against the area of her ribs, sealed off by the corset. "I haven't found it, yet."

"Unfortunate."

She nodded.

"May I offer my assistance?"

"Please."

He got down on his hands and knees, apparently caring little about the black pants he wore and the effects of the dirt and grass he was about to crawl in. Jane, who had been searching from an upright position, hesitated. Then she told him, "It's a little difficult for me to get down on the ground. I don't seem to be able to manage it very well." Her fingers itched to undo the dress and rip the corset right off. *Who* had invented a thing like this? No doubt a man—who, of course, didn't have to wear it.

Curran glanced up. "Ah, yes. Your clothing would make it such." He seemed unfazed that they were talking about the instrument of torture known as her corset. Points for Curran. "Perhaps if you were to tell me from above where to look?"

She gave him a relieved smile. "Teamwork. I like it."

He turned back to the task at hand. They worked in companionable silence for a few minutes, Jane inching along behind him and pointing out suspicious rocks. At one point, she moved too far too fast and her skirts covered his hands and nearly his head. Quickly, she drew back, hoping he didn't see how thrilling she found his nearness to her legs. He looked up, but didn't say anything.

After a few more minutes of silence, Curran asked, "How are you finding our author's tale?"

She pondered her answer for several seconds before she turned her gaze to the top of his head and said, "It may have a flaw or two."

His own eyes remained focused on the ground. "Ah," was all he said.

"What do you think of it?"

"It is her tale to author."

Oh, no. He didn't get to ask her and then not tell her what *he* thought. Carefully, she lowered herself, corset and all, until she could sit on the ground beside him without too much danger of toppling over. "If you really thought that, you wouldn't have asked for my opinion."

Curran halted his forward progress. "Perhaps."

"There isn't any perhaps about it. I know you were upset with the last scene between you and James. I got the distinct feeling that you wanted it to go very differently. And, oh, by the way, I've met your father."

He turned and sat back on the ground, gaze darkening as he rubbed his hands together, loosening the dirt. "My father."

"He's not all bad. Gruff. Demanding. Narrow-minded. But not all bad."

A shadow crossed Curran's face.

"He claims that all of your character traits come from

your mother, but now that I've met him, I think I actually see a lot of him in you."

He drew his brows together. "I disavow such an idea."

Disavow away, Jane thought. *Doesn't change that I saw a determination in Benton Dempsey, beaten down by illness though it was, that came pretty close to matching yours.* "Would it be such a bad thing?"

"You have made the acquaintance of my father." This time, he didn't sound quite so convincing about disavowing any connection.

The guy was fascinating. A brooding Heathcliff one minute, a complex Heath Ledger the next. "If you're not like him, then he must be right. You're like your mother. Can you tell me about her?" Jane asked.

His eyes turned unreadable. "Undeserving of the fate she received at his hands." Nothing unreadable about his terse, tight voice.

"Was he—Did he hurt her? Physically, I mean?" She pictured Curran as a toddler, watching the shadowy figure of a younger, healthier Benton Dempsey strike his mother. No wonder the illegitimate son would turn into a villain, seeking revenge.

Though Curran's eyes fixed on her, they didn't seem to see her. "She was young, little older than your sister Anne, when first he chanced upon her out walking." His words gathered speed, anger. "He bought her fine things. Things she could only dream of. And dangled them before her until she succumbed. Then he abandoned her. As her family had earlier."

Indignation stirred and rose within Jane. Too damn early for laws that prosecuted older men for preying on minors. Too bad, or Benton Dempsey would have been thrown in jail, where throwing a dish at someone wouldn't even be an option. "So you two had only each other."

"She was little more than a child herself when I was born."

Jane shook her head. A child raising a child. By herself, in a time without any social programs to help. "It must have been very hard for her."

"She died at his hands." His gaze had gone cold. Hard.

So she'd been right. That murderer, that scumbag, that—Just let her at him. She'd bring him his tea, all right, laced with something that would help to hasten the peaceful death Mary no doubt had planned for him. "Why wasn't he prosecuted?" she burst out. "He's just lying up there in his own bed, waiting to die."

"There was no prosecution to be made. The weapon was a subtle one, though a weapon all the same."

What? How do you subtly kill someone? Butter knife? "I don't understand."

"He abandoned her to the illness that claimed her life."

"He knew she was ill and didn't help?"

Curran nodded, mouth pulled tight and jaw muscles working. "His wealth could have afforded the services of a surgeon. Though it was beyond her means, the cost to him would have been a mere pittance. When at last he deigned to answer her pleas, it was too late."

She pictured Curran's mother lying in a rat-infested hole of a place, hungry child at her side. Knowing she was dying and that the one person who could help had refused. "I'm sorry." It seemed so little to say.

"I do not seek your sympathy."

"Then why did you tell me about it? I'm not the kind of person who could hear about this and *not* feel sorry for you. And your mother." She held his gaze. "I'm sure you have that much figured out."

He leaned forward, eyes boring into hers.

She'd said the wrong thing. Yet again.

"You have a most—" He drew out the words, but broke them off.

"Impudent tongue?" she finished for him. Then she looked away, clearing her throat while she tried to regain her composure. He shouldn't get that close to her. It did things to her. Things that . . . "It's not the first time I've heard that."

After a long moment, he said, "We shall resume the search." He got back on his hands and knees, brushing the ground with long, strong fingers.

At last, he seemed to feel her eyes on him. "What are the consequences," he asked the ground, "if this stone is not found?"

"I don't go home." A place she didn't want to be, but couldn't imagine living without.

He pulled himself to a standing position, extending his hand down to help her up. He wasn't asking, he was telling. She took his hand.

"Where is your home?"

"Not . . . here." She occupied herself with brushing dirt from her dress, unable to look up. If she did, he might see the fear she was certain stood naked in her eyes.

"And you want to return."

She exhaled sharply. "I don't want to *not* return." With a glance up at him, she added, "If that makes any sense at all." He didn't indicate one way or another. Instead, he seemed to be waiting for her to tell him more. She did, because there was something about his eyes, the way they looked at her, as though he *really* wanted to know. "I've sort of made a mess of things lately. All I wanted was to leave, go somewhere far away. Start again. But I didn't mean *this* far away. Without that stone, I don't have a choice. Do you know what I mean, what that feels like?" *Ohhh.* She herself might not have known exactly how it felt, until right this moment. It felt incredibly . . . frightening.

His hand reached forward, taking hers. The warmth of his roughly gentle skin on hers sent mini tidal waves washing over her and she swayed for a moment, losing her balance. He steadied her with his other hand, which didn't help her equilibrium any. "We shall find your stone."

"If we don't, Mary Bellingham may be stuck with me for good." A little hiccup gave away the fact that she wasn't doing well at trying to make light of the situation.

"Stuck with you."

She nodded.

"Then it appears as though we must ensure your future."

"No one can ensure the future. Life doesn't work that way."

"This is life as our author sees it."

"Right . . ." she said slowly, not at all sure it was right at all. "Then don't we have to wait to see what she . . . sees?"

He shook his head. "She is in need of our assistance."

"Mary is the one holding the pen. She writes the words. There isn't anything we get to assist with. I've found that much out."

"It is not an easy task, but with great concentration and determination, one may be able to guide her hand."

"Get her to write a scene differently?"

"Indeed."

"I can't! Trust me. No one wants *me* to get involved in this."

"Miss Bellingham knows little of what she writes."

Jane shook her head. "She's living in this time. Writing the lines. She knows."

"Have you that opinion as you speak the words? Her words?"

"I . . . Sure." The very best thing was the way she moved, with grace and coordination, as though she'd never been the person who socked her college's star basketball player in the eye while doing an enthusiastic cheer in the final seconds of a tied game. Yes, she'd decided to add the backflip that took her across the line, but she'd only been trying to get the crowd really worked up. Turned out the guy couldn't make the winning free throw with one eye nearly shut. Even the college president had blamed her.

Mary Bellingham would never write a heroine like that, so the woman had to be doing something right.

"She seems to be of the opinion that I would share my plans for James's downfall with James, which is nothing less than foolhardy."

That one, she had to agree, seemed a little suspect. "Not the way a true villain would go about it."

"And has my younger brother claimed your affections, as yet?"

"It's very early in the story," Jane protested.

"Does she not appear to be having trouble with that endeavor?"

"Some, maybe. Well . . . Yes. I suppose." She straightened. "But it isn't as though I have any room to criticize."

He took a step toward her, looking down, his face only inches from hers. There went that racing heartbeat again and her nose started to get in on the game, sniffing without remorse the erotic scents of woods, soap and horses that emanated from him. "If she is unsuccessful in completing this story," he said, "you and I, as well as all manner of people in this tale, shall find ourselves forever relegated to an uncertain fate."

His British accent made even that sound like not an entirely bad thing. "An uncertain fate," she repeated. What the hell did that mean?

As if he knew what she was thinking, he said, "If the story ends well, we go on, permanently ensconced in our lives. If not . . ."

"If not?" This didn't sound good. At all.

"The author may abandon the tale altogether."

Abandon. Jane Ellingson, from Seattle, Washington, in a state of forever limbo. Cast adrift in a sea of floating, meaningless words, never to be seen again.

How could a trip to Starbucks turn out like *this*?

Chapter 8

An unfinished state. It sounded like a zombie movie. The thought of all of them—Curran, James, Mrs. Hathaway, even Anne, roaming space or even the Earth as the walking dead, albeit in lovely nineteenth-century costuming—zapped into her mind. She shivered in the warm afternoon air.

Without the stone, she would end up in a state of literary limbo. Possibly tossed from one story to another, in search of a home. Oh, God. What if she ended up in a Stephen King novel? The covers alone scared her. Or she could be suspended in a sort of *Afton House* purgatory, with the words floating over her head and slapping her in the face once in a while.

"Others in the same circumstance have met a worse fate," Curran said.

"What could possibly be worse than that?" It would be like always seeing only half the movie or reading half the book, forever left to wonder what had happened.

"The hearth."

Hearth? Hold on a minute. Translate that to *fireplace*. "You're telling me an author would throw the pages in the fire? How *could* she?"

"It happened such to three prior tales she sought to write."

"No," Jane breathed. "She just—?" Making a tossing motion with one hand, she finished, "Tossed the whole thing into the fire?"

His nod was abrupt, but there was no mistaking the meaning.

"I can't believe it. What happens to the characters—the *people?* She makes them up, gives them a life and then takes it away, just like *that?*" Jane snapped her fingers. "Can't even be bothered to see it through, work things out. No." She began walking, back and forth, her feet making soft thuds on the grass. "Has to take the easy way. Boom. Into the fire. Done with that one! On to the next. Is that what you're telling me she did?"

"I cannot imagine it was easy for her."

"No? She did it, though, and in the end, that's what matters." Her pacing picked up momentum. "We have to do something. We can't let that happen again. Not to us. Not to the others. No one deserves that, including the author." Her voice rose. "She only wants to write a good book. There's nothing wrong with that."

"Precisely."

"We have to help her." She slapped the fingers of one hand against the other's palm. "*Effort,* Curran. That's what we need."

"Pray tell me more." His voice was dry. Amusement danced in his eyes.

Yes, well, it had been his idea in the first place, but now that she was onboard, things were going to happen. They weren't always *good* things, but faced with a situation like this, what choice was there? She jammed her hands on her hips, thinking. "She's never been a villain, so she doesn't know anything about being one. You'll have to help her with that."

"So it comes to me, does it?"

"Think, Curran, *think*," she implored him.

"Indeed, I have been doing little else these last hours. And I find it quite the pleasure that you would deign to join me."

The amusement in his eyes had turned to downright hilarity. So glad he found it funny to be one Little League toss away from a fiery death by author. She took a deep breath in and out while thumping her index finger on her forehead. "I know," she said, snapping her fingers. "We'll write it down."

One eyebrow rose.

"We'll figure out things that could happen and write them on paper that we place in the room. In big letters, so that Mary can't miss them."

"Miss Bellingham determines what room we are to be in and what is to be in the room, well before we begin."

He had a point. Damn. She hated when that happened. "So . . . Plan B, then."

"I do not—"

"Understand. I know. It's . . . you know, an American term."

"Perhaps if one were to—"

"Write it down *while* we're in character . . . No." She shook her head. "That would involve finding pen and ink and Mary would have to have that right there . . ."

Curran also shook his head. "If, however, one were to . . ." He pointed at his head.

She squinted up at him. "Use his head to . . . ? Oh!" Clasping her hands together, she said, "To concentrate. Hard enough that the words don't just come rolling out the way Mary wants them to."

"It may well be impossible." Curran lifted his shoulder.

"But we have to try. I think I almost may have done it when she had me playing the pianoforte. My attention wandered and I stumbled over the notes." She nodded with the energy of a bobblehead doll. "Did it once and I can do it again. And so can you. You're going to help steer her in a villainous direction and I am going to show her what romantic means."

"Romantic?"

"She has James telling me about walking his mother by her favorite flowers. That's very sweet, but it doesn't stir anything in me, if you know what I mean?"

He looked as though he did. She made a mental note to mull that over later and went on. "She has had him ask me, a couple of times, if my accommodations are comfortable. No compliments on my dress, my eyes, *whatever*. No moonlight rendezvous. No stolen kisses . . . Well, there was *almost* one, but Mary wasn't writing it." Her hands moved up and down, punctuating her words.

"A nearly stolen kiss?"

"It didn't happen." She brushed that aside. "James thinks he has lots of experience, but his experience is, in the truest sense of the word, coming from Mary and she doesn't have much. We've already established that. So she's trying to *imagine* what it would be like."

"You, however—"

"*Have* had experience with dating and with love." She paused, with a small sigh, to give that word the weight it deserved. "So I could help. Without actually doing anything that might, you know, not go as . . . expected." She bobbed her head again, hoping he wouldn't ask what she meant by that. "To do this, we're going to have to get James to cooperate."

"A request you will make."

"Oh. Of course." She nodded. "Absolutely right. I'll talk to him. He'll have to understand that it's in his best interest, too." Relief flooded over her. She could help the author, make sure this story went well, that everyone got their happy ending, and still have the grace and coordination of Book Jane. "I'm glad we talked about this." Impulsively, she threw her arms around Curran's neck, her senses assaulted by his clean, woodsy scent, the feel of his whiskers against her cheek and the rumbling sound of surprise he made in her ear. Talk about stirring things. Things that hadn't been stirred in what felt like a long time were waking up and jumping right into the Mixmaster.

She let go of him, suddenly awkward with her hands, which seemed not to know what to do. Finally, she grasped them hard behind her back to keep them out of trouble.

His face hardened and then he looked away, refusing to meet her eyes. "Madam," he said, "you would do well not to place your trust in me."

A tiny part of her melted at his gentlemanly attempt to put distance between them. "I won't," she said, not meaning it at all. A girl had to like a villain who would take the extra step to warn you away from him. "I was thinking the same thing." Which she wasn't, but he didn't have to know that.

"Very well," he said with a formal half bow. "Then we shall see where the course of the tale next takes us."

Or where *we* take *it,* Jane thought. But as quickly as the resolve appeared, a familiar sense of dread began to steal over her. Every time she took matters into her own hands, they ended up going unimaginably wrong. The trick would be steering Mary's story while letting the author continue to keep a tight hold on the reins.

Sure. No problem. I have such a great track record with tricky situations.

Curran strolled through the garden after Jane made her exit to Afton House, his eyes upon the ground, still searching for the elusive stone. Moments later, he realized he was not, however, searching with either attention or resolve.

Instead, he saw green eyes before him, eyes that were as compassionate in one moment as they were sparking fire the next. Full breasts straining at the constraints of her dress. Hair that became appealingly mussed, as though its owner cared little that it be tamed into submission. A pink bow of a mouth that looked as though it would stand up to a man's, causing him to quite lose his head.

And he must have lost his, to even be thinking of her such. She was, after all, the heroine of the story, intended for his brother. The villain could be with such a woman under only the most vile of circumstances. And he was, perhaps unfortunately, a villain too honorable to entertain such an idea.

He clasped his hands behind his back, head bent. Jane Ellingson had an irreverent manner of speaking, of voicing thoughts he believed existed only in his own head. She seemed to hold nothing back nor have any regret afterward.

It was not Mary's intent to create such a heroine, that he knew. He had had the distinct impression that, had he not been there, Jane might have undone her dress to rip that confining corset right off and fling herself to the ground to search for her stone.

The idea had nearly undone him as well.

Possibly he should find such character traits deplorable, exhausting. Or frustrating, as he suspected James did. Yet he found them quite the opposite.

He sighed. A passing fancy was all it amounted to. And pass it would. He'd ensure it.

Jane opened her eyes to find herself standing before the entrance to Afton House, dressed in a matching

cloak, gloves and hat. Beside her stood James, looking
every inch the picture of the well-dressed man in a tall
hat, finely tailored pants, white shirt and jacket.

"I am so pleased, Jane, that you are accompanying me
on a carriage ride," he said. "I am anxious to show you
more of our grounds, which are a thing of beauty this
time of year."

She heard herself say, "Oh, yes. I quite like the outdoors," at the same time as she was thinking, *You could
have told me I was a thing of beauty*. She had to figure out
how to get the message to Mary. How to do what Jane
and Curran had decided must be done.

"I knew it," he beamed. "As soon as I laid eyes upon
you. And fond of horses, are you?"

Was she? "Indeed, sir. I have favored that fine animal
since I was but a child." Good to know. *Real* Jane had
never set foot in a stirrup.

"I am proud to say that we possess the most lauded stables in all the county," he said, casting a modest eye
downward. "You must give me your opinion and I shall
hope it to be the same."

"I would be most pleased to do so and am eager to
make the acquaintance of your horses."

"Make the acquaintance," he sputtered. "Of my horses.
Oh, Jane, you are a funny thing. I confess it gives me
pleasure to be in your company. Think of it. Horses as acquaintances to be made."

"Do you not think so, sir? Have you never engaged in
conversation with a horse?"

"Why, only look at you!" he cried. "The very sparkle in
your eyes at the idea. Now, Jane, I'll tell you I do have a
favorite steed. And upon occasion, I have chanced to say
a few words to him. So there you are."

Her lashes swept down and then up. "I can only

suspect, sir," she said, "that he is as honored by your attentions as am I."

James's answering smile bathed her in warmth. "It is I who am honored, Jane, to spend time in your company." He extended his gray-clad arm. "Shall we be off?"

She took his arm. After a somewhat rough beginning, this scene seemed to be going a little better, Jane decided. Mary was at least allowing them some light flirtation.

With a great show of courtliness, James helped her into the open carriage. Every movement she made felt graceful, confident and not at all inclined to trip and fall. In this moment, it was good to be Jane.

Once they had both settled into the leather seat, James took charge of the reins and with a small jolt, the carriage set off down the dirt road, the horses making a steady clip-clop sound that resounded through the still-ness of the afternoon air. Jane checked her cap but found it firmly tied in place. It wasn't going anywhere.

They rode along, with James the one to carry the conversation. When Jane was allowed to contribute, it was to murmur an impressed "Oh" at the different sights he pointed out, though all she really saw was land. Lots of it. With trees and rolling hillsides that often had the carriage listing to one side or the other. They were sitting far enough apart, though, that their legs didn't end up touching. Too bad. They needed a really good pothole or something, to send her sailing right onto James's lap.

Mary must think it best for a woman to be seen and not heard. To sit carefully smoothing her skirts and brushing tendrils of hair from her eyes, while managing to look admiring all at the same time. Easy job.

And damned ineffective, if you asked Real Jane.

James pointed out a spot to her left. When she turned to look, she was caught by the sheer beauty of it, a bank of lush green grass along a small lake of deep blue water.

Two large trees bent toward each other, beckoning an invitation to an area that looked perfect for a lazy picnic, a game of tag, a . . . romantic interlude. It was the prettiest sight she'd seen so far.

Mary *couldn't* miss this opportunity. Really. She couldn't.

She felt the expected "Oh" comment bubbling in the back of her throat. Before she even realized what she intended to do, she fought to suppress it, to keep it from making it out of her mouth. *Not this time, Mary. Trust me. I have a better idea. Stay with me, Mare.*

It wasn't easy, fighting with her mouth for control, but she was determined. In the end, she could manage only one word and it emerged in a shout. "Stop!"

"Why, Jane, whatever is the matter?" With a jerk of his wrists, James halted the horses.

"It's . . . It's . . ." *Damn, Mary. Let go for a minute.* "Such a lovely spot. *May . . . we . . .* stop?" Though she could feel herself outwardly remaining calm, with only the barest of smiles tickling at her mouth, inwardly she gulped huge amounts of breath at the effort.

James looked concerned. "It is your wish?"

She concentrated. "Yes."

"It is a place I am myself quite fond of. I should be only too glad to show it to you." He dropped the reins and stepped out of the carriage, coming around to the other side to help her. She placed her hand in his, keeping firmly in check the triumph she felt at getting through to the author.

Once on the ground, James strode and Jane glided toward the spot on the edges of the lake. The branches of the trees bent, she noticed, in a shape that looked very much like a heart. *How* could Mary have missed this? It was a wonderful day, overcast and mild, with a hint of moisture in the air. As they came closer to the water, she could hear its gentle ripples, feel the peacefulness that seemed to dwell on the shore.

Okay. They were here. Now what would Mary do?

She slowed her steps and stopped, reaching down to brush her fingertips against the petals of yellow flowers growing wild among the grasses. Carefully, she broke the stem of one and lifted it to her nose, inhaling the soft, subtle scent. James also stopped, beside her. She looked up at him from beneath her lashes.

He stood, watching the water, one leg in front of the other, hand on his hip. His chin lifted, showing his classic profile to its best advantage. A high forehead, long, sculpted nose, mouth with just the right amount of fullness.

Everything she should want. More than she should ask for. All this and coordination, too. How could she go wrong?

As Mary kept her standing, silent, Jane did an internal check of her pulse. Normal. She checked for goose bumps. Missing. Nary a bump, goose or otherwise, to be found.

Time to push the issue.

She worked to form a single word on her tongue, which seemed to have found new muscle strength. At last, she freed it. "James," she burst out.

"Yes?" He turned to look at her.

Intense concentration. More tongue gyrations. "I feel a . . . chill." Too bad this much exercise didn't work off any calories.

One brow lifted. "Indeed?"

So, okay, the day was pleasant, with no cold front moving in. Still, he didn't have to look as though he didn't believe her. Then, as she watched, trying to drag some sort of meaningful signal into her eyes, she saw the gentleman in him take over. "You must allow me to offer my jacket." He shrugged his arms out of the sleeves. "I

shall lay it over your . . . cloak." He did, but with less certainty than she would have liked.

She sucked in a breath. This next suggestion was going
to take all she had. "Perhaps," she said, "your arm, placed
around my shoulders, would better serve to warm . . ."
She focused her energy on her left foot, managing to
make it take a step toward him, though that meant she
dragged the more reluctant right foot behind it like a
deadened limb. Probably not the most romantic picture.

Wow. Mary was *strong*.

Alarm crossed James's face. "Jane," was all he managed to say before the invisible hand released and the
shoulders of both of them sagged. Neither said anything
for a couple of minutes, following that unspoken pact
that meant they waited, quietly, until the author chose to
again pick up her pen.

Then James raised his palms, pivoting on his heel. "Are
my affections to be challenged in such a manner?" he implored. "This cannot be." He faced her once again, directing a question at her with no small degree of horror.
"Are you, Miss Ellingson, now shown to be a—a *cripple?*"

She laughed. Couldn't help it. Tried, but she couldn't
help it. His reaction was so over-the-top ridiculous, how
could anyone take him seriously?

Oh. Mary did. And the anger that now spread over
James's features told her that was an obstacle to be sur-
mounted. "Am I to understand that you find amusement,"
he inquired with tightly drawn lips, "in this turn of events?"

Real Jane would shout out a *yes*. Book Jane, the one
who followed a straighter path, wouldn't dream of it. She
turned up her own two palms and glanced at them. It
was a choice, at least at this minute. She lifted first one
hand and then the other, weighing the alternatives.

"Miss Ellingson," he demanded in the most formal
of tones.

She let her hands drop to her sides. "James. I need to talk with you."

"Undoubtedly." He clasped his hands behind his back and raised his chin. "I stand prepared to accept your apology for making light of a serious matter."

"My apolo—? No. That's not it."

"Not *it?*" The emphasis he placed on that last word had to have hurt him.

"Well, no. I can't apologize for laughing when it was just because you . . ." Her voice trailed off. He looked so offended. "Obviously there's nothing wrong with my leg. Mary and I were only having a difference of opinion. She was trying to have me say one thing and I wanted to say another and—" She broke off at the sight of the storm clouds gathering in his face. This line of reasoning wasn't getting her anywhere. "I mean, I'm sorry."

He blinked hard. "You questioned our author?"

"I think you were doing that, just a minute ago. When you thought I was crippled." She waited for him to say it. She knew it was coming . . .

"I am the hero. Entrusted with certain responsibilities."

And there it was. "You alone can argue with her?"

"I carry a great deal upon my shoulders."

Good thing they were padded. Jane began pacing back and forth before him, the words coming out faster than she could control them. "Mary doesn't know what to do here. It doesn't look as though she has much experience with a woman being swept off her feet. We have to help her."

"As indeed I have beseeched you to do. Helping our author is far different than fighting her."

She made a sound of frustration. "James. Listen to me."

"If only you would deign to follow the lead I have so capably set, you would at last allow yourself to feel the true extent of your feelings. This alone would assist Miss

Bellingham in bringing the story to a most satisfying conclusion. I tell you, Jane, I have had far more experience in matters of the heart. You must trust that I know best."

Facing him with her hands on her hips, Jane tapped a toe. As she replayed each of his words in her mind, her toe tapped harder. And harder. Far more experience. True extent of her feelings. So far they only extended to: *What the hell are you going to do here? Wait until we're married ten years to kiss me?*

"Jane?" he inquired mildly.

"I disagree, James," she bit out, which should have been enough to warn her that Demure, Obedient Jane had run for cover and Real Jane was about make an appearance. Too late, she tried to stop, to convince herself to keep following Mary's lead. Mary, who wielded a pen that made certain Real Jane wouldn't mess things up, for the fourteen-hundredth time. But Mary couldn't—*Oh, to hell with it.*

"*You* wouldn't even put your arm around me when I said I was cold. Perfect opportunity, but you stare it in the face and say no, thanks. Do you think I'm going to fall hard for you when you never even touch me? When you don't take advantage of a romantic place like this to shower me with compliments, with endearments, with— I don't know—tender smiles? When you don't make it your business to get to know me, be *interested* in me? For who and what I am? You don't know anything about me, except that I'm supposedly fond of horses." Her chest heaved up and down. "Which, by the way, I'm not."

"I confess I find your behavior most alarming, Jane. You are reminded who you are addressing yourself to and that you are talking about our author. Your father would surely—"

Before he could finish, she'd closed the distance

between them and reached up to hold his head between her hands.

Startled, he drew his breath in sharply.

Maybe he thought she was going to smack him. Furthest thing from her mind. Jane closed her mouth over his surprised lips, kissing him for all she was worth.

Sometimes, you had to grab the bull by his horns. Or, in this case, the gentleman by his ears.

Chapter 9

Jane could feel alarm and surprise radiate through James, which only made her kiss him harder and with more determination. He was going to kiss her back and, in the process, discover what a truly great heroine she could be. Not because it was "the very thing to do," but because it was the only thing to do. They, together, were going to move this story along to a happy ending very, *very* far away from any fireplaces.

If it killed her.

Whoops. Too far. That's what she was trying to *avoid*.

He had nice lips and a clean-shaven face, which was a plus. She'd always thought Victorian men had long side-burns and other facial hair, which she'd never particularly liked. Give her a man with a smooth face, and just a hint of bristly whiskers, any day. Only a hint, though. Who needed whisker burn? Not an attractive look on a woman.

All right, so . . . kiss-*ing*. Kissing hard.

Hold on. He was kissing *her*, bringing his hand up to tip her head back and give him the dominant edge. Perfect. She wanted him to take charge, to make her forget about any other man she'd ever loved or hoped to love.

To make her think only about him and his . . . As her fingers ran through his hair, she noticed it wasn't quite as full and thick as she had once thought . . . Oh, that's right. She had noticed it that one time and wondered if he would go bald early in life. Not that it mattered. *That* much. It's just that it was definitely thinner than, say, *Curran's,* which looked like a woman could run both hands through it and love the way it felt, the way it curled just a little at the ends . . .

Now this could be bad. Thinking about Curran while James was doing his very best to kiss her oblivious at *her* invitation, no less. Something like that could take her right out of the moment, spoil the intent of this whole thing. But Curran—

Not going to think about Curran Dempsey. Any. More. To make sure, she leaned into James with purpose and focused on kissing him so hard, he would forget about everything else. And then wonder how in the world he'd become so lucky as to have a heroine like Jane. So lucky.

He pulled his lips back, a fraction of an inch, for just a second. "Now, Jane," he murmured, sounding pleased.

Good. Very good. That was half of this happy couple reacting well. She only had to work on getting herself as into it. Again, her lips closed in on his.

But she put a little too much of her body into that kiss, apparently. In the next instant, she lost her balance. James stumbled, too, trying to remain upright, which only made her trip over his feet and tangle both of them up until she landed squarely on top of him in a heap of skirts, her head going over his shoulder to meet the grass.

The air went out of him when he hit the ground and he made a sound something like *"Oof"* that was partially drowned out by her short, sharp scream. She didn't weigh much, but with all this paraphernalia she had to wear, not to mention a corset that looked deadly even when it was off her, it seemed entirely possible she might have damaged him. Hurt something.

Wouldn't that be her luck when she let Real Jane come out and play. To damage the hero beyond repair. What would Mary do about that?

She shoved the cap thing that had dropped over her eyes back up on her head so that she could look at him, and spit out the pieces of grass that had managed to attach themselves to her mouth. "Are you okay?"

His expression moved from disbelief to anger and back again. "Are you quite mad?" he asked, sounding as though he already knew the answer.

"No, I—"

"Kindly remove yourself from my person." With each word, his tone grew more vehement.

She would have to forgive the fact that it wasn't the most romantic thing to say. She had, after all, just pushed him onto the ground. "We could laugh about this?" she suggested hopefully. "Roll around in the grass a little?" Yeah. Even she wouldn't want to go for that. It was so hard trying to clean up after the Jane-isms that were a part of her everyday life. She'd thought she could be safe from them here.

She sighed.

He frowned. "Have you finished?"

"Oh. Sorry." She put her palms against his chest and pushed against him to lift herself up. As she did, she felt a vibration coming from the ground. A moment later, a sound. She turned her head to look. Not far away, a horse and rider, coming closer.

James heard it, too, and struggled to get up, brushing grass and dirt from his clothing. Jane stumbled backward but managed to right herself and shove the cap farther up on her head, puffing at a piece of hair that seemed determined to position itself only in the middle of her face.

James had just straightened his shoulders and given a tug on his jacket when the horse and rider arrived in a flurry of hooves, drawing to a stop. She heard the horse's neigh and saw a flash of his eyes before she realized who was riding him.

A tall figure all in black. Curran.

Scowling mightily.

She didn't know why. She was only doing what they had agreed on, wasn't she? Making this story move along, romantically speaking. Given that James was looking out of breath and rumpled, with bits of grass clinging to his hair, a person might think she was doing exactly that.

Curran's gaze moved from James to her and back again. "Your presence is required at the house," was all he said, in that low, rumbling voice of his that would make anyone who heard it stop whatever they were doing to pay attention.

James seemed to think it important to challenge his half brother. He glared. "I shall be there presently."

"Mary Bellingham has arisen and breakfasted. From the worsening condition of our father, it appears she may make his demise her next endeavor."

"I anticipated as much."

Jane cast a sidelong gaze at James. He had folded his arms across his chest.

"Then you already knew you would be needed at the house." Curran's gaze swept pointedly over his brother's grass-stained clothing.

"I shall be there presently," James repeated, this time barely moving his lips.

With no visible sign, Curran urged his horse to go, taking off in an impressive show of hooves, man and sheer power.

Dirt clods kicked up by the horse landed on James's jacket. He brushed them off with sharp jerks of his hands. "Now you have done it," he huffed.

"Done what?" she asked. Always good to have clarification of how much trouble you were really in.

"Because of this—this situation, I was not at leisure to hear Mary Bellingham as she awoke, to know that she again sought to write. That my presence would be needed." His hands stabbed at the air, punctuating his words. "I do not understand, Jane, how you could choose to take this tale into your own hands with so little regard for the possibility that you will ruin us all with your insufferable meddling."

"Meddling?" She yanked at the tie on her bonnet, pulling until the hat came off her head. "That's what you call it?"

"You would find another term more apt? I confess I would doubt it." A twig had lodged itself in his sandy hair, sticking straight up.

"Tell me that you didn't enjoy our interlude there a little more than our last few scenes together that Mary wrote." She folded her own arms across her chest. "Go ahead, James. Tell me. But remember that I was there. I felt the way you kissed me back."

"Our author will take the story in the direction it is meant to go."

Straight to a chaste wedding. And a tasteful, subdued marriage. She decided to soften her approach, venturing a playful smile. "You haven't answered me."

He took a step toward her, putting his hands on her elbows. "I found it pleasurable. You enjoyed my kiss."

She tried to remember. "Just promise me you'll also help Mary when she writes the romantic scenes. We could have more kisses like that, with her writing them."

His chin lifted high in the air. "It is with my help that

Miss Bellingham possesses the ability to write at all. I am the reason she picks up her pen."

Self-esteem was great, but this might be taking it a little far. She reached out to pluck the twig from his hair. "But what happens between the two of us is the only reason she has a story."

He stared at the twig in her hand and then exhaled, looking down at the ground.

"Please just try to give her the benefit of your . . . experience," Jane went on. "Don't wait for her to think of something touching and affectionate to say or do. She might not be able to. Help her come up with it."

Slowly, James raised his gaze to meet hers. "I dwell in her memory. A living, breathing enactment of the man she once knew. Whose image and manner she can never forget and indeed would never choose to. She would sooner cast me out altogether than allow me to behave in a way she has not herself had occasion to witness."

"But she's writing fiction."

"Ah, but fiction is only the writer's particular view of facts."

A slam against imagination and creativity, if she'd ever heard it. And if what he said about dwelling in her memory was true, this was great. Just great. Mary Bellingham was writing a hero she knew. Probably the one who had thrown her over for another woman. Mary wasn't going to write him as anything but the way she remembered or she wouldn't have a true sense of satisfaction at ending up with him. Even if it was just on paper. So now Jane didn't just have to contend with an author's imagination. She had to overcome the author's truth.

One thing she could say for sure. Fictional characters *earned* their keep.

* * *

Jane opened her eyes to the sound of sniffling and the writer's firm grip on her rigid spine.

"I hear he grows so weak," said her aunt, standing next to her, "that he can hardly lift his head from the pillow." She honked loudly into her handkerchief and then waved the balled-up white fabric in front of her face. "Yet he is determined that guests should be entreated to stay. That all should go on as it has."

"Mr. Benton Dempsey is the most unselfish of men," Jane agreed. "To think only of his guests and his son and daughter, when he is himself ill."

"You would be fortunate to marry into such a family," Mrs. Hathaway said, dabbing at her eyes. "For I know they would treat you well and you would be the happiest girl alive."

"And you would send for your sister to visit you often," piped up Anne, from Jane's other side. "For you would miss her most dreadfully."

"Indeed I would," Jane heard herself say. "And now, my dear sister, how have you been occupying yourself? For I have seen little of you."

A guilty look crossed Anne's face and she looked away.

"How has she been occupying herself?" Mrs. Hathaway grumbled. "By making a most dreadful nuisance, that is all I can say about the matter."

"Anne," Jane said with gentle reproach. "You must tell me that you have only been a helpful, obedient girl, for I would wish to know nothing else."

Her sister's eyes widened in innocence.

"Wandering about the grounds of Afton House by herself," said Mrs. Hathaway, both chins bobbing, "until I have to send the servants to search for her. Quite unconscionable. I cannot imagine what thought your father must have had in his head to allow her to accompany us."

Jane turned to Anne with a smile. "My father knew

that I would miss my sister and long for her company."
She received a shy smile from the girl in return. "But
now, Anne, you must promise you will give Aunt Hathaway not another moment of worry. This dear lady has
been through quite enough." *Dear lady.* Not exactly the
term Real Jane would use to describe the woman. But
she liked Anne, who had a glint of something that didn't
look like Victorian obedience in her eye.

"I can only hope that will be so," wailed Mrs. Hathaway, "for I am nearly at my wits' end with the girl."

The end wouldn't be that far to go was the thought that occurred to Real Jane as Book Jane bestowed on her aunt
a look that felt suspiciously like sympathy.

"Mr. Dempsey!" cried her aunt.

Jane whirled to look, suppressing an irrational sense
of disappointment at the sight of James. Who did she
expect, Benton himself? Curran? She shoved that
thought away as quickly as it appeared.

James's clothing was in its usual pristine condition,
without any sign of the tumble they'd taken in the grass
by the lake earlier. Come to think of it, if she could just
look down to see if *hers* . . . No luck. Mary held a tight
grip on both her head and the pleased look Jane turned
on James.

"Mrs. Hathaway, Anne," he acknowledged. Then he
bathed Jane in the warmth of his approving smile. "Jane.
May I dare to hope that you will once again play for us
this evening?"

"It would be my pleasure, sir."

"Then it is decided."

At least something was.

Jane took advantage of a lull in Mary's writing to go for
a walk with her younger sister. It felt good to be outside

again, drinking in the sweet air and letting the occasional sunlight brush its warmth across her forehead.

She may not be able to pull on a pair of comfortable jeans and a T-shirt, but at least she had managed to leave the ever-present lace cap thing in her room. Next, she planned to see what she could do about the corset that tortured her nonstop. A smaller waistline was not worth it. At all.

She and Anne walked together companionably, along a path that led past the gardens and along the back of the house. "So when are you to have your . . . coming out?" Jane asked. She was pretty sure that's what it was called, anyway.

Anne looked at her in surprise. "You know, Sister, that it is to be one year hence."

"Of course," she agreed. "I do, but I had forgotten. So this is sort of a scouting trip? I suppose the Dempseys might invite eligible men to dinner for you."

The girl turned to her in bewilderment. "Your manner of speaking is most—"

"I know," Jane hastened to say. "Unusual. I'm, uh . . . based on an American friend of the author's. So when she's not writing, I'm . . . Well, you'll get used to it."

Anne looked doubtful for a moment but then nodded. The good thing about being young, Jane reflected, was that it came with a certain amount of being able to accept things on the surface. Not question them too deeply.

"I know you're my sister, but there are some things the author hasn't filled me in on. What"—Jane paused to think how to phrase the question in a way the girl would be more accustomed to hearing—"activities do you enjoy, Anne?"

The girl kicked a small pebble in the path, once and then twice. One quick scrutiny assured Jane it wasn't the one she was looking for. "I am fond of reading," Anne said. "*Not* fond of the pianoforte nor the embroidery that our mother insists I undertake. She knows how tiresome I think it, yet she pays no heed." Her voice rose to mimic what Jane presumed to be their mother's. "'An accomplished lady, Anne, must endeavor to make herself useful.'" She sighed, heavily and with no small amount of drama. "As if playing a song could somehow alter life itself."

Jane grinned. Spoken like someone who had never had a rock song ingrained into her memory for all time. She looked closer at the girl, noting the profile of a nose a bit too large, a chin a little too receding, freckles sprinkled across her cheeks and hair determined to burst from its restraints. Anne seemed to spring forward as she walked, something like a terrier Jane had once known. A far cry from the dainty, restrained steps Mary forced on Jane. "And what else do you enjoy?" she asked. A person with this much energy had to channel it somewhere.

"Stories."

"Stories? Writing them?"

Anne nodded. "When my pen meets paper, it is as though all else ceases to exist." Then she ducked her head, looking embarrassed, as though she wasn't sure how the admission would be received.

A niggling suspicion began to steal over Jane. Could Anne, she wondered, actually be Mary, in character as a younger girl, before the disappointments of a suitor who chose someone else? Jane could see Anne accused of being less than pious in a few years. Mrs. Hathaway had said as much now.

Interesting. "I think that's wonderful," Jane said carefully. "That's a talent you should nurture."

Anne darted a look over at her and then away, the hint of a smile playing at her mouth. "It is not the limit of my accomplishments."

"What else?"

Without warning, Anne moved off the path to a clear-ing of grass nearby. Jane followed her, curious.

Anne shot her arms in the air and hopped up on one leg, turning what looked to be a perfect cartwheel, though the tangle of her skirts obscured much of it. She emerged, flushed and grinning, hands still in the air.

Jane broke into applause, to the apparent surprise of Anne, who seemed to have expected shock and maybe a scolding. *Ha. It's going to take a lot more than that to shock me, Sister.*

The girl brushed her hair back from her face, clearly pleased.

"Very nice," Jane said. "But can you do this?" Hands on her hips, she looked behind her to take the measure of the ground, hiked up her skirts and called on the inner cheerleader she knew still lurked inside somewhere. Then she put her arms up and prepared to launch into her trademark three-rotation backflip. *Ow.* She hadn't quite bent over when the corset practically cut her in half. Stupid thing. She pulled herself back, stumbling to catch her balance.

"Jane?"

"I'm fine. No problem. Just—give me a minute." She looked around. Over there, not far away, a grove of trees. Could she . . . ?

Never mind whether she could or could not. She *would.*

She walked quickly to the trees, ducking behind a par-ticularly leafy one.

"What are you doing?" called Anne.

Jane raised her voice only enough to be heard by her sister. "Just getting rid of something. Keep an eye out for me, okay? Make sure no one is coming." Her last words were muffled as she ducked her chin and reached behind her to try and undo the dress. After a few fruitless tries, she gave up. She'd never be able to do this by herself. Victorian dressmakers had apparently seen to that. "Anne! Come here, I need you."

The girl came swiftly to her side.

"Help me get out of this, please. I have to get this corset off before it kills me. Literally."

Anne's eyes were doubtful. "But your dress . . . ?"

"I know. It might not fit. We'll just have to make it work."

With Anne's help, the dress and the corset came off, leaving Jane in the odd chemise and drawers that served as underclothing. "Quick," she urged the girl. "Get me back into this dress." No one else had come along or she would have had them both dive for cover.

It wasn't easy, fitting Jane back into the dress. The corset apparently took an inch or two off her waist. Luckily, the dress was cut such that she was able to squeeze into it with Anne's help.

"There," Jane pronounced, hands on her hips. "Much better."

Anne held up the corset. "What shall we do with this?"

"Leave it on the ground. Maybe wild animals will drag it away. Use it for a nest."

The younger girl held her hand over her mouth as a giggle turned into a full laugh.

"Now," said Jane. "I'll show you what *I* can do."

Back into position in the clearing, her hands in the air. And . . . launch. It felt good sailing through the air again with carefree abandon, even if her skirts did cause a big problem with her flexibility and the now-tight waist of her dress didn't want to give an inch.

One flip, whoa . . . skirts over the head. *Heavy* skirts. Keep going. Two flips . . . She hadn't let herself do this since college, when she'd caused that huge fiasco at the basketball game. The basketball star with all the promise had never made it to the NBA. She'd always secretly feared it was her fault. Humiliation, she could take. But causing someone else to lose their dream? That, she couldn't take. And . . . threeeee flips. Except that, on her way down, she caught those skirts she'd managed mostly to avoid on the first two and ended up with them over her head, pinning her to the ground, her backside sticking straight up in the air.

"Oh!" She heard Anne's muffled squeal and felt footsteps rushing toward her. Anne's hands pushed and pulled at the unwieldy fabric at the same time Jane's did, until Jane finally managed to sit back on the ground and claw her way to the surface, flushed and laughing.

Anne's eyes had lit up and she was giggling uncontrollably, placing her hands on Jane's shoulders. "Oh, Sister, that was so very—however did you do it? You must teach me. At once!"

"I daresay there are other things you should seek to learn, young Anne," said a voice from above. A male voice, deep and terse. Sounding as though he couldn't believe what he was seeing. Jane squeezed her eyes shut and then mustered her courage enough to look up and meet the shocked stare of James Dempsey.

"At least . . ." she attempted, "I'm no longer crippled?"

He didn't laugh.

But Anne did.

Chapter 10

By the time the servant arrived to help her dress for dinner, Jane decided she'd had enough of allowing Real Jane to show up. This was her life and all she'd ever done on her own was mess it up. She had a chance, one chance, to get it right, through someone else calling the shots. She was taking it.

Besides—and she didn't want to allow herself much time to think about this—without that stone, she might be stuck here for good. In a story where, if she didn't marry the handsome master of Afton House, she could end up a pitied spinster, shoulders bent with the weight of broken dreams, like Violet. Dependent on the good-will of her brother. Did Book Jane even *have* a brother? She had no idea.

And how would she support herself? Women without family money or husbands in this age were servants or—or—governesses. She'd never been around children much and that was probably a fairly necessary qualification for the job. And if her piety had to be put to a test, might as well say right now that she'd fail miserably.

Okay, then. Not much choice but to suck it up and go along. Strap the corset back on, in more ways than one, and be cooperative. Influence Mary where she could without wreaking havoc. *Don't think. Just cooperate. Effort, Jane, effort.* She slapped her palm, startling the servant who carried her dress.

"Sorr—" She drew in a breath. "Please. Forgive me." Time for this Victorian woman to begin acting like one.

The servant, a different pale, skittish girl with her dark hair scraped into a white cap, bobbed a half curtsy, nearly dropping the dress. "Miss."

"Allow me." Jane took it from her and spread it on the bed. This time, the fabric was a pale yellow, sprigged with rows of white lace. It was pretty, in a dress up, doll kind of way. And maybe that was exactly what she was supposed to be. She closed her eyes and waited, hands on her hips. The picture of a lady.

She could still do what she and Curran had talked about. But without giving it her own Jane-like take that never worked. For anyone.

When at last she was dressed, she smoothed the fabric with her hands, held her chin high and took small, deliberate steps toward the door.

"Beautiful, miss," said the maid, in a tiny squeak of a voice.

"Thank you." This wasn't so hard. She could do it, even when Mary wasn't writing. She opened the door carefully and made it through without bumping either side. Small victories. They counted.

She could be on her way to a coordinated life.

When Mary began writing, Jane was once again seated at the dining table in a room awash with the dancing glow of candlelight, from sconces on the wall to extravagant candelabras. Flowers graced the long table in large urns. Mary apparently liked setting scenes at dinner. Maybe the woman was fixated on food.

There was plenty of it on Jane's plate, slid silently in front of her by a servant who then stepped away. Jane only glanced at it as she lifted her fork to take a dainty bite and then turned her attention to James, seated on her left at the head of the table.

There seemed to be a difference in his approving look this time, a hesitation that hadn't been there before. Great. Mary may not have written in the backflip, but James knew it had happened. He'd been there to see Jane's Victorian underwear flashing the sky on that third rotation. He probably now doubted her suitability as a wife, which would definitely not help in moving along a romance.

She had to get through to him that she had reformed. That the earlier incident had been a temporary lapse. That it wouldn't happen again, if she had to duct tape Real Jane and fold her into a carriage bound for London.

She would listen carefully to the words Mary wrote for her. Put her heart, her whole being behind them. Provide subtle hints, suggestions even, but only in a Victorian-appropriate way. She would help the author develop this book into something wonderful. Yes, she would.

"Miss Ellingson has agreed to again play for us this evening," James announced to those seated nearest them. "We await hearing her with much anticipation."

"Indeed," nodded Mrs. Hathaway. "For our Jane plays with the touch of an angel, does she not?" She beamed at Jane. "Would that she could stay here and play for you every evening, Mr. Dempsey."

And that would happen by way of . . . ? At least the woman seemed to get away with her blatant matchmaking. James gave a polite nod.

"My sister is a woman of many accomplishments," contributed Anne.

As Jane slowly, gracefully turned to her sister, she felt a jolt of panic. Anne *couldn't* be talking about the backflips, could she? What if—What if Mary decided the heroine of this story had some sort of mental defect that resulted in her performing gymnastic stunts and . . . Mary wrote her out, sending her off to a mental institution, in favor of someone else? One of these other women, maybe. Jane couldn't get her head free enough to look at them, but she knew they were there, dressed in beautiful silk dresses with their hair up and gracious smiles fixed in place.

"My sister, I fear, is not impartial," she murmured. "And she is quite unwilling to talk about her own accomplishments."

"Which her older sister raises only as a sign of her own generous heart," pronounced Mrs. Hathaway.

Was the woman earning a commission from brokering this marriage?

Jane swallowed another bite of virtually tasteless food. A vegetable of some kind, cooked until every vitamin had to have been eliminated. Good thing she didn't feel all that hungry. Either Mary was writing her with a full stomach or the corset remolding her ribs didn't allow enough room for food. But she could get used to the thing. She *could.*

"Have you your dress for the ball, Miss Ellingson?" whispered a female voice next to her.

Jane turned to see a young, heart-shaped face framed by glossy brown ringlets. "Yes, Miss Ashby. And you?"

"*Mama* was quite beside herself. The dressmaker fell ill at a most inopportune time, when my dress was not yet done by half." Miss Ashby's eyes widened with the drama of it all.

If this was the worst problem the woman ever had, she'd live a charmed life. But Jane heard herself reply, "How vexing. Whatever did you do?"

"We arranged for another dressmaker and the gown is now finished. No thanks to the first. What could she have been thinking?"

Jane pictured an impoverished dressmaker, lying on her sickbed barely able to move, lamenting the money she would not earn because Pampered Ringlets couldn't imagine what she was doing having the nerve to become ill. *Never mind,* she told herself. *You can't march in and change things here. Just go along with Mary's words.*

But Miss Ashby was already rushing ahead, without waiting for a response. "Oh, it is the most beautiful gown I have ever seen," she gushed. "Tulle over layers of pink satin. And the *lace,*" she breathed. "It is spectacular."

Mary had Book Jane say something bland in reply, but Real Jane wasn't quite listening. James had turned to Mr. Stonewalter and begun a low-voiced discussion of recent expansions of the right to vote. Mention of the Chartists hurtled her straight back to a college English history class. Fascinating. Reforms in England were happening right now, not in a textbook.

"It is preposterous," said James. "Any man with a household income of ten pounds granted a vote."

"Beyond belief," Stonewalter grumbled in reply. "Such a person has not the most basic understanding of what is to be discussed in Parliament. The decisions that are to be made. Mark my words. It is the end of all rational thinking."

Right, thought Jane. What would happen next? Giving women the right to vote? Just *think* of the implications.

Stonewalter's voice dropped even lower. "Next they will propose that females vote."

Both men chortled at the absurdity.

Jane longed to turn, to lean forward and join in this conversation. Hello? Little did they know that Britain's first female prime minister would be along in a mere hundred years or so, *and* Jane herself had been elected freshman-class president in high school *and* had voted in every single election since she'd turned eighteen—

"Miss Ellingson?" Ringlet Girl asked. Her tone had a knife's edge to it.

Jane could have sworn she'd been talking back in some form of shadow conversation, hadn't she?

"We were speaking of your gown," Miss Ashby prompted.

Jane opened her mouth. Nothing.

She tried again, to no avail. A second later, all at the table froze, the man on the other side of Miss Ashby in the midst of lifting a forkful of food to his mouth. Then the invisible hand lifted and Jane's shoulders sagged. She glanced at James, but she couldn't read his expression.

Jane ventured, "Has she tired?" She moved one hand to the back of her chair, fingers crossed. This would not be a good time for James to find out she hadn't been co-operating, had let her attention wander. His patience, she strongly suspected, was more than a little worn.

He didn't answer at first, pressing both of his palms flat on the table and surveying the assembled group. At last he said, "All prepare."

Ummm . . . What?

A moment later she had her answer, finding herself at the pianoforte, playing before a group that looked to include all those who had just been at dinner. As though nothing else had just happened. As though she hadn't gone from the table to the drawing room, without a single footstep.

A ripple of apprehension began in Jane's stomach and

made its way through the rest of her at lightning speed. Curran had tried to warn her about this. The woman who wielded the pen also wielded the ability to stop, start, erase. Obliterate lives.

There was a huge price to be paid for causing trouble. When would she learn? Mentally, she thumped her forehead, even as her fingers continued to dance across the keys.

Lonely spinster, anyone? She could already see bits of herself withering away and dying from lack of human companionship. Maybe she and Violet could become best friends.

At that moment, Jane's gaze happened to land on Violet, who sat stiffly in her chair, fingers clenched together and her mouth set in a narrow line of defeat. She didn't look like someone who would kick off her shoes, kill a bottle of wine and share confidences.

So, maybe . . . not.

Focus, Jane. Focus. Happy endings take work.

A hero. A heroine. One plus one equals two, right? If only it were that easy. Oh, God, if her anxiety level ratcheted any higher, she'd fall right over in a crash of curls and jarring notes. End up with keys etched permanently into her skin. Never mind that. Mary wouldn't let it happen. Mary. Who had no idea how to create a romance. Who needed help.

Because of a stone and a wish made in a moment, or maybe a *lifetime,* of desperation.

James led the polite applause and murmurs of appreciation when Jane finished her piece. As she rose, she let her eyes meet his, trailing her long, now apparently musical fingers across the wood of the instrument. So far, so good. But, what was this? Mary was having her drop her gaze. More of the demure stuff. *No, Mary.*

Jane fought. Not hard, just *firmly.* Keeping her eyes on

James, working to curve her mouth into the beginnings of a smile. *Not* shying away. It was an effort. But Mary seemed to be letting her do it. There was an invisible line here. She just had to be sure not to cross it.

One of James's brows began to lift. As she passed next to him, she concentrated on her hand, needing just . . . the *fingers* to . . . okay, this was tough, but she could do it . . . and there it was, her fingertips lightly brushing his sleeve. Saying nothing, hopefully saying everything.

Ye-e-s. If she could have, she would have run a quick victory lap around the room, but it felt like winning a race and then having to hope they didn't do drug testing. As she sank gracefully into her chair, skirts behaving admirably, she slid a glance toward James.

His chin was high and pointed straight ahead, but she could see him looking at her from the corner of his eye.

This could work. It could. Mary hadn't released them, yet. She was still writing. Jane concentrated hard, forcing her lips to open. Then she made them come together to form the first letter of the word she wanted to say. "P—Perhaps we might . . . take a stroll," she managed at last, nearly panting from the effort, though Mary allowed nothing to show.

James didn't hide his surprise. "A stroll?"

Mary. Let go of my tongue. "It is . . . a beautiful . . . evening." And she promised not to bring up anything about women voters. Or ask about the Chartists even though she was dying to. Or grab James and throw him to the ground in a frenzy of kisses. She would behave herself, but she had to get him alone. Did Mary really think he would propose in a room full of people?

"Indeed," he murmured.

She focused every drop of strength in her body on one area. Her tongue. "I fear I feel a bit faint. The air would surely do me good." *And, again. Concentrate.* "Will you escort me, sir?"

He rose from his chair, extending his arm. "Most certainly. I am distressed to learn you are unwell."

A little formal, a little distanced, but she'd take it for now. Jane also rose, laying her hand on his arm.

"Mrs. Hathaway, I am sure, would accompany us." He turned, mouth opening in the direction of the woman, who was chatting merrily with Mrs. Stonewalter.

"No!" The vehemence of her whisper startled even Jane. Mary must have backed off, decided to watch and see what happened. Why not? The author could cross out things, throw the pages in the fire. Ouch. Briefly, Jane wondered if that would hurt. She shook away the thought. "Please, James. Let us go outside."

He had a way of looking at her that said she was half out of her mind, but because he was a gentleman, he would be nice and go along. *I'll call that look,* she thought to herself, *and raise you one possible romantic moment.*

She had no idea if she could muster one up, if she could find some sort of feeling, passion even, for this man. But she had to try. There had to be some reason the author had fallen for the person she had based him on.

As they walked through and out of the room, with James trailing a wake of explanations, Jane began to mentally list his good qualities on a giant list. First . . . um, manners. Yes, he had them. Definitely. Second, looks. She didn't want to seem shallow about this, but she wouldn't be realistic if she didn't acknowledge physical attraction had *something* to do with romance. Or even a lot to do with it. And James was handsome. Very. He had a face that could grace the cover of a romance novel. The kind of guy that, in a picture, you might suspect his image had been altered with PhotoShop because he looked so perfect.

Chiseled features, eyes that could gaze meaningfully into the distance or, better yet, into a woman's. Tousled hair that, even though it *might* be showing the first signs of thinning, looked as though he'd just stepped out of a hairdresser's chair. A gallant, confident kind of walk, even if he did always seem to be trying to be taller. The way he lifted his chin as if striving for another quarter inch . . .

Anyway. Points for handsomeness. Moving on.

He had money. Piles of it, apparently. And an entire estate, coming to him because he had the right birth circumstances and gender. And on that subject, how could that sort of thing go on? It was so unfair, so—

Out of place on James's Good Qualities list.

He had financial security. Points for that.

They had reached the front door. James opened it for her and they walked out into the cool night air. A bright moon shone overhead, casting its light around them.

"Are you chilled?" he asked. "Would you like me to fetch your cloak?"

Concern for others. Had she added that to the list? Wait. She took out her giant mental eraser. She'd already given him credit for manners and he hardly showed even a pinky finger of concern for his brother. Or sister. *So only a quarter of a point on concern.*

They emerged from the house into the night air and stood by the solitary outside light, side by side, for a moment. Then James said, "I often like to ride in the darkness of evening. When it is cool and damp and the creatures of the night have come out from their hiding places of day."

Interesting. So, any points for a sense of adventure and daring? She considered it. Okay, one point. Maybe. On the other hand, he could be shooting those innocent nocturnal creatures for sport. She didn't want to know. Change it to half a point.

"There is much to be said for the solace of the night," Jane heard herself say. Really? She'd never found much solace in being alone at night.

"Solace it can be, indeed. With my horse as true and faithful companion." He turned to her with a smile. "Perhaps, Jane, you would find my horse a more talkative creature in the evening hours."

A couple of points for something that veered toward a sense of humor. Unless he was *serious* and would rather be with a horse than with a woman? Impossible. Mary wouldn't write that in a hero. At least, she hoped not. Victorians could be a strange bunch.

Change the humor category to half a point, too. He had very nice white, even teeth. Had she already considered . . . ? Yes. He had points for good-looking. Plenty of them.

"I am certain, sir," she said with that half-sweep of lashes, "that I should welcome the chance to find out." Then she concentrated hard on the sentence she wanted Mary to let her say. "And what would your horse likely confide to me about you?"

His eyes widened and his mouth twitched in apparent amusement. He stepped away from her, his shadow long and narrow on the ground. "Perhaps he would assert that his master is a reasonable and fair man who sits a horse well and on occasion favors a hard ride through the blackness of night."

As a warm and cuddly description, that one didn't quite make it. But if a person wanted to read some sort of double entendre into his words . . . Jane did a quick check on her pulse, heart, stomach. Not a single quiver, shiver or tingle. Mary needed a nudge. A big one. "And what," she said after some effort, "would he tell me about the heart of his master?"

Could not get a better setup than that. Here was the

chance for him to tell her how much he longed for a
woman at his side, to be his partner, his lover . . . well,
however that sort of thing was said in Victorian terms,
anyway. It was his chance to flatter her, take her in his
arms. She moved toward him, laying a hand on his arm.

He looked down at it and then into her eyes.

This was it. *It.* Now it would happen. She waited, resist-
ing the urge to shake him.

He parted his lips. "He would say—"

Yes, James. He would *say* . . .

"That is—" Again, he broke off, taking a deep breath
in and then letting it out. "He would say that his master's
heart is true and strong."

Eh? James seemed to be having quite the struggle
here. She dug her fingers into his arm, trying to force the
words from his mouth. She couldn't go too far, though,
or Mary would cut this scene right off. "Is it not true that
his master would . . ." Keep going. "Welcome the companionship of . . . a wife?" she prompted.

He glanced down at his arm and she released him
with the guilty realization that she'd probably hurt him,
since her fingers had nearly gone numb. This wasn't
going well. At all. How did she get him to literally and
figuratively sweep her off her feet, vow that he needed
her, that he longed for her, that—

Oh. *No.* She had just managed to get Mary to write
essentially what she'd said to Byron. No wonder this
wasn't going well. *How could it?*

Mentally, she shut her eyes and waited. For the whole
fragile world, built on words, to come crashing down
as James tiptoed from the moonlight air to disappear
forever.

Of course, according to Mrs. Hathaway, this marriage
deal was all but signed, sealed and delivered. Mary might
forgive her bold move. She allowed her eyes to creep open.

James leaned forward so quickly that she gave a small jump. His finger stroked her cheek, lightly, gently. Then his mouth closed in. Full lips pressed against hers with an intensity of purpose, as his hands gripped her shoulders and held on tight. James, her hero, was kissing her. He wasn't doing a bad job of it, either.

She'd managed to get him to make the move, with the suggestion they walk outside into the moonlight, where romance danced in the cool air. By not giving up, by staying determined to maneuver Mary into the things that needed to happen to move this courtship along, Jane had done it. The author had even forgiven Jane's throwing the Wife word right out there into the open. Possibly even used it.

The kiss. One *he* had instigated. And Mary had written. At last.

And she didn't feel a damn thing.

Chapter 11

James drew back. His hands fell to his sides and he stood watching Jane, his face shadowed in the moonlight. "We are," he said at last, "at a pause."

"She's quit writing?" Jane asked in a whisper. The freedom of her tongue told her the answer as soon as the words were out.

He nodded.

"So . . . how was it for you?" She tried joking, but there was a catch in her throat.

"Forgive my boldness, but it had to be done."

It *had* to be done? Well, he was right. It had taken him long enough. She shook her head. "Nothing to be forgiven." *Except the fact that I cannot seem to work up one iota, one little microscopic drop of simple lust for you.* What would that mean for her, for James, for everyone? Being a heroine carried a heavy burden. One she apparently wasn't ready for.

A half smile curved at his mouth. Or . . . No. It wasn't close to a smile. It was more of a . . . smirk, really. *Now* the heat began to rise in Jane, for an entirely different reason.

"I gave in to your wishes. Perhaps sooner than would be

wise, but it shall suffice for our purposes nonetheless." He gestured toward the door. "Shall we rejoin the others?"

Rejoin the others? A simple enough question, but with all the bleeped words rolling around in her mind and crashing into each other, it was a little hard to think straight. The only answer she could come up with was, "Are you out of your mind?"

He blinked. "Jane?"

"*You* gave in to *my* wishes?" She had begun to pace now. Back and forth, three steps one way, three steps the other. Never a good sign.

"Did you not ask me to accompany you into the night air, to a place where we would be alone?"

"Yes, you *imbecile.*" Oh, this was so not the way to talk to her hero, but he was leaving her very little choice. How could he make it sound as though she'd practically begged him for a kiss? As though she were some sort of nineteenth-century charity case. Or, spinster. She'd tell *him.* Her shoes pounded into the dirt. "Because you were not doing a single thing to move this story along. Because you apparently don't have a romantic bone or inclination in your body."

"This is most—" he sputtered.

"The most truth you've probably heard in a long time," she finished for him.

"Truth," he repeated. His tone turned sarcastic. "And are you no longer feeling faint?"

"Oh, for God's sake, James. I had to do something. *You* weren't."

His mouth formed a round *O* of shock. "Within all that is proper—"

"A hero isn't always proper. *That's* what makes him interesting."

James took his turn at pacing, hands gripped behind his back, boots kicking up clouds of dirt. "I took you into my arms. Kissed you, though it may have been an unforgivable action, given that we are not engaged nor have we even yet declared our regard for each other."

She stopped and turned to face him, jamming her hands onto her hips. "About that kiss."

"You cannot fault me. You implored me to do so. Yet you now judge me as though I have committed an act you find unacceptable. I would remind you that you yourself did such a thing not two scenes ago." He stopped and raised his palms to the sky, pleading with the moon. "How am I to understand the contrary ideas of a woman?"

Different era. Same cop-out. And it had the same effect it had had on her in the past, causing her to second-guess what she'd said, what she'd done. Maybe *she* was the one who didn't know what was going on here. It was either that or the guy was a pompous jerk who wouldn't know a romantic moment if it sat up and smacked him across the face. *Mary. How could you do this?* She dug her fingers harder into her hips, ordering herself to maintain control of her colliding emotions. "That kiss—" she began.

He took a step toward her. "You need not extend your apology."

"My *apology?*" A virtual runaway freight train of anger ran straight toward him, taking out overhanging trees and entire landscapes in its path, villagers running screaming for the hills. As anger shrieked through her veins, she struggled to find enough control not to shake him. "I felt nothing from that kiss. Do you understand me? Nothing."

His eyebrows lifted and a wrinkle of confusion appeared on his forehead. "Perhaps if you were to give more eff—"

And there it was. The word that was going to make her turn a chamber pot over his head at the first available opportunity. "*Effort?* Are you *really* going to say that word to me, when I have been doing everything humanly possible to make this story work?" Pacing again, this time in short, sharp steps that made her toes hurt. "No. You are *not* going to do that."

"Miss Ellingson!"

The sharpness of his tone made her whirl around, facing him again. She was not a five-year-old to be scolded. She was a grown woman, who had just been kissed, and badly, by a pompous ass. She sucked in a breath. "We have a problem."

He shook his head. "I confess myself quite unable to comprehend your demands."

That was one way to look at it. His way. The freight train picked up speed again, whistle blaring in one long and steady, piercing scream. She pressed her fingers to her forehead, shutting her eyes. "I don't know what to do here."

"It is simple," she heard him reply, though she hadn't invited him to. "We await the author's pen."

But Mary had to have known that kiss didn't go well. Or she would have had Jane swooning in his arms, swaying from weakened knees. Something. Even if Jane hadn't felt it inside, there would have been a physical reaction. Some sort of clue. "That's what I'm afraid of."

She felt a pat on her arm, meant apparently as reassurance. "A female commonly has fears," he said, as though he knew anything at all about women. "There is, however, no need."

No need. Right. Because all-knowing, all-powerful James was here. A groan, low and frustrated, escaped from her.

He ignored it. "Shall we rejoin the others? I am certain they would take great pleasure in hearing you play once again. And it would no doubt calm you, as well."

Her eyes flew open. She stared at him, her breath

coming in furious puffs. In that instant, she did the only thing that kept her from derailing in a blinding crash of words and fury, leaving the wreckage strewn all over James.

She pushed her way past him and ran into the night.

The moonlight, at least, made it easier to barrel through the darkness, skirts forming a protective cushion on all sides. Behind her, she heard something that sounded like an oath from James, but she didn't hear sounds of him following her. He would have to, of course, because what kind of a gentleman would go outside with a lady and not return with her? *That* would be an explanation worth listening to.

At this moment, she had to be anywhere but with him. Someplace where she could sort out the mess she seemed to be making of a life that was scripted for her. Where all she had to do was play along and say the words to win a nice, safe existence, free of accidental wrong-saying and wrongdoing.

If she couldn't even manage *that*, she was a bigger failure than she had thought.

She rounded the corner of the house and stopped, pressing one hand to the rough-hewn rock wall and another to her stomach. Been a while since she'd been to the gym. Last time, she'd managed to run straight off the treadmill when a very good-looking guy smiled at her. And here she was, running straight into the darkness, where anything could happen.

Yet even as she offered up the excuse, she knew this ache in her middle had little to do with her athleticism. Or lack of it.

In the distance, she heard James's voice, calling out. "Miss Ellingson?" Back to formalities. And he wasn't exactly in hot pursuit.

Peering into the night, she saw the outline of buildings a short distance away. Stables, possibly. Maybe she could dive under a stack of hay long enough to bring her thoughts into synch, to come up with a plan of action. With any luck, after a cursory look around, James would come up with a plausible excuse for her absence and give up looking.

Of course, if Mary ever caught wind of that kind of behavior, he'd be a hero with a *z* instead of an *h* and they'd all be doomed.

Think. She had to think.

She picked her way across the path that led away from the house and then scooped up her skirts to run through the grass in what appeared to be a more direct route to her destination. As she came closer, she saw it was actually one building, in the shape of an *L*, with high stone walls and small windows in the upper part of the center section.

She stopped and reached up, pulling her hair from its restrictions to let it tumble around her shoulders. It felt good. Free. With her breath coming hard and her feet hitting the ground with as little sound as possible, she ran toward the building. When at last she reached one end, she ducked into the tall shadows it cast to watch for James, her fingers against the wall.

It took only a minute or so for her to see him, illuminated at the top of the hill. "Jane?" he called into the stillness. "Are you there?" He stood there, waiting, while she held her breath. When no answer came, he retreated back toward the house.

She exhaled, as relieved as she was disappointed. He could have tried a little harder, even if she didn't want him to. Then she allowed herself to take a few deep breaths while she tried to get her bearings.

Alone. In the night. Light-years away from all she knew. In another country. Another century. Dressed in yet another torturous corset with enough layers of fabric on her to make an entire summer camp of yellow silk tents. Running from the man who was slated to be her husband for the next fifty years or so.

Might take a while to get those bearings. She'd pull a Scarlett O'Hara and think about that tomorrow.

Emerging from the shadows, she took cautious steps around the corner and heard a gentle whinny coming from inside the building. So she'd been right. It was a stable.

One door loomed directly in front of her, with two high-arched ones to the left. After a brief hesitation, she chose one of the arched doorways and inched her way into the stables.

Jane paused, allowing her eyes to adjust to a darkness relieved only by slivers of light coming in from the moon. On either side, she could make out stalls with wooden doors. In the one nearest to her, she saw the outline of a horse's head, his ears up.

She made herself as small as possible, creeping along on tiptoe. No need to sound the horse alarm, letting James know exactly where she'd gone.

A pungent mixture of horse, fresh straw, dirt and manure assaulted her nostrils, making her wrinkle her city-girl nose. It wasn't a bad aroma, just sort of earthy. Still, someplace *clean* to hide would be a good thing.

She'd just reached the end of the row of stalls and followed a turn to the right when she heard a man's voice. Quickly, she flattened herself against a stall, drawing interest from its occupant, who gave a small whinny from above her.

The male voice stopped for a moment but then resumed in tones too low for her to understand the words. After several seconds had passed, she allowed herself to look closer. She knew that voice. Knew its rumble. Her pulse had recognized it before her brain had. Curran.

As she watched, he raised a hand to run it along the side of a horse's face, blowing gently on its nostrils. The horse shook his head and gave an answering snort, earning a smile from the man. It was a gentle side of the normally fierce Curran that she'd seen only glimpses of earlier.

Jane debated whether to show herself or to slip back into the night, but before she could decide, the horse on the other side of the wooden stall did it for her, bringing up the volume on his alarm this time.

"Who's there?" Curran demanded.

Jane stepped into the faint light. "It's me."

"Come closer."

Not a good idea, given her current escalating heart-beat. But Jane had never considered herself someone with exceedingly good judgment. And right now, she was on the run. She did as he asked, stopping a foot or so away from him. "What are you doing here?" she asked.

"That inquiry is mine to make."

Hard to argue that. "I was out . . . walking."

"Surely not alone." Exasperation circled the edges of his voice.

Much as she hated to admit it, the idea of a man concerning himself with her safety had its attraction. If he wanted to mount a fiery steed and defend her honor while fending off potential attackers, who was she to stop him? Unless she was taking this line of thinking a little further than he had actually *intended*. "James was with me. He decided to go inside."

Curran dropped his hands from his horse's head. "Leaving you to wander the grounds unaccompanied?" He took a step away. "Irresponsible lout. I shall find him at once."

"No." She put a hand on his arm. "I left. I just— wanted time to myself."

He stared down at her hand.

She withdrew it slowly. Right. The villain.

Curran turned back to his horse.

"Must be yours," Jane said.

"He is."

"Do you like to ride him at night, hard and fast through the dark?" Her tone didn't sound quite as casual as she had hoped it would. Her pulse quickened.

His eyes held hers until Jane had to drop her gaze to stare at the floor. Did he think she was suggesting . . . ?

"In indulging himself in such foolhardy activity, my brother has broken the spirit of one bold horse and the leg of another." Jane looked up to see his eyes glinting in the near-darkness. "James has a recklessness that too often soundly defeats reason."

She fought a sense of disappointment that had nothing to do with James and his recklessness. "I think I've known a few people like that in my life." She moved toward the horse, lifting her hand. "May I?"

In one smooth motion, Curran drew her to him. "From his side. He must be able to see you. To know your purpose."

She followed his instructions, approaching the horse cautiously at first and then relaxing enough to enjoy the feel of his mane against her fingers. It was better than thinking about the way the nearness of his master seemed to rob her of her breath. "What were you doing earlier? Blowing on his nose?"

"Horses often greet each other in such a manner. I am told it expresses respect."

"What's his name?"

"Alfred."

She tipped her head, thinking. "A good, strong name."

"It was my mother's surname. The name I bore at birth." With a pat for his horse, he stepped back from the stall and waited for her to do the same. When she had, he pushed the top part of the door back in place and began to walk away. She followed.

"Do you miss being an Alfred?"

"One cannot miss what is not gone."

"What were you talking about with Alfred?"

Even in the shadows, she could detect his surprise at the question. But it disappeared quickly, his features regaining their more practiced, unreadable expression. "Simply the words of praise any master would give his horse at the end of a day. Before the start of the next."

Jane was no expert on human-to-horse communication, but she'd bet it wasn't quite as simple as that. She'd opened her mouth to say something to that effect when she heard another voice, from not far away, calling her name. James. From the sound of his boots, he was getting close. She grabbed Curran's upper arm, holding on tight. "If he finds me right now, I'm going to have to hurt him."

He barked a laugh, quickly stifled. "Not precisely the action your hero might seek."

"Just don't tell him I'm in here. That's all I ask. I will go back and everything will be fine. Just not now." She looked from one side to the other, scampering ahead, skirts hoisted, to find somewhere, anywhere, to hide.

Then she found it, an empty stall with what smelled like fresh straw. Turning back, she hissed one final word of entreaty over her shoulder. *"Please."* She held her breath, closed her eyes and dove into the pile, covering herself head to toe with the straw. And waited, hoping the effort at deception would be worth it. The straw was already beginning to make her itch. Who knew what kind of bugs or . . . other things might be lurking in it.

She heard James's voice and boots. Coming close. Very close. "Curran," he snapped. "Have you seen Miss Ellingson?"

"Do not tell me you have misplaced her, James."

The younger brother's answer was terse. "Kindly do me the favor of a reply."

"The lady in question has, I am given to believe, returned to her bedchambers."

"Are you quite certain of that?"

"It is what she indicated."

A pause. "So you are the last to have seen Miss Ellingson."

Hey now. What was James trying to establish here? That if anything bad happened to Jane, Curran alone would be responsible? Would be fingered by the police as the "last to have seen her"? Let's go back to that list of James's Good Qualities. Minus ten points for callous disregard.

"She appeared in the stables briefly."

"Her aunt, and indeed her father, would be most distressed to learn it."

"Then I suggest they do not."

James cleared his throat. "I must determine she is safely returned. I shall have the maid check to see that she is in her bed."

All right. Add back five points for follow-through . . . Never mind. This whole list was making her head hurt.

"It would be wise," Curran agreed.

What? No, it wouldn't.

"I am returning to the house myself," he added. "I shall accompany you."

Jane remained perfectly still, even as she heard creaking from the floor above. Servants. Another creak of floorboards sounded, prompting a ripple of panic up her spine. Being a stable servant probably didn't require references. Or a background check. The sound of Curran and James's voices, and their boots, faded as they walked from the stables. She would be left alone. Her, the horses and the suspicious servant element.

So much for defense of her honor and person. She

pushed her head up, spitting bits of straw from her lips. Great. Now she had to hightail it back to the house and into her bedroom before James discovered she wasn't there, sounded the alarm and organized a search party, complete with lanterns of fire.

What did a girl have to do to get a minute alone around here?

Chapter 12

She knew she should have bolted from the stable stall, boots flying, to get back to the house before James did. But instead, Jane remained sitting in the midst of straw and skirts, running through a mental assessment of her current status in life. She had never had much success at being Scarlett O'Hara, no matter how many times she tried it. The things she didn't want to think about until tomorrow, or *never*, always came surging back to hit her in the face and demand attention. Now.

In the twenty-first century, she'd ruined her chances with her job, boyfriend and social life. In the nineteenth century, she didn't even have much hope of gainful employment, couldn't seem to get on compatible footing with her alleged almost fiancé and any social life that didn't include the pianoforte was a pretty remote possibility.

But she had one important constant in both centuries. No matter what, Jane was still Jane. And that didn't seem to be a particularly good thing.

Giant tears formed in her eyes. She felt one begin to roll down her cheek, while the other remained stuck, turning the vision in one eye blurred and watery. She sniffed, sinking into a quicksand of self-recrimination and pity. The tear spilled out at last, rolling down her other cheek.

Some people knew all the right things to do, without even having to think about it. *They* weren't so accident-prone that people joked they didn't want to sit too close to their water glasses. Or walk too close to their stilettos.

Those people didn't blurt things out and two seconds later want to frantically push DELETE. Or just plain make a mistake and want to hide in a closet, arms over their heads, once it had been realized. No. *Those* people always knew what to do and how to do it right.

The virtual quicksand began to close in, reaching her neck. She was going down. And who would miss her? Her cheeks were wet, tears splashing. They would reach her dress soon. Then the straw. She was drowning in defeat and self-pity.

Some heroine. Mary Bellingham needs to have her writer's license revoked. At the thought, Jane gave an even louder sniff, wiping her sleeve across her face. Of all the people out there in the world who could have picked up that stone and made a wish, why had she been the one? Nearby, a horse stirred and sputtered.

"Unless you have a way out of this mess, keep your opinions to yourself," she choked out.

She heard a rustle. Then, "You have frightened my horse." The voice, deep and familiar, came from above her head.

Jane's chin whipped up. She raked both sleeves over her eyes, frantic to wipe the flood damage from her face. The lantern Curran carried moved to illuminate her cheeks before she could succeed. "I didn't—didn't mean to."

Most of his face was hidden by the shadows, while hers felt glaringly exposed. Pushing against the floor with her feet, she scooted backward, away from the light.

"I am quite certain you had no such intention, but there you have it, all the same."

His matter-of-fact tone caught her off guard, disarming her instincts to duck and run for cover. Pressing both palms into the straw, Jane turned her head in the direction of Alfred's stall. "I don't know how to calm a horse."

"It is simply a matter of assuring him that the noise will soon cease." He moved the lantern closer to his face. As the beams lit the strong planes of his features, she could see that his eyes held concern. "Would that be true?"

Jane took a deep breath, straightening her shoulders, and then let it out, feeling the weight of a weariness that seemed to penetrate to her bones. "Yes." She didn't mean it. As soon as he left, she'd be crying her eyes out again. But while he was here, she could manage to contain it. Maybe.

He extended his hand.

She hesitated and then took it, allowing him to help her to her feet. His hand felt strong and comforting and the feel of his skin, pressed into hers, sent tingles of heat shooting from her fingers to her shoulders and all the way to her toes. She cast her eyes down and brushed bits of straw from her clothing, determined not to let him see what his touch did to her.

If the same thing had happened even *once* when she was with James, there wouldn't be a problem. She pressed a hand to her forehead, looking at the stalls, the equipment hanging from hooks on the wall, the floor. Looking anywhere but at Curran. "How can you tell when Alfred is frightened?" Get the conversation away from her and the fact that her eyes had to now be rimmed with a less-than-attractive red. And on to anything else.

Curran hung the lantern on a hook near his horse's stall. "It is much the same as when a person is frightened. There is a look in his eyes, certain sounds that emerge and a reluctance to be approached." He reached out to pat the horse and then looked over at Jane.

A silence hung in the air between them, one that she hoped he would fill with words, so that she didn't have to. She wasn't sure she could trust herself enough.

But he didn't say a word. Finally, she folded her arms tight across her ribs and said, untruthfully, "I'm not frightened."

From behind Curran, Alfred gave a snort that sounded like disbelief.

"You stay out of this," she said to him.

Then she turned back to Curran. "I'm not." Jane brushed hair from her eyes with a jerk of her hand. "I'm frustrated."

Still Curran didn't speak. He just put a hand on the wall and leaned against it, his eyes on Jane. "Okay, maybe I'm a *little* frightened," she admitted. "You would be, too, if you didn't know how you got here or what was going to happen. Especially when there's a writer you've never seen or heard who supposedly holds your entire life in her hands and *she* doesn't seem to have a clue about what she's doing. And you don't know if you can keep it together long enough to keep from messing everything up because that's what you *always* seem to do no matter how hard you try *not* to." She took big, heaving breaths.

A furrow appeared between Curran's thick, dark brows. He reached for the lantern, took her elbow and began steering her away from the horse's stall. "Come with me."

She did. There was a huge difference between the way he said it and James's no-questions-asked *Come* command. Speaking of which . . . "Is James going to raise an alarm when he finds out I'm not at the house?" It wasn't as though she had a cell phone to call him and say she'd be late, not to worry. And the last thing she needed was a search party descending on her.

"James allowed himself to be convinced that you have retired to your bedchambers with an unfortunate headache."

Jane suppressed an irrational feeling of disappointment. It was what she wanted him to do, right? She walked with Curran down the wooden floor of the hall and out through the heavy door, hearing the occasional shifting and sputtering of horses they passed on the way. Jane darted a look up at him as they emerged into the cool night air. "I guess I should be glad he won't be coming after me."

A slight dip of his chin. No comment.

"So he let his villainous brother tell him I'm fine and not to worry." She shook her head. "He needs to work on this hero thing."

They continued walking for several minutes, Curran leading the way with one hand holding the lantern and the other on her elbow. She liked the feel of his hand, protective and confident. Not that it would do any good to think about that right now. Or any time.

"It seems desperately important to you to know precisely what is to come," he said.

"Only in these circumstances. Because so much depends on things turning out well." And that was different from life . . . how?

"One can never be entirely certain of what is to happen, under any circumstance." There was a hint, but only a hint, of resignation in his voice.

She searched what she could see of his face. "You've had to deal with a lot of uncertainty in your life."

"No more than any other."

"But you—" She broke off, for once choosing to listen to an inner voice that piped up from the cheap seats. *Not yet,* it warned. *Don't make it about him.* After a pause to regroup, she tried again. "So would you like to hear about *my* brother?"

"Yes." He nodded.

Her inner voice, shocked beyond belief at having been listened to, sat down and slapped virtual high-fives with the other instincts she never paid any attention to.

"He's not at all like yours, but he can sometimes cause as much trouble. Troy's a great guy. I love him, really I do. But he's practically perfect in every way." She paused, sliding a glance over at Curran as she wondered if he would get the Mary Poppins reference. Uh, no, a little after his time. She went on, "That can be just as hard to take. Especially when you're me. Potentially disastrous in every way." A small gulp.

"He is critical of you?"

"No."

"Demands that you be as perfect as he?"

She shook her head. "No. Of course not."

"Then perhaps the trouble, as you call it, lies with you."

Cold. She clenched her fists. "That's the whole point." He didn't have to be so blunt about it.

"If you were to ask your brother," Curran said in a low voice that brushed across her like a gentle breeze, "I suspect he would answer that it is tiresome to be thought of as perfect. It would leave so little to be accomplished in life." He pushed out his bottom lip, thinking. "When one is less than perfect, there is much yet to be achieved."

If that were the case, Jane would have a whole world of opportunity at her feet. She found herself telling him about growing up with Troy, the fun times they'd had as kids on the family road trips that seemed endless at the time but seemed great when looking back. "He used to *sell* me Pepto-Bismol tablets when I got carsick," she said, laughing. "Until one time when I refused to pay and threw up all over him. After that, the Pepto-Bismol was free." She told Curran about her father and her mother. He listened to it all, nodding, asking questions. It felt good.

Then she asked, "Tell me about your mother." When his mouth opened, she added, "Not about what happened to her, but about *her*. Who she was as a person. I'd really like to know."

Curran's chin lifted and she watched as he ran his tongue along his upper lip, apparently considering her question.

His tongue. What—What was it she had asked him? Her mind had gone blank, able to focus only on that tongue. And what it might feel like inside her . . . mouth. Whew. It was getting warm in the night air. She fanned at her face.

"I was a small boy."

Right. His mother. Thank God he'd put away that tongue. "What does—" She stopped to clear her throat, which seemed awfully dry all of a sudden. "What does the small boy remember about her?" She reached over to lift the lantern to see his face.

He looked at her then and she thought she could see his mask of careful indifference slip. For just a second. As a TV character on a show she'd once loved had often said, *"Have mercy."* "He remembers a very beautiful woman," he replied, "who smelled of flowers." The shadow of a smile curved his lips. "And had a voice that sounded like music."

"She sounds wonderful," Jane whispered.

He tipped his head. "A small boy believed it so."

In that instant, her heart melted for the boy that lived within him still.

He must have seen it on her face because his own quickly became unreadable again and his tone firm. "There is no certainty to be found in life."

True. But there was certainty. And there was *certainty*.

"I had a very different life than this. Before. Maybe a day, a week ago? I've lost track of time. And even though I could never tell what was going to happen in that life, I *really* can't tell with this one. There's so much that's out of my control. I have no frame of reference for living in Victorian times, nothing to hold on to. And . . ." She sighed so hard, her toes curled. "No way back."

"Ah," he said. The lantern, once again in his commanding grasp, cast its swinging rays of light before them. "As you have said. If my memory is to be trusted, this may well have something to do with the stone you seek."

"*Everything* to do with the stone."

"How is that so?"

"I made a wish . . . on the stone, to be out of there. To go someplace where I could start over, where no one knew me." She shook her head. "I meant someplace like Vancouver, maybe. *Not* England. *Not* more than a century in the past." She looked up at him. "What year is it, anyway?"

"It's 1849."

"Of course, 1849. Makes all the sense in the world." Again, she heaved a sigh. "*I* live in 2007. Do you see the problem?"

His mouth opened, but he closed it again, without reply. He saw the problem. She was pretty sure of it.

They reached a small grove of trees. Holding the lantern high, Curran pointed the way to a place that appeared to be one huge tree, but upon closer inspection turned out to be two, with a hollowed-out flat spot nearly the size of a small sofa at the intersection of the roots. He set the lantern on the ground and with his hand, indicated the area in the trees. "Shall we sit?"

"Sure. I guess so." Okay. This wasn't strange. An old nursery rhyme slipped into her head. Curran and Jane, sittin' in a tree. K-I-S-S-I- . . . She pushed her hand against her mouth to stifle the half-unhinged giggle that threatened to spill out. While it was an appealing idea, there was virtually no chance she'd be kissing Curran in the tree. The heroine and the villain? No way. Probably. *Sleep, Mary. Sleep well. In fact, sleep in.*

She sat, settling her skirts around her. Then Curran sat down. *His thigh is touching mine.* The sensation had her so zeroed in on her right leg and his left one, it took a minute for her to realize he was talking. "I'm sorry." She gulped. "I didn't hear you."

To say the least.

He settled against the part of the tree trunk that formed a back of sorts. "Though you may have a different history, in some manner of speaking, you are the author's invention, as are we all."

The author's invention. Pulling her mouth in tight, she chewed on her bottom lip. In a way, she wished they could stay here forever. Where the air, cool and clean, drifted to her nostrils, the worn tree roots cradled her bottom comfortably and Curran's thigh pressed against hers in a most un-Victorian way. If she didn't say anything, didn't move, didn't do anything at all, it was possible she wouldn't take this moment out in a blinding flash of accidental ineptitude.

"The characters an author creates," he said, "are hers alone for that piece of time. She will do with them as she likes and if all proceeds to a satisfying conclusion, the characters continue on past the final page to live as they choose, free of constraint."

"So, as long as there's a happy ending, everybody can do what they want after the book is done."

"A happy ending? Not always. But it must be satisfying."

A tiny sprig of hope pushed its way up and out of her mouth. "Does that mean I don't have to end up with James?"

His hand reached out and his fingers turned her chin toward him. "You do not understand this author."

"Then make me understand." *Make me do anything but think about how good your fingers feel on me, how appealing your mouth looks in the moon and lantern light, how I never noticed you have that small bump on your nose that looks absolutely kissable. Make me think of anything but that. Curran and Jane, sittin' in a tree . . .*

He dropped his hand. "My brother James is the love Mary Bellingham was not allowed to fulfill. And I am the one who ensured she was unable to marry him."

That one took a minute to make its way in through the flurry of her senses on high sexual alert, but it finally did. If James was the one Mary wanted and Curran was the one she held responsible for not being able to marry her true love, that didn't bode well for any role reversals. This time, it was Jane who said, "I see." And Curran who stared into the darkness. "It must be difficult to know you're the one the author . . . doesn't like."

"It has much to do with the reasons she renders me largely unsuccessful in my endeavors to keep James from inheriting everything. I must be, in some respects, incapable."

"An incapable villain doesn't make for a very compelling story. Unless it's a comedy."

He stared hard into her eyes. "That is true. And while I am many things, comedic is not one of them."

Jane gave a little snort and then, realizing what she'd done, clapped a hand to her mouth.

This time Curran actually smiled.

The effect on her was as devastating as the tongue incident had been. *Focus, Jane. Focus.*

No response from the brain cells assigned to focusing. She raised her brows and tipped her head, trying to cover for her trembling mouth. "Or, it could be that

Mary doesn't have an evil bone in her body and doesn't know what to do with you. Doesn't know how to be devious." She brought her face closer to his. "I'm not convinced you know how to be evil or devious, either."

"Entirely untrue." Stiffening, he drew his shoulders back and turned away, face set. "And I shall assist the author in making that occur."

He wasn't getting off that easy. "I've seen you with Alfred."

"The capacity for evil does not preclude kindness to animals."

Or kindness to Jane, for that matter, but she decided not to point that out at the moment. "James doesn't seem to have the same feeling about the animals in his care."

He made a disparaging sound. "Childish foolishness."

"You're wrong!" she burst out. "It isn't just foolishness. He's selfish. He thinks so much about himself, he doesn't have the time to think about anyone else. And when his selfishness hurts others—" A shock rippled through her as she realized that what she'd just said *might* not apply only to James. Selfishness. That hurt others.

She dropped her chin, staring at her hands in the darkness. Could it be that—? She might have been a little selfish about wanting to get married, about wanting someone to find out about the senator's hypocritical stance on drinking, a little jealous of . . . Holly's shot at forever-after happiness? *Oh, no.*

Maybe she and James weren't such a bad match, after all.

"Every character in a tale has the capacity for both selfish and heroic action," Curran said. "It depends on which the author chooses to emphasize."

Too true. But they'd been talking about him and his less-than-villainous nature. Right now, she didn't want to think about anything else. *Couldn't* think about anything else. "You're stalling."

"Stall—? I confess you baffle me, Miss Ellingson." He didn't make it sound like a good thing.

"So you, Curran Dempsey, are a *villain*." She aimed a skeptical look at him, folded her arms and nodded. "Really."

"We had best return." He made a movement as if to rise.

Jane's arm shot out to stop him. "Prove it," she said.

"*Prove* it?"

It was in her head and then out of her mouth. Even she couldn't believe she'd said it. And she could feel an entire virtual row of all her best instincts slinking down in their chairs, covering their eyes. She had to speak again, if only to cover the fact that her heart was beating so loud, he had to be able to hear it. "An actual villain, the real thing, would kiss me right now. Would try to take the heroine away from his brother, the hero. *That* would be a downright evil thing. Something a villain would do."

His eyes bored into her.

"But you're not doing it," she said lightly, though her voice was starting to shake. "So I rest my case. You're not a villain." What was she *doing*?

His face moved to within a few inches of hers, so close she could feel his warm breath caressing her mouth. "Were I to kiss you," he rumbled, each word clearly articulated, "it would not be for the sake of proving my worth as a villain."

Heat flooded through her. Were he to kiss her. Omigod. *Were* he?

Jane struggled to think straight, an impossibility as it turned out, because Curran's lips, the same ones that had rendered her useless at the sight of his tongue running along them, were very, very close to hers. He . . . Oh, God . . . What? He's said something about . . . What? Shivers ran up her arms and raced down her back. And her

ordinarily steady heart turned things over to a marimba
band on fast forward. "I—I—" Um . . . What was the
quest—question?

"Jane."

"Yes," she breathed, then cleared her throat. "Curran."

"How is it you plan to ensure James wins your heart?"

How did she plan to . . . ? Hold on. The shivers halted
and the marimba band stopped playing midnote. "What?"
If there had been an *s* in the word, her hiss would have
shot saliva all over him. For the best, then. That never
helped a romantic moment.

He drew back. "We have agreed the author must re-
ceive the help she needs to bring the story to a satisfac-
tory conclusion. I shall influence, in any manner I am
able, her writing of the villain. You must have an influence in James's courtship."

Still shrouded in the fog induced by the close proximity of his mouth, she narrowed her eyes and gave her
head a shake. "When did I agree?"

Now he was the one to narrow his eyes. "We discussed
it earlier and have just discussed it now."

The fog began to clear. "I don't think so. We discussed
the fact that you wouldn't kiss me just to prove you're a
real villain."

His facial muscles relaxed at that and he turned a half-
lidded gaze on her that set off the marimba band again,
playing triple-time. "Indeed we did."

"Well, you know what?" she asked lightly. "I may just kiss
you to prove that *I* am." As her inner voice threw up her
hands in despair and sank to the ground, Jane put her
hands on either side of Curran's face, tipped her head
and kissed him.

She seemed to be doing that a lot lately.

Chapter 13

Curran's lips fulfilled their promise, Jane discovered seconds after she had landed the unauthorized kiss on them. But that was as far as she could manage to think before she melted, body and soul, into the touch of their mouths and tongues. His, warm and urgent, pushing farther, deeper. Her heartbeat quickening until she couldn't breathe. Everything going black until she could feel nothing but him, think of nothing but him.

After a minute or ten, she felt him pull back. Then he grasped her arms, struggling for his voice. "This will not do."

"Yes, it will," she rasped. "It just *did*."

He released her abruptly and stood, leaving the hollowed-out spot in the tree to pace back and forth. It took everything she had not to follow, throwing herself back into his arms.

"You must understand." One hand raked through his dark hair. "This"—he gestured at first himself and then her—"will endanger the story."

Deep breaths. Lots of them. *Reclaim your brain, Jane. It's in there somewhere.* "The story has a lot bigger problems than—" Breaking off, she also gestured to the two of them and turned her mouth into an if-you-can't-see-that-you're-blind expression she hoped would hide the hurt and fear beginning to whirl at full force inside her.

Hadn't he *felt* it? Couldn't he at least acknowledge it?

Curran stood motionless in the shadows while Jane gripped her fingers together and contemplated a run for the house. Duck and cover. It worked in earthquakes and this situation had definite similarities. Her inner voice began squeaking, but she firmly clapped a hand over its mouth. If there was one thing she couldn't take hearing, it would be that she'd been wrong. That Curran hadn't really kissed her back.

Because he *had.*

"It is true enough there are problems with the author's story," he said. "You and I have agreed upon that and also that we will attempt to help Miss Bellingham in resolving them." He began to pace again, his words falling into the night air. "And it is true that only a villain would make love to the woman his brother is intended to wed. I am, however, *not* such a man."

Hearing the words "make love" come out of his mouth, in direct association with her . . . The picture they formed in her head . . . It was hard to concentrate on what he was saying instead of watching his thighs ripple when his feet pounded the ground. She'd never been this powerfully attracted to anyone, even Byron, the one she'd thought she'd spend the rest of her life with.

She tried her best to regain her dignity and carry on a seminormal conversation. One that didn't involve tongues or the idea of a certain man naked, *making love.* To her. Whew. Not so easy. She blinked. Hard. "So . . ." she said, crossing her legs and leaning forward, "you would cheat him at cards or . . . maybe put something in his drink, but you wouldn't take his woman. Do I have it right?" So much for dignity. The sarcasm oozed out of her like a lava flow.

He stopped. "Not precisely in those terms, but I suppose it is close to the truth, yes."

"Uh-huh." Jane nodded her head. "Sort of a code of honor among villains that they don't do that kind of thing." Rejection. It stung. A lot.

He remained silent. Too silent.

Her inner voice was now pummeling fists against her rib cage, trying to get her attention. Jane gave in and snapped her mouth shut.

Curran strode back to her and stood, looking down. She looked away, unable to meet his gaze. Putting his fingers under her chin, he attempted to lift it so that she would look at him. Reluctantly, she did, hating that she could feel her bottom lip quiver.

"There is a part of me that would choose to stay here with you on this night," he rumbled. "And another that knows there could be no worse choice to be made."

"Thanks." She tried to be offhand, but it didn't come out that way. If he gave her one sign, the very slightest inclination that he meant what he said about staying with her, she would jump into his arms, wrap her legs around him and demand that the willing part of him be the only part he listen to. His inner voice had to be as hell-bent on being obeyed as the one that lived inside Jane.

Of course, the difference was, she usually ignored hers.

"If we choose a path the author cannot abide, we endanger ourselves and all in this story. Once discarded, characters rarely again emerge. They are doomed to a life only partially fulfilled. One with no future. No hope of happiness."

Sounded something like her life already, but if she said that, he wouldn't understand. She looked down.

A gentle tug on her chin. "I could not be responsible for that. Do you understand me?"

Too well. She gave him a rueful smile. "You know, you really need to work harder at being a villain. So far, you're not that good at it."

"I intend to." He gave her a half smile of his own. Then he lowered his voice and dipped his chin low enough to put him at eye level with her. "Though I venture to say *you* would be a resounding failure as a villain, despite your willingness to attempt it."

It wasn't fair, the fact that his touch sent shivers of anticipation running all through her, that with just a look aimed in her direction, he could send every thought she had scurrying in a dizzying race to leave her head.

She wished she had an effect like that on him.

He straightened. "I will accompany you to the house. You must slip through the back entrance and into your chambers undetected."

"Why don't we stay here for awhile?"

A girl could ask.

"Miss Ellingson, you will come with me." Apparently not. His voice was ominous, *almost* villainous, if she didn't know better.

She stood, with all the grace she could muster, considering she had to be dragging twenty pounds of dead weight around with all the fabric in her skirts. "I believe I'm ready to go in now."

He crooked his arm and offered it to her. She had just laid a hand on it, enjoying the feel of his arm beneath the jacket, when he stiffened.

"What is it?"

"Pay heed. There is not much time."

Jane stifled a groan. "She's writing again?"

He whirled to face her. "You must attempt to persuade James—"

* * *

His last words were lost in a rush of colors and light that stilled as quickly as it came.

Jane's eyes opened and she found herself seated at the pianoforte again, fingers hovering above the keys. Didn't Mary Bellingham know anything *else* to do with her? She began to play, all the time sighing so hard mentally, her inner voice clapped a hand to its forehead in despair.

Above her, James stood smiling. "I find your playing soothing, Jane," he said, loud enough to be heard over the music. Didn't take that much. She wasn't exactly launching into a rousing rendition of anything. And soothing. Okay. That explained why he didn't look close to grabbing and ravishing her here in the drawing room where they were . . . alone, she noticed, looking around.

Attempt to persuade James, Curran had said. That would take some doing. She concentrated hard, focused on stilling her hands. No time like the present. It took a minute, but at last, her fingers extended straight out and came to a rest on the keys.

James looked at her. "Another song?"

This time, it took everything she had to suppress the words forming on her tongue and instead say, "No." She kept her gaze on James.

He waited, a baffled expression making its way across his face.

Again, she focused her energies. "Perhaps we might . . . *ride.*" Geez, the effort on that one had her nearly out of breath.

His mouth opened, but it took a minute for his reply. "I shall call for the carriage."

She steeled herself for another fight. Mary didn't disappoint. "No," Jane finally managed.

"No?"

"I . . . prefer . . . a horse." This time, she wanted to slap the table with her hands to regain her normal breathing, though nothing seemed to show on the outside.

"But, Jane. Surely . . ." His voice trailed off. Apparently he didn't know what he surely meant.

She waited. For him. For Mary, for *somebody* to decide what to say.

A pause and he again said, "I shall call for the carriage," as if he hadn't said it just a minute ago.

She concentrated, willing her tongue into . . . "No. I would prefer"—those *f*'s were hard—"to ride a horse."

No *"But Jane, surely"* this time. Instead, he said, "Very well. I shall have the horses brought around."

Since she couldn't exactly celebrate, pumping her fist in the air, Jane settled for the polite smile Mary allowed her. Just wait until she got James alone, riding their horses through a secluded romantic field. Then she'd persuade him to—

Do what, exactly?

Curran returned to the sanctuary of the stables, steps hammering along the path, knowing that a scene was at that very moment being played out between Jane and James. A scene he had no part of. Though he could have lingered in the background, watching from a position safely out of sight, he refused to give in to such a weak inclination. He would have to hope Jane was doing her best to help the author with her story, just as they had discussed.

She should not have kissed him. More important, *he* should not have kissed *her*. If he were merely drawn to her soft curves, to her pink mouth, it would present problem enough. But he found himself both enchanted and infuriated by the manner in which she spoke her mind and seemed to somehow know his, asking questions about matters he had hidden deep inside.

But then, perhaps the answers to those questions helped to move the story along. It had most certainly lit a fire within him to fully remember his mother and what Benton Dempsey had done to her. How he had brought Curran here as a small boy, ordering him to renounce his birth name and become a son of the house.

Though that was all the further it had gone. He had never truly become a son of the house because of the two who refused to accept him as a rightful brother. And the father who had bowed to the wishes of his wife.

Curran had kept the name Dempsey and remained in the household, though he had never truly been a part of it. He had been educated separately and treated like a distant cousin whose presence could not be helped. Were it not for the times his father had spent, outside the knowledge of his wife and children, schooling Curran in how to sit a horse, handle a gun and other necessary skills, he would have left this place.

Benton Dempsey considered him a son, of that he was certain. It was James who stood in the way of Curran taking his rightful place. Not only for him, but also for his mother, whose sweet, lilting voice had been brought back to him vividly today. She could no longer fight for herself, but he would be glad of the chance to do it for her.

He would do all that was required to take this estate from those who had treated her, and him, as though they did not deserve it. *All* that was required.

And as for Jane Ellingson . . . While he could no longer convince himself that Jane was little more than a passing fancy, he *could* steel himself to resist the temptation she offered. Were his brother to learn of the embrace in the darkness, he would never allow the romance to go forward, despite the consequences. Curran knew his younger brother, and his misplaced pride, well enough to be certain of it.

Which meant the fates of many characters depended on Curran's resolve.

He would keep it, at all costs.

The horse brought around for Jane had a wild look in its eye, she thought nervously as James helped her up and into the sidesaddle. But then, since she knew nothing about horses, maybe they all had wild looks. Her character didn't seem to have any problem with it, gliding into the saddle with ease, and sitting, back straight and proper, while James mounted his horse.

The deep ocean blue of her skirt spread across the reddish brown horse in the sunlight, leaving her looking much more confident and assured than she felt. The sidesaddle felt precarious, at best. As though she could easily slide off and right onto the ground in a heap of humiliation. But Mary was writing and Mary didn't write a lack of coordination. Thank God.

As soon as James picked up his reins and began to ride away, she did the same, following him. They set off down a long path leading away from the house. Jane wanted to ask where they were going but couldn't sap her energy by fighting with the author so early. Better to save it up for the important stuff.

Reins held oh-so-daintily in her hands, she rode, side by side with James, but a few paces back. A sign of deference? "It is a beautiful day," she said in a voice so sugary sweet, it could have caused cavities all by itself.

James gave a nondescript reply, albeit with a brilliant smile, that Jane didn't hear because she was thinking too hard about her next move. They could ride all day, saying lovely little polite things to each other, and never accomplish anything worthwhile. What would Mary have James do, ask for her hand in marriage like he was asking her to pass the bread at dinner?

So romantic. She'd accept while spreading butter on the roll, they would smile again and somehow the whole courtship would fall apart because neither one of them wanted to be with the other. She could see herself now, being stood up at the altar, maybe not actually saying bad words, but thinking them so hard, they ended up written on her face. The vicar frowning at the nonpious display. Fury emanating from her pudgy little aunt (What *was* that woman's stake in all this, anyway?). And Mary Bellingham, throwing up her hands and chucking the whole manuscript into the fire, where they would all be doomed to . . .

She gulped, choking off the sentence she had apparently been in the middle of speaking.

"Jane?"

"Forgive me, sir. I am afraid I lost my thought."

He laughed. "Oh, Jane."

If he said she was a funny little thing again, she was going to use some of the energy she was saving by riding sidesaddle to smack him right across the—

"You are a delightful creature," he said.

Okay. She'd take delightful. For now.

They were riding past a small pond of water on their right, with wildflowers and grasses along one side. No one was about.

A perfect place to do what she had to, what she'd agreed to do. "Please," she managed with some effort. "May we stop?"

James nodded. "Why, of course, Jane. As you wish."

They turned the horses off the path and toward the pond, stopping when they were near the water's edge. Jane waited for James to help her down, which he did with all the assuredness and ease of a gentleman. He had it all, some people would think. Looks, money, social standing. And then other people, like Jane, might think he had almost nothing.

Nothing that *really* mattered, anyway.

But Curran had made it clear she had to try. So had Benton Dempsey. If for no other reason than sheer survival. It wasn't just her life. It was everyone else's.

Besides, if this all worked out, *maybe* she could say good-bye to James as soon as Mary wrote "The End" and, well, pick things up with . . . someone else.

When her feet hit the ground she held on to James's arms with her gloved hands and didn't let go. "My Jane," he said, a teasing look in his eyes. "You are my Jane, are you not?"

"If you wish me to be, sir," she said. A little too primly, Jane thought.

"Is it not true we thoroughly enjoy each other's company?"

She heard herself respond, "I find you a fascinating companion, sir." At least she smiled this time.

James smiled back, but there was no adoration to be found in his gaze. Zip. Zilch. Nada. No wonder. She'd called him a fascinating companion. Not exactly the kind of praise to go straight to a man's heart, causing him to pledge his undying love.

This called for drastic action. Book Jane might not be able to release her inner vixen, but Real Jane could. At least, she thought she could. She hadn't really ever tried it, but—Oh, forget it. Now wasn't the time to second-guess herself. She'd already done enough of that for two lifetimes.

Hold on. There seemed to be a little problem with her eyes. Mary was working hard on closing them. To hell with that. Jane needed to *see* James to seduce him. If she concentrated hard on forcing them open, she'd have . . .

half-lidded. Ta-dah. Seductive. Or, at least something close to it. Then she raised her hand, apparently catching Mary by surprise, and managed to trail one finger down his arm. "What . . . have . . . you . . ." Not easy here. "Thoroughly . . . *enjoyed*, James?"

The answering narrowing of his eyes, paired with a sly smile, implied he'd be willing to play along. "You play the pianoforte well," he began, drawing out the words.

She let her finger trip back up his arm before it began another descent down. Slowly.

He watched. "And you are . . ."

Jane used her other hand to sweep a tendril of hair from her face, arching her back slightly. "Yes?" The effort it took to get the one word out almost took her breath.

". . . quite a handsome woman."

Handsome. Took her a second to translate that one. Then . . . yes! She'd managed to get him to compliment her. Score one for the heroine. She aimed her best come-hither gaze at him, not sure how well Mary was letting it come through. Seemed to be some sort of a contortionist struggle going on with her face muscles. *Keep it steady . . . There. Whew. That one took some work.* Much more of this and she'd collapse on the ground in a heap of exhausted heroine. And not for the right reasons.

James looked a little puzzled, but after a few seconds his expression turned to one of cautious interest.

All right, then. She'd take one ladies' man, well done, with a side of thighs. The thought nearly caused her to laugh out loud, a dangerous idea since Mary seemed to be loosening the reins. "Thank you," she managed to say and then threw in a wink that must have caught the author unawares because it went off without a hitch.

"Shall we stroll?" James asked, offering his arm and a smile.

"Oh, yes. Please." This wasn't bad at all, knowing she

would walk without stumbling and falling into the pond or accidentally pushing James in. Marrying him, she could be a woman of leisure, money, social standing. With coordination by the buckets. And maybe even a title of some kind thrown in somewhere.

She glanced at James as they walked and gave him a warm smile. Her head held high, all her wishes coming true. A chance to start over, where no one knew her. No one would ever know about the proposal to Byron, the wine on the wedding dress, the press release about the senator. Everything she'd hoped for, coming true. Right here, right now.

How in the world could everything so right feel so incredibly wrong?

"Jane," said James, coming to a stop. He turned and took both of her hands, holding them up and tightly in his grip. "I have something important to ask you."

This was it. The big moment. Time for lightning bolts, birds singing, a marching band striking up. Something. At least her heartbeat should run a mile or two over the speed limit.

Nothing. She sucked in a deep breath. He hadn't asked her yet. That's all it was. He had to ask the big question and then she'd go into crazy-in-love—or at least willing-to-like—mode.

"Jane."

"Yes."

A sound like a roar came from the right. After a second or two of confusion, Jane recognized it as galloping hooves. Bearing down on them. Fast. She turned toward it, mouth open, to see a horse, streaking the air with black, and nearly upon them.

A shout from James pierced the sky and he grabbed her around the waist, throwing them both to one side and on the ground, out of danger. Terror coursed through her veins as the horse pounded past them in a rush of air. She was smashed into the front of James, the fabric of his jacket covering her face and her legs somehow wrapped around his. She lay still, afraid to move. After what seemed like forever, the sound of the hooves became fainter. From pounding to mere thudding. Somewhere other than in front of her.

She lifted her face a few inches. "I—I—" she sputtered.

James began to rise, keeping his arm around her. Once he'd made it to a sitting position, he rose and then helped her up with a great show of chivalrous care. As she brushed at her rumpled skirt, he pointed in the direction the animal had gone. "That beast," he announced, "is my father's pride and joy."

Jane's hand flew to her mouth. "And he has escaped." Turns out she was shocked by this.

James's mouth pressed into a tight line of anger. "I know who has done this. Even as our father lies on his deathbed. It is the ultimate insult."

"Who, James?"

"None other than Curran Dempsey." Now his angry gaze turned in the direction of the house. "It is he who has done this. Unforgivable."

"What shall you do?" Jane was feeling a little less than horrified about this whole thing, truth be told, but she went along with what Mary was writing. At the moment, she had other concerns: one leg and an elbow were beginning to ache. A person didn't get thrown to the ground every day. Bound to be some consequences.

He grasped her shoulders and looked intently into her eyes. "First, Jane, my dear, are you injured?"

"Please do not trouble yourself with me at such a time." What? He'd been about to ask her to marry him. Who *else* should he be troubling himself with?

He nodded, expression grave. "It is I who must rescue Lord Thunder. For the sake of my father."

Lord Thunder? *Really?* And why did she feel as though there should be superhero music building to a crescendo? She forced her eyes to his shoulders, suspicious that he'd suddenly grown a cape. "And your brother?" she heard herself squeak.

"I shall never again allow him to be called such. He has gone too far this time. Even my father will at last see it to be true."

Somebody should go after that horse. As fast as the animal had been traveling, it should be somewhere in the next county by now. And Jane didn't see any high-speed chase vehicles nearby.

"You are to return to the house at once, while I attend to this." He began walking rapidly toward their horses. "Come, Jane."

Come, Jane? The only time she was *coming* was when . . . Well, never mind that. It certainly wasn't going to be when James lifted his pinky finger and beckoned. She fought to keep her feet rooted in place. But Mary fought harder and Jane's feet began to move.

And then, a long pause. Jane's shoulders sagged in relief. Mary had quit writing.

One very serious conversation was going to happen. Right about . . . now.

Chapter 14

"I'd like to talk to you," Jane tried telling James as he bundled her up and onto her horse. "I'd like to *talk*—" The last words fell into the air because he'd already moved away from her and onto his own horse. "Hey!"

He nudged his horse into action and motioned impatiently for her to follow.

"But Mary isn't writing now!" she tried to protest.

"We must hurry," was the reply he tossed over his shoulder.

She barely caught it, he was moving so fast.

Good thing her horse seemed to know what to do because she'd quit that sidesaddle thing as soon as James had turned around, and thrown her leg over just to be sure she remained astride. It hurt. There was that *thing* in the way and nothing was the same on one side as it was on the other. Not that it mattered as much as the condition her back end was going to be in as it thumped against the saddle.

Riding. She was *horseback* riding. Any kind of an accident could happen. And probably would. Unless . . . being the heroine came with some sort of immunity? Wouldn't do Mary much good to have a heroine with broken limbs.

Although . . . if it were her legs, no one would ever know because the damn *skirts* kept them completely out of sight, anyway. What was wrong with a woman having legs, anyway? Hers weren't perfect, but she'd always thought her knees and ankles were relatively nice.

Ow. That *thing* didn't feel great thumping against her thigh. "James!" she called.

He didn't answer.

"Hey, you," she said to the horse. He ignored her as well and continued his determined pace toward home. It seemed no more than a few minutes of bumping, thumping and otherwise lumping before they were riding up to the door of Afton House. Jane blinked hard and coughed as the dust swirled and settled around her.

James jumped down and was swiftly at her side to help her down. As he reached up, he frowned. "What the devil?"

She glanced down. Her skirts didn't hide the fact that she'd thrown her other leg over the horse, and she was now hanging on for dear life, her knees pressed so tightly into the saddle, he might have a few bruises of his own. She gave him an awkward pat, feeling bad about that. As if in answer, he shifted his weight from leg to leg, waiting. James continued to frown.

"It seemed like I'd be able to ride better this way," she said with an innocent shrug. "Ride fast, anyway. We were going very fast."

"Jane." He held his arms up again.

She nodded and then attempted to descend the way Book Jane would: gracefully and with a skill that said she'd been doing it for years and expected nothing, at all, to happen.

But then . . . She wasn't Book Jane at the moment. One leg hung up on the saddle's pommel, helped along by an abundance of skirts, while the other leg slid toward the ground and Jane's head fell back toward the rear portion of the horse. Only took a few seconds for her to be dangling, half-on, half-off the horse while James sputtered and tried turning her first one way and then the other. He barked out a command to a nearby groom, who also fumbled with getting Jane off while she struggled to hold her skirts down so they didn't fly over her head. After all, there was shocking. And there was *shocking*. Another groom held the horse's head, keeping him steady.

From her nearly upside-down position, it seemed that at least three people and one horse were annoyed with her. Somewhat smaller than the usual count.

After a minute or so, they managed to get her down from the horse and right-side up on the ground. Having had a certain amount of practice in the area of recovery after embarrassing incidents, she calmly brushed back her hair and straightened her skirts.

"Jane." He stated the fact of her name.

She cleared her throat. "Yes?"

"I am off." With that, he covered the distance to his horse in a few quick strides and mounted, turning the horse and urging it into pursuit. Of the esteemed Lord Thunder.

Jane turned to the two grooms. "Thank you," she said, with all the dignity she could muster. "You may return my horse to the stable now." They didn't need to know her heart pulsed with disappointment that, without Mary's pen at work, Jane would be Jane.

The house seemed deserted, except for servants, when Jane began to roam the halls. She'd taken off her riding clothes and changed into the closest "something more comfortable" she could find among the dresses that seemed to be hers. The corset had remained, simply because it didn't seem much more comfortable to wear a dress that was too tight without it.

She had taken one un-Victorian liberty, though, by discarding her shoes to walk barefoot. It felt good, even a little decadent, to have just said no to the odd boots that seemed to be everyday wear. She let her toes wriggle into the wooden floor as she padded down the hallway.

Before long, she found herself near Benton Dempsey's chambers. As she came to the portrait of the woman with the heart-shaped face, she stopped to look at it again. On closer inspection, she thought she saw a resemblance to Violet, though the woman in the picture didn't have the resigned look of defeat that permeated Violet's delicate features.

This woman looked gentle, even hopeful as she posed. But there was that pinky finger sticking straight out and away, as though its owner longed to follow. "Did *you* get your happy ending?" Jane whispered. "Maybe you knew how to navigate your way through an author's head." There really should be road signs of some kind. WARNING. DANGEROUS PLOT AHEAD. YIELD TO AUTHOR'S WILL.

"Who's there?" she heard an imperious voice call.

The guy might be sick, but his hearing was intact. Jane walked down the hall until she reached the open door to Benton Dempsey's room. "Jane Ellingson."

"Come to see if James is a wealthy man, as yet?"

As though that was first and foremost on her mind. "Once again, you don't look close to death to me."

"A matter of some disappointment to you, I presume."

She lifted a shoulder. "I think it's more disappointing to you, actually. Are you waiting for your big, dramatic death scene?"

He looked startled for a minute and then chortled, ending with a coughing fit. When it had finished, he acknowledged, "It is a bit tiresome, being confined to bed with this miserable cough until such time as our author sees fit to put me in my grave."

"May I come in?"

Impatiently, he motioned her inside. "Provided you are not that wretched nurse. She may not enter here."

"What if she suddenly brings a miracle medicine because Mary has decided you shouldn't be written out, after all?" It could happen. She thought.

This time he gave her a look that clearly branded her naive.

She decided to regroup. "The picture in the hallway. Of the young woman in a white dress, who looks like Violet. Who is she?"

Something in his eyes melted, but then was gone in a flash. "My wife."

"She was lovely."

He nodded, as though that was a given. The wife of Benton Dempsey could be nothing but lovely. It occurred to Jane that it was pretty easy to see where James came by his pompous side.

"You were married for quite a while. And had children together."

Again, he nodded. "James and Violet."

"So when did you start up with Curran's mother? Before or after you were married?"

His eyes widened and his face hardened. "Young woman, you have—"

"I know. An impudent tongue," she interrupted. "But there's no reason to waste what time you may have left by dancing around the edges."

Benton Dempsey made a sound between a groan and a growl, lifting his palms. "In my final days," he complained to no one in particular, "I am to tolerate such impertinence from a woman whose future is dependent largely on me."

"I have a future," Jane protested, hoping it was true.

"Indeed you do, *if* you wed my son."

A little thrill ran up her spine until she reminded herself that he meant James, not Curran. She pulled over a chair and sat down beside his bed. "We were talking about your mistress."

He gave his signature *humph* and looked away.

"Fine." She stood. "I would think it gets pretty lonely up here with no one but the nurse to throw things at because I *don't* think your children are coming to see you. But if that's how you want it, I'll gladly leave."

An impatient wave of his hand. "Be gone."

"I am. Right now." She turned to leave.

When she'd nearly reached the door, he called out, "So that is how you would have it? An old man left to his bed, with none but the nurse to occasionally jab at him to see if he is yet dead?" He added a fit of coughing at the end, for good measure.

Jane stopped, stared at the door for a minute and then slowly turned. "You want me to stay."

"It is of no consequence to me. It is you I would think unwilling to behave in such a deplorable manner. Your father would not approve."

With a sigh Jane said, "I'm not worried about the approval of someone who would put me on the marriage auction block. Sell me to the highest bidder."

Benton's razor-sharp gaze belied his illness. He indicated the chair. "There is but one bidder."

Ow. A shot straight to the heart. "You don't have to be so blunt," she mumbled, walking back to the chair and slumping into it.

"I believe in stating the facts of the matter. As you yourself say, there is little time."

For some reason, her thoughts zeroed straight in on Byron and the memory of that last night with him. Had she thought there was only one bidder for her then? Had she climbed right up on that marriage auction block and practically begged him to take her? It was an awful thought.

She deserved better than that.

"Are you distressed, Miss Ellingson?"

She shook off all thoughts of Byron, and bidders, turning her attention back to the sick old man. "No," she lied. "No reason to be. No reason at all." Jane got up and began to pace back and forth. Her determination built with each step.

"Entirely true—"

"I mean, here I am, in Victorian England, where my future rests with a woman who writes me as articulate, graceful, beautiful . . ." She cast a narrowed gaze at Benton. "She *is* writing me as beautiful, right?"

He gave a grudging acknowledgment. "No more so than—"

She put up her palm. "No comparisons to dead wives or mistresses. Please."

After a brief cough, he shrugged agreement.

"I should never have to worry again about what I'll do or say because I'm close to perfect, am I not? I wouldn't be the heroine, otherwise." Her steps were getting faster now, her pacing more brisk. "And because I'm the heroine, she'll pay attention if I can somehow make her see what I see."

"You are causing my head to spin," complained the man in the bed. "Stand in one place, if you please."

She'd nearly forgotten he was in the room. "I don't please," she said, but not unkindly. She pulled to a stop, though, and began tapping her finger on her chin. "There *is* someone here who's better for me. I just have to make her see that."

From the corner of her eye, she caught sight of

Benton Dempsey trying to sit up straighter, an eyebrow raised in what looked like hope. "Oh, no you don't," she said, wagging her index finger at him. "You've already put two women in the ground. And you don't even seem that broken up about it."

As soon as the words were out, she regretted them. The man was dying, for God's sake. The thunderclouds forming on his face looked a lot like a storm front she'd seen moving in on Curran's a time or two. So much for the theory that the Devil side of the oldest son all came from his mother. "What I *meant* to say is that you're a key part of the story. She wouldn't change your circumstances just for the heroine." How many times had she begun a sentence with *"What I meant to say"* and seen the same skeptical look Benton was aiming at her right this second? "And I didn't mean—I'm sure you miss your wife and the . . . other woman. Curran's mother."

"Do not be quite so certain." His tone had a loftiness to it that almost made her smile. Almost.

"You still haven't answered my question about her. Why would you have a mistress when you had a wife right here, taking care of the life you'd built together?"

"You presume to know much about the life of others."

"I'm not presuming. I'm asking."

He sighed, turning his face to the wall. "It was simply a matter of fire and water."

Jane absorbed this, trying to understand. "And that means . . . ?"

"My wife Lydia was raised to be a lady. Her task was to put fire out wherever she found it. To drench it until nothing remained."

Not a very pretty picture of a lady, Jane thought. "Curran's mother was the fire."

"She was that. And he just like her. But while fire provides the heat we need to survive, it also injures. Destroys."

Jane stayed quiet, hoping he would go on talking, even if it was to the wall.

After a few minutes, he did. "Lydia discovered the existence of Curran's mother—"

"Why don't you ever call her by her name?" So much for remaining quiet.

He turned to look at her. "I made a vow to never again speak her name."

"But Lydia is gone now." She kept her voice low, gentle.

"I am a man of my word."

That did it. Benton Dempsey was just a little too holier-than-thou for Jane's taste, given the situation he'd single-handedly created with his three children. *Three* children, not two. "So you kept a promise to Curran's mother to raise her son as your own and you kept a promise to your wife to never speak the name of Curran's mother and to not treat Curran as your own son. Do you see a conflict between the two? You weren't keeping your word to either of those women, were you?"

The old man's face contorted, with what looked like both pain and anger. "I shall give you the benefit of my years, Miss Ellingson. Listen closely."

He'd gone back to addressing her formally.

"Yes, Mr. Dempsey?"

"Regret," he said, his mouth twisting on the word, "is something you can not turn your back on. It remains with you each day of your life, as a black hole that can never be filled, no matter how you attempt to do so."

"I—Oh." She drew back, not sure how to respond to the vehemence of his words.

"You would do well, Miss Ellingson, not to allow your heart to get the best of you, to give in to weaknesses that will only hurt you and those around you."

He *knew*. Somehow he knew what had happened between her and Curran. No. He couldn't. He had to be guessing or just giving advice because he thought she had asked for it. Or because she hadn't. *Regret. Choices.* She didn't want to hear this right now.

"What is wrong? You have gone quite pale, Miss Ellingson." There was a deliberate sting in his voice, she could hear it.

"*Nothing* is wrong. You're the one who is pale—"

She stopped when a by-now familiar feeling came over her, lifting her chin and straightening her shoulders. A flash of light and she found herself in the hallway outside Benton's bedroom, behind James, who strode into his father's bedroom.

Jane stayed at the doorway, hands clasped in front of her. Obedient fiancée-to-be.

"Father."

Benton Dempsey, who a moment ago had been sitting up and feeling scrappy enough to engage in verbal swordplay, now lay back against the pillows, his face pinched with illness. "James," he whispered.

"Sir, it is my duty to inform you that Curran today attempted to make off with Lord Thunder."

Make off with the horse? Curran wouldn't have done that. And besides, he hadn't been anywhere near that horse when it bolted past Jane and James, hell-bent on escape. What was James doing, setting up Curran for punishment? Inventing a lie and then tattling about it? Anger formed in Jane's stomach, aching because she was powerless to do anything about it. Mary had a firm hold on her. She could only stand and watch and she suspected the expression on her face was dead-on supportive of James.

The older man's eyelids fluttered and he struggled to pull himself upward.

Immediately, James was at his side, reaching toward him. "Do not, Father. You mustn't strain yourself."

Benton's movement stopped and he turned questioning eyes on his son.

"The horse is recovered." James drew himself up to his full height, which didn't exactly have him towering over the bed. "I have gone after him and he is again safely in the stable."

Relief crossed the father's face. He whispered something Jane could not hear.

James bent over him and then straightened again. "You are most welcome, sir. I shall ensure that Curran is never again near Lord Thunder."

When he turned away from the bed and strode back toward the door, the look on his face was one of concern. But Jane looked harder at him. She, after all, had the bird's-eye view the author didn't. There was something else in his face. Confidence.

And an almost, but not quite hidden triumph.

Chapter 15

Jane walked to the gardens of Afton House to begin searching the grounds inch by inch. She hadn't found the stone earlier, she decided, because she hadn't been thorough enough. Instead, she'd allowed herself to become distracted and only look in stops and starts.

Not going to happen now. She *had* to find that stone. There was only so much time, since it didn't seem Mary was one for a lot of sleep.

The day was mild and calm, with hardly a breath of air stirring. It appeared she had the gardens all to herself, which was surprising, she thought, since they were really very beautiful. Maybe in this day, people took a place like this for granted. Coming from the cramped city life of Seattle, where she had one small terra-cotta pot of flowers on her three-by-four-foot concrete patio, she didn't.

The flowers and shrubs in the gardens were meticulously tended and laid out in rows of deep green, with colorful flowers as exclamation points and a placid pool of water at one end. It would be a place as comfortable with reverent pageantry as quiet reflection. Or a frantic search.

She zeroed in her gaze on the ground, inch by inch. Examining every blade of grass, each rock. Since the corset was again cinching her flesh in epic proportions, she suspected she was going to have to throw herself down again and drag herself across the ground, dress be damned. *Not* finding the stone was not an option.

She'd gone only a few feet when she heard someone come up behind her. Turning, she saw Anne, shoulders hunched and hair in tangles, her face distraught. "What is it?" Jane asked.

"I have," the girl wrung her hands, "committed a grave error." Her voice sounded small and far younger than her fifteen years.

Little did Anne know that she'd come to the inventor of grave errors. The diva of unintended drama. The— never mind. "It can't be that bad." She laid a hand on Anne's arm.

The girl nodded miserably. "But it can."

"Tell me what's happened."

Anne's gaze dropped to the ground. "It was meant to be amusing."

Jane waited.

"I had no intention to—Was most certain that—"

"Trust me," said Jane. "Whatever it is, I've done worse."

"*You,* Jane?"

"You don't know everything about me, Anne." She tried giving the girl an encouraging smile. "Remember that I'm American when Mary is not writing me? I have a life other than this. A life where I do some pretty stupid things. On a regular basis." Harsh. She amended it to, "Once in a while."

At last, Anne admitted, "Lord Thunder." She screwed her eyes nearly shut as she looked at her sister.

A bad feeling began to steal over Jane. "Benton Dempsey's horse."

Anne nodded. "He—We—did not intend for him to leave the enclosure."

Jane went from laying a hand on the girl's arm to gripping it tightly. "You let him escape?"

Unshed tears sparkled in her eyes. "It was not to have happened. It was merely a game. To let him loose where James would discover him. But there was an opening. One I did not see."

Sympathy stabbed at Jane's heart. She knew that look, that sense of foreboding and remorse. Knowing, but not wanting to know, just how badly things were going to turn out. Still . . . "Why would you want to leave him where James would discover him?"

The girl let her eyes flutter closed and then opened them. "Matthew and I—"

Jane did a rapid-fire search of her memory. She didn't think she'd heard that name before. "Matthew?"

"The stable boy. He is well acquainted with James's temper. Indeed he has been on the receiving end of it, far too many times. And I—Mr. James Dempsey is—is—"

"Arrogant?" Whoops. She shouldn't be putting words in Anne's mouth.

A nod, given to her shoes. "We thought it would be amusing to . . ." Anne's voice trailed away.

"Amusing to watch James have a fit over the horse being let out of his stall," Jane finished for her.

Anne nodded again, her misery evident. "Lord Thunder is high-spirited. Matthew says that James wants the horse most desperately after his father—But Matthew thought James should see that Lord Thunder is perhaps more horse than he is suited for."

"This was Matthew's idea?"

"No," Anne rushed to say. "It was me."

"I get it." Jane nodded. This hero seemed to have more than one person putting him to the test. She put a hand to the girl's tangle of curls. "Pretty big problem. That's horse theft, which is something I don't think they look lightly at around here. But you're telling me that you didn't mean it. That things turned out a lot differently than you thought they would." Didn't they always.

A contrite nod.

"I don't suppose Matthew is . . ." What was the word for *cute* in this era? "Attractive?" No, not the right word. "Appealing? Handsome?"

Anne's mouth formed a circle of shock. "Oh, no, Sister," she rushed to say.

"He's not?"

"It is not that."

"Good. Because that almost never turns out well. Doing something you know you shouldn't because you're trying to impress someone."

"The idea was mine alone," Anne admitted. Now she looked confused. "Impress Matthew?"

Right. A stable boy would have no chance with a girl of Anne's social standing. What had Jane been thinking? She dropped her hand from her sister's arm. "I know you feel bad about what happened," she said softly. "But what you did was—" No. She couldn't do it. Jane couldn't even address her own selfishness in this kind of thing, let alone help this teenager see hers. "I know you feel bad, but at least Lord Thunder is back and no one was hurt."

The girl's shoulders sagged, relief shining in her eyes. The admission of guilt had been hard for her, Jane realized. She wondered if she should launch into some kind of a lecture about the risks that were involved with what Anne had done. As quickly as the idea popped into her head, she popped it back out. Anne knew. She didn't need to be reminded by an older sister who, more than anything else, seemed fixated on having the younger girl act older than her years. At least when Mary was writing.

"So, what to do," Jane mused, taking a step across the grass.

Anne fell in beside her. "You are quite different, Jane, when our author is not writing." She spoke hesitantly, as though she weren't sure how the words would be received.

Jane grinned. "That much, I've been able to figure out." She sighed. "I don't think Mary would know what to do with the real me. She writes what she thinks I should be. Who knows, maybe I'm who she hoped to be at some point in her life."

"Perhaps." The girl nodded. "Our author would then enjoy writing you."

Jane screwed up her face at that. "I'm not sure 'enjoy' is the right word to use."

"I cannot believe that I am anything but a trial to our author."

Jane stopped and turned to Anne. "I think you're there to remind Mary that not everyone has to be proper in this society. A person can still have some fun, even if you have to be under the age of eighteen to be allowed to do it. Mary could have been a huge practical joker when she was young. Who knows?" She quirked an eyebrow, looking for Anne's agreement.

The girl gave a reluctant grin. "I have heard it said that she favored mischief upon occasion."

"There you go. You're probably her favorite character." Jane clasped her hands together. "What I wouldn't give for a little fun right now. While Mary isn't writing."

"I have found a place," Anne volunteered.

"What kind of a place?"

"With a swing. A magnificent one."

"On the estate?" She didn't see the Dempseys as the sort of people to have, and use, a swing.

"Yes. Though it is hidden. I do not believe it has been used for some time."

"Perfect." Jane looked back over each shoulder and then pointed a finger at her sister. "Show me. We'll go there, have some fun, and figure out what to do about this mess you're in."

Anne needed no further encouragement. "It is this way." She indicated a direction to the right and they set off together, steps in synch along the path. After a few moments, the girl ventured, "I believe this is the worst I have ever done."

"I know that feeling, except that I usually seem to top the worst I've ever done with something else later. Like I said, I've done some pretty bad things myself. Without ever intending to."

"Could that be so?" The expression Anne turned on Jane said she wanted to believe it but didn't think she could, leading Jane to wonder what sort of invincibly proper aura she was giving off as heroine of *Afton House*.

"Let's see . . . where to start." The list was uncomfortably long. "Well, here's one." She steeled herself for a confession, which never came easy. "I spilled red wine down my friend's beautiful white wedding dress. Only a couple of days before the wedding." She squeezed her eyes shut, reliving the moment. "Red wine does not come out."

"Oh," breathed Anne. "Yet you did not intend to do so, surely?"

"Of course not. No." Jane opened her eyes and shook her head. "But it was horrible, all the same."

Anne nodded. "I once spilled ink on our mother's treasured white lace. She swooned so greatly, I feared she would injure herself." She paused. "Do you recall?"

Jane shook her head. "No. But maybe that's a good thing!"

Her sister gave her a shy smile that disappeared a moment later. "Lord Thunder could have broken his leg. Never been found. Hurt Matthew."

"Or hurt you."

Anne shrugged. "That does not concern me."

She may not worry about being hurt physically, but there was a whole other element to this kind of an awkward life. One she suspected Anne knew something about already. Jane squared her shoulders, looking straight ahead. "I made the mistake of asking a man to marry me, because I thought he felt the same way about me that I did about him."

"You proposed marriage?" Anne's eyes were wide, disbelieving.

"I did." Jane nodded ruefully. "And he didn't. Feel the same way, that is." Ow. The memory still hurt, but not as much as it had before. Maybe because she could now share it to help someone else feel better: JANE ELLINGSON'S LIST OF TOP TEN THINGS TO DO TO SCREW UP YOUR LIFE. Everything for a reason, her mother had always said. Jane, however, rarely found a valid reason. So this was a first.

"Oh, my poor Jane. You must have been devastated."

"I was," she admitted. Past tense. Hmmm. Her own heart seemed to have moved past weeping, although it was still sniffing pretty loud.

"But the proposal only came from your heart. Which is not to be faulted for its feelings."

"It did, yes. But I think . . ." No. She didn't really think that, did she?

"You think?" Anne prompted.

"I may have . . ." Go ahead. Say it. "I may have known he didn't feel the same way. And I may have been thinking only about me and what I wanted. There was a business trip he had just taken to Mexico. I *think* he could have taken me with him, but he didn't. I was, okay, a little upset about that." She took a series of deep breaths, afraid the admission had taken a tremendous amount out of her. It hadn't, though. Felt more like throwing off a rock that had been sitting squarely in the middle of her shoulders.

"He did not ask you to accompany him."

"Right." It sounded lame, even to her.

"Perhaps you were only making such a proposal to assure yourself of his regard."

"So instead, I asked him to marry me. See, I told you I had done worse things than you." She gave Anne a grin that wobbled.

"I did not know about this."

"You wouldn't have," Jane rushed to assure her. "It happened when . . . well, when you wouldn't have known."

"When you had gone to visit Aunt Hathaway?"

Oh, God. Had she? That must have been some visit. She was saved from answering by Anne's announcement that they had arrived at the swing. Following the girl behind a stand of trees, Jane saw a small clearing. And a large swing. A *very* large swing, with a wooden slat for the seat, hung by ropes from the branches of a tree in the center of the clearing.

It looked inviting. And fun.

"Race you," Jane said, with a wink at her sister.

She took off first, Anne following close behind. It felt good, her feet pounding through the grass, each step landing harder than the last. As though all of this that surrounded her was somehow more real with each physical connection she could make. Jane drank in the clean, fresh smell and the sun pouring down on them from above. In Mary's England, the sun shone often.

Jane slowed up to let the younger girl pull ahead. When they reached the swing, each of them held on to one of the ropes with both hands, panting. Jane cursed the corset once again, which seemed better at reducing her lung capacity than anything else was, and the fact that Mary must not have her character doing the equivalent of Jane's every-other-day routine at the gym. "How about if you go first and I push you?" she offered when they'd recovered.

Anne nodded and then carefully sat on the swing's wooden seat.

Jane gave her a starting push. "So what are we going to do to make this right?"

"I have confessed the truth of the matter to you. Is that not enough?" The pleading in the girl's voice told Jane that Anne knew it wasn't.

"I don't think so. Someone else has been blamed."

"You are the only one who knows of the mischief. And Matthew, of course."

"Yes. Matthew." In between pushes, Jane tapped her finger to her chin. "Is he likely to tell anyone?"

Anne shook her head, vehemently. "He would lose his position."

"Right. Of course."

Anne began to drag her feet on the ground, stopping the swing. "I shall push you," she said.

They changed spots.

"Still. This isn't right, Anne. We have to figure out something. When I really screw something up . . ." Forget that. She'd never done the right thing in her entire history of accidents. "I suppose we could—" She shook her head. "No. Don't think we can rely on Benton Dempsey to clear you. It was his horse."

"Mr. Dempsey. I could not." The girl looked mildly terrified . . . for a prankster with near-professional status.

"He is mildly terrifying. I'd hate to see a plate hit you." She looked back long enough to see Anne's quizzical look. "I've seen him throw—Never mind. You don't want to know." She snapped her fingers. "I've got it. We'll go to Curran."

"Oh, Jane, he frightens me so!" Anne, with an alarmed

expression on her face, stepped around so that she could see Jane.

Jane made a don't-worry-about-it gesture. "Nothing to be afraid of. Curran is miscast as a villain." Funny how her heartbeat sped up at the mere mention of his name.

"No! He is—The way he looks at a person—I could not bear to confess such a deed to him." Anne shivered. Didn't look entirely like fear.

Oh, yes. The way he looks at a person. As Jane thought about that, she had to fan her face with her hand. Then it occurred to her that Anne might be having a similar reaction, even if she was too young to recognize it for what it was. This was the Victorian era. She doubted Jane's mother had ever had one of *those* talks with her.

"Yes," she said. "When a man looks at a woman like that, she might feel odd things. Might even seem scary at first. But it's not really the man, it's, well, a woman seeing an attractive man and thinking . . ." Thinking incredibly provocative thoughts about him, imagining him beside her, doing things that—Wow. Face fanning again, double-time.

Anne's eyes widened.

"The *point* is," Jane continued, "a man like Curran has a certain . . ." How could she phrase it, without giving herself away and embarrassing Anne to death? "A certain sensuality that just *emanates* from him." She stopped, realizing she'd said the words aloud.

Anne looked interested. Very interested.

Jane cleared her throat and stood straighter, trying to buckle down and get this right. "Matthew might sort of, you know, make you feel that way sometimes, too."

Anne looked away.

"And that's okay," Jane rushed to say. "Absolutely normal."

"He is . . ." Anne began to admit, then recovered herself quickly. "Mr. Curran Dempsey is not a villain? But he must be. Our author has declared him such."

Jane thought about this. No sense in tarnishing Curran's reputation, so she decided to take a different approach. "If he's such a villain, he'll understand what you did and not judge you, right? He has to have done things much worse."

Anne blinked.

"Come on," Jane said, looping her arm through the younger girl's. "We're going to find him."

"But our father. He must not ever discover what I have done."

"Something tells me he wouldn't be that surprised." Jane tugged at Anne's arm.

Anne looked down at the ground, watching her feet scurry along beside Jane.

"I'm pretty sure he doesn't have to find out," Jane reassured her. "Curran isn't going to tell him, so let's not think about that right now."

And let's also not think about Jane's growing suspicion that the reason she was moving so fast to find Curran had more to do with a legitimate excuse to talk with him than the need to put things right about the horse.

She hoped that wasn't the case. Because if it was, how much more unheroine-like could one person get?

Talk about miscasting.

Chapter 16

Jane had Curran's whereabouts right on the first guess. She and Anne found him at the stable, preparing to mount his horse. Walking with purpose, she led Anne to Curran and then came to an abrupt stop, suddenly feeling uncomfortable and out of place by the light of the day in this all-male domain.

The two females found themselves surrounded by dirt, dust, horses, leather. And men, who faded into the background when they approached.

Curran paused, his hand on the saddle. "The Misses Ellingson," he acknowledged with a nod. "The two fairest ladies in the county. To what do I owe the honor?"

He sounded charming, but Jane noticed he wasn't smiling. "Mr. Dempsey," she said by way of greeting. "Alfred."

The horse eyed her with suspicion.

Jane seemed to be having some trouble keeping her knees from buckling. When she looked at Curran's mouth, she relived the moments when it had been on hers. So she switched her gaze to his eyes, where she didn't fare much better.

He waited. Anne waited. Jane brushed a tendril of hair from her face and took a step forward, her eyes on a point somewhere over Curran's shoulder. "Anne has something she would like to tell you."

Nothing happened. Anne, she saw with a sideways glance, again looked terrified. "It's all right," Jane coaxed. "Mr. Dempsey will not be angry."

She hoped not, anyway. The crease between his brow had made a return appearance.

Anne stood mute, her hands grasped so hard in front of her that her knuckles turned white.

Curran looked slowly from Anne to Jane and back again without saying a word.

Jane decided she'd better help get this confession started. "It's about Lord Thunder," she began. "As it happens, his getting out was all a simple accident." She lifted a palm and shoulder, as if to say, *"Who knew?"* Then she made a gesture down low at her side, urging Anne to chime in.

Instead, she saw Anne's gaze veer to the right. Following it, Jane saw why. The stable boy standing at the door, behind Curran, had to be Matthew, Anne's cohort in crime. The fear on his teenage face matched hers. But there was something else on his face. If Jane was correct in interpreting it as a longing for the younger of the Ellingson sisters, he wouldn't be climbing far up the career ladder.

Curran also shot a glance over at the stable boy, who took a step back into the shadows. Jane didn't blame him. She debated whether or not to hide Anne behind her and slowly slink away herself. But then Curran's half-lidded gaze returned to linger on Jane. In it, she saw something meant only for her—recognition of the agony of a teenage crush.

She dipped her chin, the smallest bit, in acknowledgment, feeling a tremor begin inside her that had no business being there. *He's the villain, Jane. The villain.* It would help if he would act like one on occasion.

"An accident," he repeated.

"Yes." With her elbow, Jane nudged Anne.

"An accident, sir." The girl's voice melted away.

"I see," Curran said.

"And now we're not sure," Jane told him, "what to do to make things right." She reminded herself to breathe.

"We shall do nothing."

"Nothing?" She lifted her brows.

"Nothing?" echoed Anne, finding her voice.

"But you—" Jane fumbled with what to say. "Have been blamed for it. We have to do something to make sure people know it wasn't you."

In one fluid motion, he pulled himself up onto the horse and into the saddle, taking the reins. He directed his next words to the bent head of Anne. "Let us leave the explanation to what is often referred to as my careless nature. I am certain you meant no real harm." He lowered his voice, just enough to soften any sting. "What I see on your face tells me that such an event will not occur again, with Lord Thunder or any of the other horses." He gave his own a pat.

Anne's head rose. She gave a barely perceptible nod, bottom lip quivering. Then she allowed herself a hint of a smile.

Jane's heart swelled.

"There you have it, then," said Curran. He next directed a look at the stable boy, who quickly bent his own head, picking up the bucket he had set on the ground.

Curran's gaze moved back to Jane, prompting heart palpitations that had her pressing her hand to her chest. He'd taken the heat for Anne. A teenage prank gone wrong and he'd allowed himself to be the target of blame. And he'd managed to do it without embarrassing the girl.

What a hero. Oh. Wait. *Damn.*

"I have business to attend to," Curran said, "but I must talk with you, Miss Jane Ellingson, when I return."

"Of course," she said hastily. Anytime, any place. Talk. Not talk. Anything he wanted to do. "I'll be here."

With that, Curran rode, quite literally, into the sunset.

When he had gone, Anne looked over at Matthew and he looked at her. They each took a step toward each other.

"Oh, no you don't," Jane said, tugging at her sister's arm. "We have more talking to do. Important sister stuff."

With a small, furtive wave at the stable boy, Anne went with Jane, who had started down the path that led to the house. "Perhaps you are right," the girl said in a small, quiet voice, "About Mr. Dempsey as a villain."

"He doesn't make a very good one," Jane said absently, thinking of the way Curran had quickly sized up the situation, weighed the alternatives and decided to accept the blame for something he hadn't done. "Although I think he tries." He was accustomed, he had as much as said, to people assuming the worst about him. What would it be like to live like that? Even with Jane's record, people more often than not gave her the benefit of the doubt.

"He did not even scold me, which I fully deserved." Anne's voice turned to wonder. "And I think—Could he have known Matthew had a hand in this?"

"That's the funny thing about Curran. He knows a lot more than he lets on."

"Our author does not seem to understand that Mr. Dempsey is other than she would portray him."

"I think Mary and James are the only ones who don't recognize that."

"And the elder Mr. Dempsey?"

Jane thought about that for a few steps. "He's pretty firmly fixed on the way things are, that Curran can never inherit, even though he's the oldest son. But I get the distinct feeling that he loves Curran. Might even favor him a little."

"Mr. James Dempsey would not like that."

"You're telling me." Jane screwed up her mouth. "So I suppose Mary isn't going to let anything happen differently." She focused her attention back on Anne. "You didn't exactly give me the whole story with Matthew."

Pink stained the younger girl's cheeks. "I do not understand."

"The way he looked at you, I'd say Matthew might have a crush."

"A . . . crush?"

"Feelings for you. Romantic kinds of feelings."

A brief excitement played out on Anne's features before she was able to regain control. "Do not speak of such things. It is quite impossible, as you know."

Yet when hormones and emotions took over, Anne could find herself in trouble. Never mind that she wasn't the only one who could find herself in trouble with an impossible man. "I know," Jane said slowly. "Sometimes the impossible relationships are the ones you want the most."

They walked in silence until Anne volunteered, "He wanted to carry the blame for Lord Thunder himself, to protect me from the wrath of Mr. Dempsey."

"Mmm." Jane nodded. "Protective. Don't you hate it when they do things like that?"

"Hate it?" Anne sounded baffled.

"What I mean is, you *don't* hate it. Which makes it even harder to say no—" She broke off when she realized this conversation was not going as planned. Good thing she'd never become a teacher, tasked with imparting sex education. There would be a population explosion. "Just . . . be careful, Anne. I guess that's all I wanted to say."

"I shall," the girl promised solemnly. "And Jane?"

"Yes?"

"You won't tell anyone that . . . ?" A helpless gesture followed. Anne couldn't bring herself to say the words.

"I won't." Jane assured her. "Your secrets are safe with me, Little Sister."

Anne's answer was to fold her in a quick, heartfelt hug.

When Mary next began writing, Jane found herself in the drawing room, seated at a table around a game of cards with Mrs. Hathaway, Violet and Curran. Across the room, James stood before the fireplace.

"Won't you play, Mr. Dempsey?" trilled Mrs. Hathaway. "This table is, I daresay, far too female. We need a gentleman's quick mind."

Oh, now. There was way too much that could be said in this situation, none of it properly Victorian at all. But Mary kept firm control of Jane's mouth. She looked over her hand of cards and gave Violet, her partner in the game, the slightest raised eyebrow. The other woman, her face its usual blank mask, acknowledged the signal with the tiniest of nods.

The roller-coaster drama of a game of cards. How *did* they sleep at night?

"James does not care for such pursuits," she heard herself say to Mrs. Hathaway.

From the corner of her eye, she saw Curran's jaw muscles working furiously. He appeared to be holding himself back from saying something. Or wait. Was he actually *trying* to say something? Though her hand reached for a card, her attention was riveted on the man to her right.

At last he remarked, "On the contrary, my brother cares for . . . such pursuits far too much."

Yaaay, Curran. Jane wasn't the only one giving Mary trouble. She felt like breaking into applause, an impulse that stilled when she saw the round *O* of Mrs. Hathaway's mouth, the look of shock on Violet's face and, worse, the tight-lipped fury on James's face. That couldn't be good.

"Have you something to say, sir?" James demanded.

Curran closed his eyes and then opened them, appearing to concentrate hard. "Only that I have been told your debts are mounting fast at a certain establishment." He bit hard on his bottom lip before managing to force out, "Take care, Brother, that you do not gamble away an inheritance not yet yours."

"Preposterous," shot back James. "I shall do no such thing. I do not—How could you even suggest—"

"It is no suggestion. I myself have witnessed your activity on many a late night. Perhaps if your skill were greater than the hand you were dealt . . ."

Behind Jane, the fire crackled. Mrs. Hathaway gave a nervous, apologetic cough. Violet's face looked carved of stone.

"My skill. Shall I suppose that *you*, of all people, are offering to teach *me*?" James's tone dripped with sarcasm.

Not the greatest comeback in the world.

A pause, then a flash of light and Jane was standing before the fireplace with James while Violet, Mrs. Hathaway and Curran played cards at the table. Across the room, Anne sat in a chair, fidgeting with embroidery.

Okay. So Mary didn't much care for that last little bit. James's love of cards must be a sore subject. Good to know.

"I have written to your father, Jane," James was saying in a low voice. "And I am pleased to say he has responded, giving his blessing to a marriage between us."

A marriage between them. How desperately romantic. And wait a minute. Had she missed something or had James never even asked *her*? A technical detail, but one she was more than willing to debate.

Excited words of pleasure balanced on the tip of her tongue, ready to launch. She could feel them, could nearly wrap her mouth around and smother them. But then, as fast as she was ready to fight saying them, they were gone, melting away into the oblivion that was unspoken words, thoughts, feelings.

With surprise, Jane felt Mary's grip on her lighten. The author still had pen in hand because Jane's shoulders were erect and her chin up, but her mouth felt oddly relaxed. As though the author was waiting, as much as Jane, to see what would emerge.

She looked at James, an expectant and pleased smile on his face. And then at Curran, who had risen from his chair and stood, waiting. Back at James, whose smile was beginning to show a bit of strain and at Curran, who might possibly be working up to a smile.

James. She felt nothing. Curran. She felt . . . But she couldn't. Could she? Was it possible Mary would allow her to be with a man who made every one of her senses stand up and pay attention? When she was within a room's length of the man, she could barely think. He drove her crazy at the same time he drove her to him.

It was not because he was unattainable. It was because she had to have him. Big difference. Huge.

Of course. The author was just now waking up to the fact that her characters, once created, had to be able to take over and live. *Finally.* Jane was beginning to feel a kinship with Mary Bellingham, a bond that could happen only between author and character. That trust that comes from knowing Jane would act in a heroine-like best interest of the story. And she could do that. She could. Just as soon as she figured out what that might be. *Thank you, Mary.*

She looked back at James again. And then her gaze shot to Curran, with a dizzying sense of exhilaration that she really, truly might have a chance at real happiness, with someone who made her toes curl and didn't cringe at her accidents, which, by the way, she didn't seem to have when she was with him.

That made her pause. The accidents, the bane of her existence for as long as she could remember, didn't happen when he was around. Odd. But even if they did, he, as opposed to nearly every other person in her life, wouldn't be put off by it. For whatever reason she couldn't explain, she was sure of it.

Could it be? Really? He liked her the way she was. Accidents and all.

Mary. We have a winner!

Curran's eyes locked on hers. For one spectacular moment, all else faded away, the drawing room, the people, the card game, everything.

And then the pause that meant Mary was lifting her pen. *No,* Jane wanted to cry. *Let this play out. Let's keep going.*

They waited, until James raised his finger with great dramatic flair. "She is . . ." Then a look of disbelief, swiftly followed by a growing horror, spread across his face. "Take heed!" he shouted.

"What is it? What's happening?" asked Jane.

Anne dropped her embroidery to scurry to her side. "I'm frightened," the girl whispered.

Jane put an arm around her and pulled her close.

The drawing room grew warmer. And warmer still. Jane could feel beads of sweat forming on her forehead, all over her body, as the room became increasingly hot. James held on to a chair while tugging at his jacket. Violet's blank expression turned to confusion. Mrs. Hathaway fanned herself with her hand until she collapsed against the chair and Anne, nestled in next to Jane, began to whimper.

Curran took a step toward them just as Jane spotted something orange in the corner of the room. "Look!" she yelped, pointing.

A flame, climbing upward, licking at the walls. Then joined by another.

She clung to Anne harder, as though she could somehow protect the younger girl with her body. Fear pulsed through her veins until she thought her heart would pound nearly out of her chest. *Think. Remember. What to do in case of fire.* "We have to get to the door," she said to Anne, hoping her legs would carry the two of them there. *Damn these skirts.* She wanted to rip them off to leave her free to move. "Curran!" He was moving toward the flames, instead of away from them. Then she saw why. James was staggering to the corner, a pillow in his hand, his cheeks red and glistening with sweat.

This couldn't be. The beautiful estate. On fire. Mrs. Hathaway began to scream in a high-pitched wail and Violet sat silent in her chair, stunned. Anne had buried her face in the bodice of Jane's dress.

"Get everyone out!" Curran shouted back at them as he and his brother both picked up pillows and began beating at the flames, which were only growing in intensity.

"Violet!" With her free hand, Jane began shaking the other woman's arm. "Come on. Get up. We have to get out of here. Now."

To Mrs. Hathaway, she barked, "Quiet!"

Startled, the woman clapped her mouth shut. "I'm frightened," she mouthed.

"Follow me. And you, Violet. Come!"

Both did as they were told and the four women crossed the room swiftly to the door. But as they reached it, Jane saw something that caused her heart to sink to her toes in despair. Flames. Licking at that wall as well.

"We shall be killed!" wailed Mrs. Hathaway, swaying and collapsing against a chair.

"No we won't!" answered Jane. She had not lived twenty-six years of her life only to die in a fire in a make-believe reality. "Get down on the floor," she ordered Anne. "Put your face to it. "You!" she said to Violet. "Water! We need water. And cloth." Jane began ripping and tearing at her skirts.

She had just succeeded in tearing off a huge chunk when, unexpectedly, the flames began to subside. Smoke filtered in, its pungent odor filling the air. Jane tore the fabric into strips and began dunking it into a water pitcher she found on a back table. Water spilled all over the wooden surface. "Here," she said to Anne. "Cover your face with this." Next she gave one to Violet and one to Mrs. Hathaway. Then she saw James and Curran, both red-faced, with singed pillows in their hands. "The fire went out," she said unnecessarily. She handed them each a wet cloth. "For your face. Use it to breathe through." She pressed one to her own face, drinking in the relief from the smoke that it provided. "We have to get out of here."

"To the garden," James ordered. "The smoke is through-out the house."

"What happened?" Jane asked, but no one answered until they were all through the door and the halls and had spilled out the front entrance into the welcoming cool air.

When they reached the gardens, Jane fell onto the grass, barely registering that her dress was above her knees in the front. Her legs welcomed the freedom. Again she pleaded, "What happened?"

James looked first at her legs and then slowly up into her eyes.

Now he gets interested, she thought.

"We were fortunate indeed," he said.

Curran nodded in terse agreement.

"What do you mean?" Jane asked.

"Our author threw the pages of her manuscript into the fire."

Shocked sounds of disbelief from the women, including Jane, who shook her head. "No. She couldn't have done that." How could it have been possible? Right before the flames hit, Mary and Jane had connected, the author showing herself willing to listen to her character, to maybe even allow her to consider another man as hero. She had. Jane had felt it, she had even—

Omigod. Jane had pushed too far. She had frustrated Mary Bellingham until the author had felt she had no choice but to throw the entire manuscript into the fire. Jane had very nearly been responsible for the death of how many people? Single-handedly.

"But . . . We're still here," she said, her voice scratchy and faint.

"Only because she risked grave injury to herself by pulling the pages out of the fire." Curran looked grim. "She is not likely to do so again."

Chapter 17

Mary was not likely to pull the pages out of the fire again. Jane let the words of warning sink deep inside her, where they sat, weighing on her heart.

She could pretend all she wanted that this story had something to do with her, but the truth was that the story was Mary's, written from her perspective and experiences. And they had to help her make it work or be doomed forever to a life that wasn't one.

As she looked at Curran, a sense of sadness washed over her, so strong that her shoulders sagged and her chin dropped to stare at the grass. Anne slipped an arm around Jane's waist.

"It is of little surprise," contributed Mrs. Hathaway with a self-righteous sniff.

Jane's chin rose abruptly.

Violet turned away. James began to pace, his hands locked behind his back. And Curran, his expression fierce, stared into the distance.

"Perhaps Miss Bellingham was not meant to be an author," Anne said. As all eyes turned in her direction, her cheeks colored. "She struggles most terribly."

Sympathy tugged at Jane. Mary's brother was the successful author. The one his younger sister would always be measured against. And try as hard as she could, she would likely never measure up in the eyes of others.

A dilemma Jane might know a little something about.

She pushed herself up off the ground and stood. With as much dignity as she could muster in half a skirt, she began to walk. Away from the others. To be alone with her thoughts, which hurtled through her, stopping and starting, careening around corners at a speed that made her light-headed. The smell of smoke, faded but still there, stung her nostrils. A reminder of the consequences for forgetting who held the pen.

The grass crunched beneath her feet, the landscape stretching out ahead with no sign of other civilization. A far different life than she'd ever encountered. One of Mary's creation. Jane had made a wish and plunked herself right in the middle of a work in progress. What right did she have to try and drive Mary's story? It wasn't as though Jane had a great track record for handling romance, or any other aspect of her life, on her own.

It couldn't have been an accident that she'd found that wishing stone in Starbucks. Hundreds, if not thousands of people must have been close enough to see it. It had waited for her. Chosen her. She'd had the greatest need for a new path, for someone to take charge. And that stone had known exactly what wish she would make. She'd bet anything on it.

Now it was gone. And she was on her own.

Be careful, oh so careful, what you wish for.

In the distance, a bird broke into song and then was joined by another. Jane fingered the remnants of the skirt she'd ripped up for cloths. Could be she'd start a new fashion trend. The thought made her chortle until she realized she was actually catching herself on a sob.

She stopped, stretching her neck to lean her head

back. No tears. No regrets. No time for either. She had to deal with the situation the best she could. If that meant helping Mary get the man she'd always wanted but couldn't have, that's what had to happen.

An author who became so desperate, so frustrated, that she threw her own work, a part of *herself*, into the fire had bigger problems than Jane did.

And that was saying something.

Curran turned and watched Jane leave, scowling so the others would not know that he would have preferred to follow her. Though her skirt was ripped and partially dragging on the ground and her legs, hands and face dirtied and smudged, she managed to walk with a dignity and bearing he'd seen in few women.

She'd kept her head in a fierce situation, when the flames and smoke had nearly consumed them all. Shown herself to be a heroine worthy of Mary Bellingham's pen.

He must do the same with the responsibilities Mary had given him.

The desire to do otherwise had begun in earnest when Jane and Anne came to him with the real story of Lord Thunder's escape. He had known, without a doubt, what he should do, in what manner he should behave.

Yet he could not.

The trust Jane had so innocently placed in him, by presenting the story and her frightened sister, had gone to his head. Rendered him useless at the deviousness he should be capable of. It would have been simple to take bold action, having the stable boy whipped and young Anne relegated to her room. Or sent home. Curran could have gone to his father and claimed the praise he deserved for his hand in exacting punishment for the sin of endangering Lord Thunder.

Yet he could not.

Two innocent and contrite young faces and one allur-

ing female had undone him to the point that his true
nature, instead of the one he fought so hard to cultivate,
had again claimed him. He wanted Jane Ellingson for his
own with an ill-advised desire that strained at both his
breeches and his heart. He wanted her in his bed, instead
of just his dreams. In his arms, instead of only his head.

Yet he could not.

She'd disappeared from sight by the time he became
conscious of a stirring behind him as the others began
to mill about.

"Whatever are we to do now?" wailed Mrs. Hathaway.

"Hush," snapped Violet, most uncharacteristically.

Curran turned, surprised. But then he should not be.
The Hathaway woman was enough to try the most patient person, let alone Violet.

James strode to him, rocking upward on the balls of his
feet, as he often did when standing by his taller older
brother. "We must act swiftly and resoundingly," James said.

Curran regarded him for a full minute or so before re-
sponding, "And what would you propose be done?"

"Our author cannot be treated with so little respect."
A sharp bob of his chin punctuated the statement.

Curran longed to shake his younger brother, repeating,
"And what would you propose be done?" But that would do
nothing to help the situation. Instead, it was time he began
taking his villain tasks straight to heart. "You are quite
right, James."

Surprise and then suspicion flashed in the other man's
eyes. "Yes." He cleared his throat, announcing loudly,
"Yes, I am. I will not have her treated such."

Curran nodded, as though agreeing, when in fact he
wanted to bore into his brother's skull that the statement
was in fact one he should be making about Jane. Perhaps
then all would be sorted out.

He steeled himself for what he must do, while ensuring

he showed no sign of the effort on his face. A practice he had become accustomed to over the years. "It is intolerable," he said, agreeing with James, "that Jane would be so uncooperative, would have so little regard for the author who labors on behalf of our tale."

"Indeed." James clasped his hands behind his back.

"Perhaps you—No." Curran shook his head, as if re-thinking.

James gave a half laugh. "Surely you do not presume to offer advice."

"Not advice. And not even well thought out, if it were."

"To be expected." James seemed to be making an attempt at teasing his brother. It did not go well.

Curran shrugged and made a move as if to turn away.

"So tell me what this barely thought-out comment would be. So that I may join you in a laugh." His eyes grew wide. James did not know how to tease. "As brothers." Nor did he do well with attempting familial ties he did not believe in.

Still, Curran kept his true thoughts to himself. "It was just that Jane Ellingson appears to be someone who would like a firm hand. A man who would tell her in no uncertain terms what is to go on."

"Ha!" James pointed a finger at him. "That is how little you know her."

Again, he lifted a shoulder. "As I said . . ."

"Not well thought out. Entirely true." James's finger still pointed at Curran as the younger brother began to walk away.

No doubt to find Jane, Curran reflected. And assert that firm hand.

This would be a treat. If he was a gambling man, which indeed he was, his money would be on Jane.

* * *

By the time Jane turned to walk back toward the house, determination was well on its way to replacing fear. She would do her part. Do what she had to. And she'd do her damnest to make sure the others did as well.

The group in the gardens had dispersed. Only Curran lingered still, standing with his back to her. He turned as she approached and her heart caught in her throat. His dark eyes burned into her very soul, wrapping her in a fierce heat without touching her body. "You know what it is we must do," he said.

"Yes." One word. An entire future.

"It is perhaps . . ."

Don't say for the best. It isn't and I don't want to hear those words leave your lips when we both know it isn't true.

He didn't. Instead he said, "I shall leave you now."

She cleared her throat, making a small squeak of a sound that seemed to echo her sense of loss. Once he moved away from her, the feeling would be gone. The one that connected them in a way Mary wouldn't. "Yes," she said again, looking at his arm, at the house behind him, anywhere but into his eyes. "I need to find James. As soon as Mary begins to write again, we have to be ready."

"You may be assured that James will devote his full attention."

"I know." Jane sighed. "It's not his attention I'm worried about."

He didn't ask what she meant or say he didn't understand. Because he did, which made things that much worse. Then she felt his whiskers brush her cheek and his lips on her skin. A last kiss, lingering long after his hand left her elbow.

She watched as he walked away. With each step he took, her spirits tumbled further down a steep, twisting staircase and the ache in her heart spread. Wrapping both arms around her stomach, she held on tight, as though she could contain the longing she felt deep inside and keep it from making a suicide leap to run after him.

He had the same determined stride with an edge to it that was distinctly Curran. But she thought she might be able to detect a slight sag to his shoulders that hadn't been there before, as though a new weight had settled in.

The weight of being a villain who was, in his heart, a hero.

"James. I've been looking for you."

He turned around. "Jane."

She'd gone in search of him as soon as she returned to the house and found him in the drawing room with Mrs. Hathaway. They were talking in hushed tones when Jane entered the room. "You and I need to talk."

"Ohhh," simpered the older woman. "Please forgive me. I am most certainly wanted in the—" Gesturing vaguely, she didn't finish the sentence before she began swishing toward the door, darting looks back over her shoulder.

Jane waited, taking care to hide her anxiety until the woman had gone. When at last the door shut, she turned back to James and jammed her hands on her hips. "We have to make this work."

"Indeed we do." He regarded her coolly.

She tried to ignore the stab of disappointment that followed his words. What had she expected, after all? That he would passionately throw his arms around her and declare his undying love? That he had been wrong not to see how absolutely wonderful a catch she was? Not going to happen.

"So we agree on that. I've been thinking," she began.

"As have I."

Oh. She hadn't expected that. "Good," she said, nodding. "Because we're going to have to work together."

He took a few steps to the fireplace and stood, rocking forward on the balls of his feet. "Jane—"

"James," she broke in, knowing she had to get this out now or not at all. "We need to . . ." This was a little harder than she might have expected. She actually felt a blush began to warm her cheeks. ". . . Work more romance into our time together. Help Mary with that. Give her the right setting, the right atmosphere, and things will be, you know, *easier* for us. A midnight stroll. A walk along the pond, talking about our innermost thoughts and feelings. A leisurely horseback ride." She stopped. "No. Scratch that. The sidesaddle thing, that's not me. A candlelight *dinner*, sharing a bottle of wine, that would be good." Better clarify that one since all the dinners around here seemed to be by candlelight. "With only the two of us."

"And this is what you would propose to do."

Her smile disappeared as she heard the thud of her ideas landing on the ground at his feet. He sounded so stern. A lot like a certain college professor whose class she had dreaded every day. The day that professor had tripped over her industrial-sized backpack, though, she'd felt terrible.

"You speak quite without thought, do you not, Jane?"

Not the you're-so-right-and-I'm-all-for-it answer she'd hoped for. And he was giving off enough ice to serve as a freezer in his spare time.

Talk about things not *doing*. This certainly wasn't. Not at all. A whitish-hot anger began in the center of her stomach and worked its way through her body with the speed of traffic on a six-lane freeway. "You *do* things with too *much* thought, James."

That hadn't quite come out as the chastising she'd meant it to be. He looked confused.

"You can't figure out why this doesn't just happen," she went on. "Why I'm not falling down at your feet madly in love. Or at least madly willing to marry you whether I even like you, or not. I should be grateful for the chance, right? Willing to do anything to be Mrs. James Dempsey?" Her words ran all over themselves, cars barreling down the freeway, careening around corners, off each other and into light posts. "Sure you have money. Sure you're reasonably good-looking—"

"Reasonably?" he thundered.

She'd hit that nerve square on. *"Very* good-looking. Is that better?"

He narrowed his eyes.

"Not the kind of man I usually go for, but you must be Mary's type because she's made it clear you're the one she wants to be the hero, whether you deserve to be or not."

Lightning bolts flashed in his eyes. *Don't question his looks or hero status,* she stored in the back of her mind for future reference.

"As the hero of this tale," he said, his voice even and his jaw set, "I shall be the one to determine the setting of our encounters. I shall be the one to decide how our scenes together shall work. We can discuss each before Mary begins, if you like." He made a magnanimous gesture, apparently to show he was the very essence of a team player. As long as everything was done his way.

And he talked about their scenes together with all the enthusiasm of making a grocery list. Jane folded one arm over the other, across her stomach. Her foot began to tap. "Why should it be you?"

He sputtered, professing his disbelief. "And who else would it be?"

"You haven't shown me much so far."

"Shown you—? Jane, this is impossible." He shook his head, walking toward the window. "Quite impossible. I have shown far too much tolerance and now I must insist upon your cooperation."

"My *cooperation?* As if I haven't been giving it?" Her

voice sounded childish to her ears and there was that nagging worry that he might be talking about her and Curran. Last night. And the way she couldn't stop thinking about him, no matter what she did.

"Your cooperation and sincere effort. I find I must demand it."

Jane's foot tapped faster and she hugged herself tighter. This was going nowhere. And she swore she could still smell smoke, lingering in the air. She drew a breath in and out. And again. Slowly.

Then she walked toward the window. "You won't get anywhere by making demands on me," she said to the view of the wide dirt path leading to the estate's front entrance.

He crossed the room and, with a hand at her elbow, turned her toward him. "The setting, as you put it, matters little," he said. There was a conviction in his voice that alarmed her. What if he was right?

As fast as that thought made its way into her brain, Jane shoved it out. He couldn't be right or they were all doomed to go up in one big blaze. And nothing right would happen if they both dug in their heels and refused to budge.

She laid a hand on his arm. "It matters to a woman, James," she told him earnestly. "And it matters even more if you really listen to me, am interested in what I say, ask questions about the things that are important and compliment me once in a while to show that you notice things about me." She held her breath, waiting for him to answer. The silence grew heavier with each second that passed.

At last, he said, "It is much that you ask of me."

"I'll do the same for you."

He looked away and then back at her. "I am not convinced."

"You may not be convinced, but at least you're not positive that it *won't* work to put a few words in Mary's mouth. A few ideas in her head. What do we have to lose by trying it?" *Don't answer that.*

"And that would repair this romance."

"Would definitely give it a fighting chance. The alternative, I would remind you, singed your eyebrow just a little bit on that one side." She pointed, but at the expression he turned on her, she dropped her hand, letting it fall awkwardly to her side.

"I have never previously encountered such demands. Other females of my acquaintance have been only too happy to comply—"

"That's because you've never met anyone like me." She didn't want to hear about his other women. Not when she was going to have to marry the guy. Just to save his life. Attempting to strike a casual but confident pose, she put one hand on a nearby table, the other hand on her hip. Sass. That's what was called for here. "I'm not demanding, but I am single-minded. When I need to be." There was a difference, right?

Unfortunately, her casual but confident hand knocked a vase to the carpet, where it crashed and rolled around in a very expensive-sounding way. Miraculously, it didn't break. Jane's eyes flew back to James.

He met her gaze. "That is true. I have not made the acquaintance of any other quite like you." Then he sighed.

Finally. They'd agreed on *something*. Of course, it would have been better if he'd made meeting her sound like a good thing.

Sitting on the grass, Jane pulled at her hair until it tumbled from its structured, absolutely proper style and fell down around her shoulders. She massaged her scalp with relief and then fell back on the ground, arms above her head. It felt good just to lie there, no one judging her, no one putting words in her mouth. Literally.

A few minutes of hope before Mary began writing again. Hope that it would all work out. Hope that everyone would be all right, would get their happy endings. Even that Mary would find hers, the one she couldn't have in real life. So Jane wasn't going to question . . . *too* much that James was the object of Mary's unrequited desire. Maybe the author had forgotten a few redeeming personality traits of the original when she created the book's hero. That would explain some things.

As she stared up at white, puffy clouds, the fresh smell of grass wafted to her nostrils, mixed with the scent of flowers and horses. No exhaust fumes or pollution hazes or other signs of twenty-first-century living. If Mary would just let her lie here for a while, eyes closed, she could get things figured out. And hey, she could come up with a plan for world peace while she was at it. The thought made her chuckle. Different time, different country. Always the same dilemma.

"Jane."

Her eyes flew open. Above her, Anne stared down, her face a question mark. "Are you ill?" the girl asked.

Jane shook her head.

"Ah." Anne nodded, pondering that for a moment. Then she said, "I shall join you." With that she also flopped on the grass and they lay side by side, one Victorian semi-lady and one almost lady, staring up at the slow-moving clouds. Very shortly, the setting lent itself to confession mode. "I was not entirely truthful," Anne volunteered, "about Matthew."

Jane nodded. "I figured that out."

"But a stable boy. It is foolish to even suppose—"

"It does appear that way." She didn't make the rules of this society, didn't even know what they all were, but she'd have to say that someone in Anne's position and someone in Matthew's position didn't often get together for any kind of a relationship.

Still, it wasn't fair. If she had turned down prospective relationships because of what the guy did for a living . . . Her mother would have been happier, but she would have been the only one. Jane had a quick flashback to the day her mother had dropped in at her college dorm and met Todd, Jane's crush, a redheaded varsity gymnast who, upon introduction, had dropped to the floor to do splits.

Jane had thought it was cute. And in those shorts, the guy's muscled legs were amazing. Her mother had been appalled but gamely reached down to shake his hand. Last Jane had heard, Todd was making his living doing a gymnastics show on a cruise-ship line. Well, if anyone could hang upside down on a moving ship, and make it work, it would be Todd.

"But don't worry." She reached over to give her sister's hand a pat. "You're not the only one. This book seems to be all about people wanting relationships they can't have."

Anne sat up. "Tell me more, Sister."

Bad direction to take the conversation, Jane thought. Confiding in Anne could make Jane feel better, but it could jeopardize the story. She'd been through too much with these people to do that.

Escaping a burning building together apparently kicked Jane into protective mode. She mulled that over for a minute while her inner voice gave a satisfied nod and sat down to wait for the next incident, which would be along any minute now. "Never mind. I just—Nothing."

Jane closed her eyes again and a lukewarm breeze gently ruffled her hair. Then she heard Anne ask, "Do you mean Mr. Curran Dempsey?"

So much for peacefulness. Jane sat up, jerking her head in denial before she had even thought of a reply. "No. Of

course not. What do you mean, Curran Dempsey?" Even
to her own ears, her protest sounded pathetic.

"He has a particular manner of looking at you."

"Ha!" She tried to scoff, but was pretty sure she ended
up looking even more pathetic. "Looking at me. I don't
know what you're talking about. He's the villain. Sure,
he's going to look at me, but only to figure out how he
can use me to get what he wants." She paused. That
hadn't exactly come out right. "And what he wants is that
James not inherit Afton House."

"I believe there is something more," Anne said lightly.

"You're just infatuated with the idea of romance." Jane
flung herself back on the grass. "And looking for *something*
to distract you so that you don't think too hard about
Matthew."

"It is not so," Anne murmured. Jane turned her head
to watch as the girl began plucking at the grass. "Can you
imagine what our father would say were he to discover I
had even talked with a stable boy? And Mama would have
one of her spells. We would not see her for months."

Jane couldn't picture that, since she had no experience with either parent.

"It would not be like with you, Jane. Never giving them
a moment of concern, as Mama says nearly every day." A
note of bitterness crept into the younger girl's tone, which
then rose to mimic someone else. "'Your sister would never
behave in such a way, Anne. Have you no thought to your
deeds, no manners whatsoever?'"

The words may have been stated differently, but they
were all too familiar. Book Jane had been cast in the role
of the practically perfect older sibling, while Anne struggled in the part of the one who never quite measured
up. Jane's heart swelled in sympathy as she watched
Anne's face, pinched with frustration. And once again

she wondered just how close this story was to Mary Bellingham's life.

Raising herself up to rest on her elbows, Jane hesitated before saying, "This may sound like a strange question, but you know that a lot doesn't add up here, anyway. You and I were raised together . . . and we weren't."

Anne nodded. "It is unusual."

"Here's the question. Why are the two families pushing for me and James to marry? Am I just the convenient unmarried woman in the next county over or is there something more? Do you know?"

Anne looked uncomfortable.

"Go ahead. Tell me." Jane crinkled her forehead. "Please?"

The girl looked over one shoulder and then the other. "I can only know what I have heard Mama and Father tell one another, when they were not aware I was listening."

Jane sat up. "Good. That should give me something to go on."

"It is believed," Anne said, "that you would be able to influence Mr. James Dempsey to give up his fondness for cards and love of liquor."

"He has a fondness for cards."

Anne nodded.

"And let me guess. I'm the pious one, the *good* girl who can make him give it all up and live life on the straight and narrow."

"I'm not certain I understand—"

Jane put out a hand. "Sorry. I was just repeating what you said, in a little different way. American, you know." She lifted a shoulder.

Anne gave her a relieved smile.

The altogether new idea of being the one to straighten someone *else* out was nudging against her consciousness, pulsing with a small, nagging what if. *What if* she could find a way to blend Do-Good Jane with Do-Wrong Jane. Would she end up with one relatively normal person? An intriguing thought.

"So why is our Aunt Hathaway so desperately interested in me marrying James? Every time I turn around, she's shoving me together with him. Or inventing things about me as the perfect potential wife."

Now Anne looked even more uncomfortable.

"Does she have something to gain if I marry James?"

A hesitant nod. Then Anne said, "Her husband, our uncle Hathaway, is ill. From what I heard our parents to say, they are in need of money."

"I don't see what that has to do with me, unless . . . Oh, no."

The younger girl made a face.

"Is she getting a commission?" Hastily, she changed the term to something more appropriate to the time. "Will our parents be giving her money if she arranges for the marriage to James to go through?"

"Yes. They said that perhaps she could ensure the matter."

Ugly. Really ugly. Made Jane feel something like a prostitute. And not only that, but one who was so unattractive, the pimp had to work to put her together with someone. "This is terrible," she said.

"Aunt Hathaway has done as much for others," Anne piped up. "For a cousin of ours in London, in fact."

Great. A marriage broker. Well, at least she now knew the woman's interest and it wasn't simply a matter of family hoping the best for other family.

Jane pushed herself up and shook herself off, as if she could somehow shed the auction block feeling. "Let's go find that swing again and we can talk about your love life. *Which*, by the way, you're too young to have. Have you ever thought that you and Matthew could just be good friends?"

Chapter 18

Some things were universal, no matter what period of time you lived in. And one of those things was a swing. Though the wooden seat and rope were rough and primitive, it functioned the same, sending the swingee high into the air, where a feeling close to what the Wright Brothers must have experienced came over Jane. The sense of weightlessness, that a person could fly. High. Leaving troubles behind to sit on the ground and watch. Or slink away. Mostly, hers watched. And waited.

Jane pushed and Anne swung. While Jane tried to keep the conversation on a semiserious note, evaluating the pros and cons of rushing into courtship, it soon devolved into a discussion of the wonders of the opposite sex. "I should like to know what it is like to be kissed," confided Anne as the swing went back toward Jane for another push. Pink stained her cheeks.

"You'll love it," sighed Jane. "As long as the guy is a reasonably good kisser, anyway."

"What is—How does one know?" When the swing came back, Jane could see that Anne's pink had moved into a full-on red.

"You can tell when you kiss him, of course. But how do

you know beforehand? Whether or not he can kiss?" She pointed at Anne. "Which in your case is important because you can't run around kissing everyone to try them out." She dropped her hand to go back to a description, giving Anne a hard push on the swing. "Well, it can be hard to tell. But if you look at him and feel like you could melt into a puddle at his feet—"

The swing was back. Anne gave a squeal at the melting-puddle idea.

"No, it's true," Jane assured her. "It happens." So, how to describe a good kiss? She pushed a couple of more times, thinking it over. "If your insides turn sort of squishy and your stomach is turning over and you just can't *wait* to kiss him, it's a good indication you're going to enjoy it." Much like she felt with Curran. Absently, she gave another push as his face passed before her mind's eye. The guy could send shivers through her without even being there. How did she explain that one to Anne?

The girl was silent for a few swings back and forth, apparently thinking about Jane's words. "My stomach does not feel any particular way with Matthew. Except in need of dinner."

Jane nodded. "That should tell you something, then."

"It is perhaps just that I favor his company. He does not look upon me as a child. Or treat me such."

Growing pains. "Believe me," said Jane, who was beginning to relish the unfamiliar role of older sister, "before you know it, fewer and fewer people will be looking at you as a child. That only takes time. It won't be long, particularly if our father has something to do with it." Look at her, talking as though she actually knew the man. But in a strange way, she felt as if she might.

Anne dragged her feet on the ground, slowing the swing until she brought it to a stop. "Now I shall push," she announced.

"Okay." Jane grinned. Enough of the responsible older sister. She was ready for some elementary school *fun.* Changing places with Anne, she hopped onto the wooden seat and backed up with her feet, as far as she could go. Then she set off through the air, bringing her legs forward and back, in rhythm with the swing. Above her, the tree branch creaked.

"Take care!" she heard Anne giggle.

Care. Who took care on a swing? Okay, maybe she should, but it felt so good to be sailing through the air, her skirts blowing up around her. Maybe she could use them as some sort of parachute. At the idea of descending through the sky slowly on a cushion of billowing skirts, she threw her head back and laughed. Benton Dempsey might have to rethink his future daughter-in-law's ability to keep James on a straight path.

"You are so high!" shouted Anne.

"It's all in the legs!" Jane shouted back. "You have to pump!"

Anne ran around to the side. "Show me. Please!" She clasped her hands together in anticipation.

Now they were on Jane's turf. This is where things felt good. "Just watch," she called. Out with her legs. Back with her legs. She pumped hard. And then harder. At the last minute, at the very second when the swing hit its limit, she decided to go for the big finish. "Watch this!" she yelled down to Anne, pushing herself out of the swing and through the air, making her signature move of spreading her arms wide. "Parting the sea," her mother had termed it. In the echoes behind her, she heard the girl's scream and wondered if she had, yet again, acted on a really bad idea.

Too late now. A thought reinforced by the force with which she landed on the ground. At least she remembered to absorb the shock with her legs, making an almost five-point landing. Well, four points for sure, given not only the handicap but the imminent danger a Victorian corset posed. After the landing, the stupid thing cut her nearly in half and made sure she fell right over in a tangle of skirts. Ow. Really, *ow*. Her boobs felt pushed up into her neck somewhere and she was afraid she might have rendered her arms completely lifeless since the corset had shoved itself up and under them. *That* would make for some interesting bruising.

But for a minute there, she *had* stuck the landing. She was pretty sure, anyway.

"Jane!"

"Yes?" She'd grabbed a fistful of grass trying unsuccessfully to save herself from toppling. So she put the other hand into action batting away the fabric, as she did checking feet and legs to make sure they were in working order. When at last she looked up, it was to see a wide-eyed, giggling Anne, hands clapped to her mouth.

"I must do it! At once!" Anne cried.

Jane grinned gamely. "Go ahead, as long as you don't have one of these things on." She pointed to her corset. "Because that will do you in, let me tell you." With Anne's help, she made it to her feet and opened her hand, letting the grass fall. As she did, something hard and shiny caught her eye. She bent to pick it up. A round object. A . . . stone. With one rough edge. "Omigod."

"Jane, look!"

Anne had already run back to the swing and was pumping her legs, as Jane had demonstrated, and sailing higher.

Jane looked at her. Then down at the stone, her ticket back. Her way out of this whole mess. It was unbelievable. She'd thought it was lost forever and here it was. *Thank God*. Relief washed over her, buckling her knees. Choices. She had choices.

A girlish shout came from the swing. "I shall jump, Sister! As you did!"

Anne. The stone—"Anne, wait!"

The girl looked down, a frown on her face.

Jane walked swiftly to the side of the swing, trailing dirt, twigs and grass, the stone clutched firmly in her hand. For it to get lost again, it would have to be pried out of her fist. "Before you do that, there's something I have to show you. Something important."

"I have no need of—"

"Yes, you do." With the stone, she could leave this place. Forever. Go back to . . . Oh. Her life, which hadn't been so great in the first place.

The swing began to slow as Anne reluctantly quit pumping her legs.

Jane shot her a look of mock sternness, as much to focus her thoughts as anything else. "Aunt Hathaway is going to have something to say about those shoes."

At last, Anne came to a stop. "I cannot think what should be so important for you to tell me. I shall only do what you did." Her chin was high, her tone huffy.

"Okay." Jane shrugged. "But if you break your neck, it won't be a good look for you, no matter how high collars get." She waited.

It didn't take long for her to get the teenage Victorian version of *fine* in return. "As you wish," said Anne, making it clear she was agreeing only to pacify Jane.

"I want to show you how to make sure you get a good landing, one where you bend your knees. Trust me, it's your friend." She proceeded to show why in small hops, complete with her arms in a swan dive.

From behind a tree not far away, Curran Dempsey watched the demonstration, listening to the gravity of the instruction and the feminine giggles that resulted from it. Skirts flew and tumbled as the two hopped and rolled upon the ground. Jane emerged to stand, her arms triumphantly in the air and her cheeks flushed.

"Thank you," she said, turning one way in a mock bow and then turning in the opposite direction. "Thank you. We'll be here all week, if this corset doesn't kill me first."

A more awkward Anne sprawled on the grass, dissolving into laughter.

"Make your knees do the work," he heard Jane say, the gravity of her pointed finger lessened by the levity in her voice. "You have to get this right."

He'd never seen a display less proper. And he'd never been more intrigued by anyone. A lady of grace one moment and fire flashing in her eyes the next. Turning cartwheels on the ground, leaping from a wooden swing. What was he to think might happen next?

He could not imagine not knowing.

Bobbing his chin with regret, Curran turned and walked away rather than torture himself any longer with wanting what he could not have. What he must help his brother, who could not possibly appreciate such a woman, to have.

And what Curran would have to do to accomplish that.

Jane dressed slowly, her body stiff from repeated leaps off the swing and corset insults the day before, despite her very best shock-absorbing jumps. She imagined Anne would not be doing much better, especially since it had taken her a few memorable crashes to get it right. But the time Jane and Anne had spent together had been worth it. The two of them, almost like real sisters, laughing and letting their hair down. Literally, as well as figuratively.

Jane, who had never had a sister, had loved it.

But there was another reason she moved slowly. It gave her time to savor the dream she'd had last night, the one

Curran Dempsey had invaded with his rumbling voice and sensuous I-could-take-you-right-now lips. The way he looked at her, the way he talked with her . . . as though she were not the perpetual screwup but instead an interesting, desirable woman.

In her dream, he *had* taken her. And she had taken him. Over and over again, until both were spent and wrapped in each other's arms.

The dream had proven to be both bliss and torture. She'd tried as hard not to wake up as she'd known she had to. And at this moment, she wasn't ready to let it go. She could hold it close in her heart, a secret fantasy she didn't have to share with Mary or anyone else.

Because that's all it could be. A fantasy.

The servant girl crept in on silent feet to help her dress. Jane wondered what women did who didn't have anyone to assist them. God forbid they would have to put their bodies through agony, and layers of clothing, all by themselves.

Today's outfit was a fetching mint-green number made of soft, delicate fabric. It was laid out on the bed, ready for her. The servant walked over, corset in hand. "Could we skip that thing?" Jane asked.

The girl's eyes went wide.

"Guess not," Jane sighed. She missed her jeans. Her comfy, tight-fitting T-shirts. Her sandals with the sparkly beading. Frappuccinos. *Grey's Anatomy*. Her list could go on.

She even missed her life in a way she'd never thought she would. Despite her always saying the wrong thing, at least she was the one deciding to say it.

The stone. It was her ticket out. All she had to do was remember the words she'd said to get here in the first place and she'd be out of here just as fast. That's all she had to do. She fingered the stone. A small object, with such tremendous power.

All she had to do was use it. So why couldn't she?

Not yet. Not while Mary's book was still heading south. She couldn't do it. Just couldn't. All those people to be responsible for. She wasn't going back to her old life, only to have to worry about this one.

It wasn't easy being a heroine.

Jane opened the door and headed down the hall. When she came to the stairs, she began to descend, eyes down. Then she heard footsteps coming from the other direction and glanced up.

Curran. The living, breathing star of her midnight dreams. Her breath caught in her throat.

He didn't waste words on a greeting. "Jane. Please accompany me."

Wordlessly, she did as he asked, following him down the stairs and through a hallway into another wing. She loved the way he walked, as though he defied any and all opinions of him, answerable only to himself.

She wished she could do the same.

They wound through more halls until at last he opened a door that led outside, to a small, secluded garden, bordered by high stone walls. In the center sat a curved bench made of stone. Big enough for two people to sit. Well, two people and one huge skirt.

Flowers and plants grew wild and colorful, lending a slightly dangerous edge to the place, as though it afforded privacy to those who might seek to do things away from the prying eyes of others.

"It's beautiful," she murmured, following Curran into the garden.

"It is the place where Mary must next write you and James." He cleared his throat and straightened. "Together."

Jane walked a slow circle around the bench, and Curran, a finger to her chin. "Yes. This would be a good spot. Especially if there was a full moon shining down. With both the light and the shadows that would bring." She paused to picture it. "Yes, it would be perfect." Of course her mind's eye insisted on Curran as the man with her, instead of James, but that was only natural. Wasn't it?

He showed no sign of thinking the same thing. "You must sit here." He pointed at the bench. "And just so." Curran sat on the bench and turned sideways, his back rigid, in a less-than-perfect imitation of a woman in a Victorian dress.

Jane put a hand over her mouth to hide her smile. This was serious business. But he looked so comical, trying to be her.

"And you must tell him that he is the most"—he paused, eyes darting one way and then the other as he apparently gave this thought—"enlightened and charming gentleman whose acquaintance you have made. And extraordinarily pleasing to look at." He nodded. "That would be the thing to say to James. The only danger is that he hears nothing else that follows."

"Mmm-hmmm." She nodded her head. "Flattery gets you everywhere with James. That much I've figured out."

"You must be sincere in your words."

So her true feelings were apparent. "Mary will take care of that." Like it or not.

"I am not certain I hold the same confidence."

"Don't worry about me. I can act. When I need to." Jane walked over to join him on the bench. Being so close to him, his knees touching her skirts, awakened a yearning so strong, it was nearly painful. Forget insides that turned squishy. Hers were pure liquid. "Why are you—" He had the most amazing eyes. She could get lost in their depths and not mind never being found again. She tried again. "As long as James goes along, too, everything should be fine."

He tipped his head back, appearing to choose his words

carefully. "Our author sheds tears until she sleeps most nights. She is finding herself unable to convey the man she once knew in the manner she wishes to. And still she longs for him, though she knows his affections are elsewhere."

Sympathy welled within Jane. "He married someone else."

"Indeed." Curran nodded. "Another, more handsome woman, with far greater wealth to offer than our author's family."

Poor Mary. Jane's heart squeezed tight at the idea of the woman crying herself to sleep at night. Second-best in everything to someone else. Her brother was considered the better writer. Her one true love chose someone else. And there was little chance of another man coming around to sweep her off her feet. The only redemption she had was in writing this book, and it wasn't going well. How awful.

Jane would do her part to help. "So you think I need to sit how?" she asked Curran, turning sideways on the bench, as he had.

He stood up and went around to the back of her. Placing his hands on her shoulders, he pulled them back and up. It was one of the few places on her body not covered in layers of fabric and she could feel every one of his fingers, strong and warm. Much as they had been in her dream. She closed her eyes, reveling in his touch.

Then he took her hand, arranging it over the other in her lap. He leaned down to say in her ear, "You must have on your face that smile that says you know far more than you will reveal. The one that promises much, but confesses nothing."

Did she have a smile like that? Frantically, Jane searched her brain, only to find that everything it contained seemed to be short-circuiting from the nearness of Curran, from his touch, from his voice in her ear. "I—uh—" Oh, brilliant. Just brilliant.

He came around to stand before her. "I have seen that smile many a time."

He had? If he didn't quit looking at her like that, she was going to melt straightaway into a puddle at his feet, unable to even cry, "I'm mel-lll-ti-nng, I'm mel-lll-ti-nng . . ." You know, maybe they should just get out of this garden altogether. Right now. But at the thought, her inner voice was joined by a chorus of others, maybe on loan from other frustrated hearts, all shouting, "No-o-o," with a few yells of "Are you crazy?" chiming in.

Okay, then. Get it together. Get back in the game. You can do this. That had to be coming from her inner trainer, based on the voice of her high school PE teacher/quasi-drill sergeant, Ms. Malone, who made rare appearances in Jane's consciousness. Usually only when she'd gained five pounds, courtesy of all-American heroes Ben & Jerry.

Pretend he's a normal guy. Nothing special.

Yeah. Like *that* was going to work.

Jane rose from her seat, instructing her brain and all body parts to pay attention. "How are we going to get Mary to do this, to make this a setting? I have a hard enough time getting her to let me say something. She may not even know about this garden." Did her voice sound normal? She hoped so.

"She does not. So we must make her aware."

She wanted those arms around her. *Now.* Instead, she cleared her throat. "How?"

"Tremendous concentration and effort. I shall summon James. He will wait with you here in the garden, both of you intent on one purpose: entreating Mary to write."

"Sending her a mental message."

"A writer is seldom able to ignore such a message, when delivered with sufficient force."

Jane nodded. "It will get her to pick up her pen and when she does, here we are, in a place she hadn't thought of."

"Exactly. You must commit each detail of the place to memory, in detail, so that she will picture it as well."

Mary running around in Jane's memory. Not a comfortable thought. Virtually nothing in her head was Victorian, including her current focus on imagining Curran without his clothes. "Yes," she said a little more loudly than necessary as she sought to banish that thought, along with everything she wouldn't want Mary to access.

"So you will bring James here." She had to kick into project-management mode or she would never be able to pull this off. "At what time?" She glanced at her wrist, only to realize she had nothing resembling a watch to check.

"Now." His dark eyes burned into hers. "Have you any other questions?"

A million of them. Most specifically why he had to be the villain, instead of the hero. Why Mary couldn't have seen that he had far more redeeming qualities than James did and have chosen to do Curran justice instead of worrying about the peacock that had thrown her over for someone with more money.

But Jane couldn't ask those questions.

Instead, she drew herself up tall and said, "So I am to tell James that he is . . . enlightened and . . . um . . ." She frowned, searching for the other qualities.

"Charming," Curran offered.

"Oh. Right."

"And . . . ?" he prompted.

"Good-looking," she replied, exaggerating the syllables for emphasis. "Or, I mean *pleasing* to look at."

"Yes." He nodded. "We are understood."

She saw regret in his eyes that seemed to match her own. She took a step toward him. "And what should James be saying to me?"

Curran looked down at her. For a moment, neither of them spoke.

Jane could hear her breath, hear his. And nothing else.

"He should say that you are endlessly fascinating," he said, voice rumbling like tires on a gravelly road. "That you are at once beautiful and fragile, strong and fearless."

"Oh." The single word caught in her throat.

"That while some trouble of the past has clearly wounded your spirit, you are unafraid to allow your most vulnerable side to emerge."

How did he know that? Even worse, how did she deal with him knowing that, knowing her like no one else had ever bothered to?

He moved closer, until his breath tickled her nose. "That you are a grown woman who will laugh and enjoy the pursuits of childhood, with an irresistibility a man would do well to—" He broke off.

Whaa-aat? Embrace? Resist? Grab hold of? She could swear neither one of them was breathing. And her heart was going to hammer itself out of her chest any minute and leap into his hands. For safekeeping or to be tossed away. He held it. That much was clear.

"That you are unlike anyone else whose acquaintance I—*he* has ever made."

"And, um . . ." She struggled to speak. "You think—he'll be able to say all that?"

Curran blinked, hard. And took a step back, breaking the spell. "I shall speak with him on the matter. When I have finished he shall understand the importance."

Jane closed the gap between them, unwilling to let the moment go. She might never get another like it.

She took a deep breath, and a chance she knew she shouldn't. "He won't be able to say it like you just did. Won't be able to—" Her breath caught. "Mean it."

A long, agonizing silence. "He must," Curran said at last.

Chapter 19

Jane gulped. She had a wild, really weird idea, but then with the circumstances surrounding her, that could be a given. Why would she think of anything rational while stuck in the pages of a book? "Curran. Can you arrange for me to be able to talk with Mary? Like you and James do?"

He didn't answer for a minute. Then, "We do not talk with her."

"You communicate with her somehow. You always seem to know when she's writing, getting ready to write, is frustrated."

"It is not through words." He took in a sharp breath, furrowing his brow, as though trying to figure out how to explain it. "Rather it is pictures, thoughts, that pass from her mind through mine. James's experience would be the same."

"Do you push pictures and thoughts *back* to her?"

He shook his head. "It would not be wise."

Jane absorbed this information. "Did you get that from Mary?"

"An author shares with her characters only what she deems suitable."

"A lot of one-way communication going on," Jane

mused. Spotting Curran's puzzled look, she reached out
to grip his arms. "Please. Show me how. I know we've
been thrown in the fire once already and this would be
taking a very big chance, but I have to try it, for all of us.
I have to."

Curran gazed upon her earnest face and felt himself
quite willing to succumb to any request Jane might choose
to make of him. Surely there could be few things more
dangerous than a woman whose passionate heart spoke
through green eyes that held him captive in their gaze.

Yet the more characters Mary spoke through and the
more that attempted to speak with her, the increasingly
untenable the situation could become. Especially given
the author's fragile state and faint heart with regard to
the tale.

He closed his eyes, steeling himself to the task. "Jane,"
he said, shaking his head. "It is not possible."

"Please, Curran," she asked softly.

His eyes opened and his resolve weakened. "On the next
occasion, it may be the rubbish pile, rather than the fire."

"Smellier, but not as hot," Jane answered playfully, but
there was a resolve in her voice that matched his own.
He would have expected as much.

As he prepared to answer, she added, "Just tell me
how. And then trust me."

She knew not what she asked of him. His trust did not
come easily. Or, for that matter, at all. Survival came at
a cost. He had paid its price long ago, as a boy brought
to a place where he was not wanted. He knew no other
way, nor would he have it so.

Trust her, Jane said. *Trust her.*

"Come with me." He began to walk.

Jane easily fell into step at his side, once he had adjusted
his longer stride.

"Where are we going?" she asked.

"I shall take you as far as I am able." Farther than he should.

Perhaps respecting the gravity of the situation, she said nothing. They wound their way through halls and into another wing, where he stopped just before the dining room. "There." He pointed at a painting on the wall, framed in gold.

Jane followed his hand to the rendering of Mary Bellingham.

"This is our author," Curran explained. It seemed to him that he should have made the introduction with greater reluctance, but perhaps it was entirely fitting. Jane was the heroine of the tale.

She took a step toward the painting, searching it intently. He, in the meantime, watched Jane, her soft, light-colored hair glowing in the gaslight of the hall, her face anxiously taking in all the details in the painting. Then she turned to him. "I like her," she said simply, honestly. With an earnestness that pulled tight at his heart. "I will do my best to help her book succeed."

"As you should," he answered crisply. Then he spun on his heel to walk away before she could see—that, despite an iron resolve and his best intentions . . .

He trusted her.

Curran's abrupt departure left Jane feeling confused and disappointed. She'd hoped he would tell her more about the author whose likeness she saw displayed before her. Curran knew her, she suspected, better than James did. Curran, after all, didn't have the same filter of self-centeredness that James held on to so tightly.

Not that it was the only reason Jane had hoped Curran would stay.

But he had chosen to leave, she reminded herself, drawing up her shoulders. And she had her own mission to concentrate on. *Get through to Mary Bellingham.* One woman to another.

Jane closely examined the painting, determined to memorize each detail of the woman's face. If she couldn't see her, she would have to rely on the artist's impression of Mary.

James had called her "plain of feature." True, Mary's face was a bit too square, her nose too broad and her lips too thin to be called beautiful. Her hair looked as though it could not bear to curl, even though that was the style of the day. Someone had tried, it seemed, without a lot of success. One tendril in the group held a curl, while the others had gone limp in seeming defeat, leaving an assortment of straight, curled and wavy hair framing her face.

Mary had a fully upright, almost regal bearing, as though she defied those who might criticize, and her expression appeared quick and sharp. Jane suspected she could see a little of that less-than-pious nature in the curve of Mary's lips. As though there might be a joke only she was in on, but if you asked, she'd let you join in.

Her dress was properly overwhelming and subdued, revealing little about the figure underneath. And her hands were folded obediently in her lap. She looked directly at the painter with eyes that would seem to miss nothing.

But she had. She'd missed so much. Seeing only the things about James that she had admired, for all of the wrong reasons. Seeing only what she wanted to believe about Curran. The man he was based on may well have broken the couple up to save Mary from a life of disaster. It may have been the best thing that had ever happened to her.

The woman in the painting, whose gaze would say she saw everything, hadn't seen her hero for what he really was. And wasn't. Wouldn't be the first, or the last, woman to do that. And now Jane, hardly the champion of putting things right, had to make sure she did.

As a full moon shined its eerie light downward, Curran, true to his word, delivered his brother to the garden and left after aiming a razor-sharp dagger of a look straight at him. Though Jane's eyes never left Curran, he did not once look at her. She understood. He was determined to make this work. She could only do the same.

"Hello, James," she said quietly, hands behind her back.

"Jane." His tone held slightly more warmth than it had previously, but was still light-years removed from a passion that would not be denied.

Great. This was going to require performances worthy of the Oscars, from both of them. And they wouldn't even get a red carpet out of it.

No time to waste. "Let's get started," she said.

"Yes." He nodded, sweeping one gallant hand at the bench. She sat down, arranging herself sideways as Curran had requested, though she thought she knew a *little* more than he did about how a woman should sit when bent on seduction. A pang of jealousy went through her as she wondered who he had based his perception on. Some woman who had made him crazy with the way she sat? She discarded the thought as quickly as it had lodged in her brain. Enough things were making her crazy already. No room for any more.

She arranged her hands in her lap and glanced up at James. He seemed to be having some trouble with where he would stand, his face agitated as he took a step, then back and then forward again. "Right there, James," she instructed. "That's good."

He narrowed his gaze and took a step to the right.

Jane moved her hands from her lap to behind her, on

the edge of the bench. Then she drew up her shoulders and arched her back. Not too much, but just enough to make James's eyes widen. When she saw that they had, she gave him a smile. So much for Curran knowing everything.

If only it were *his* eyes opening wide.

"We need to focus now on the garden, right?" Jane asked. "So much that Mary will want to write this scene." Just for fun, she stretched her neck while re-arching her back and ran her tongue slowly over her bottom lip.

James reacted immediately, taking another step forward.

Jane put up her palm. "Stay right there, James," she said softly. "And concentrate. Hard."

This time he did as she asked, closing his eyes and then opening them again.

Focus, Jane. Focus. The flowers with their wild colors in shadows, stalks bending and lifting as though they could not be contained. The cool stone of the bench beneath her and the privacy of the wall that enclosed them. The crisp, clear full moon against a black night. Jane took it all in, committing it to memory and focusing on a setting so made for romance, Mary would have to write it. She wouldn't be able to resist imagining herself in it. With James.

James stood as still as Jane sat, apparently practicing his own brand of concentration, though she saw his eyes sweep her from head to toe, lingering in the area of her breasts, which she was doing her level best to show to good advantage.

Come on, Mary, she pleaded. *You can write this. If I can do it, you can write it.*

All remained still and quiet in the garden as she and James waited. And concentrated.

After a few minutes, he broke the silence. "Perhaps if I were to . . . ?" He moved toward her, taking her hand

and guiding her upward to stand before him. Then he slipped a hand around her waist, holding her.

Jane's chin lifted at that and she knew Mary had raised her pen to begin writing, without transporting them somewhere else in a flash of light. It had worked. They had done it.

"I find you, my dear," said James, who seemed to have a struggle with getting the words out, "to be endlessly fascinating."

Curran's words. Coming from James's mouth. She wondered what sort of threats or bribes Curran had had to make to get his know-it-all brother to cooperate. Talk about a complicated web. This villain was working at cross-purposes with himself.

"You do, sir?" she whispered, allowing Mary to take over the reins on that one. Oh, wait. She had to work in some things of her own, also per Curran's instructions. What was she supposed to say again? A glance at James's perfect features refreshed her memory. She focused on her tongue, making it say the words. "You are most pleasing to look at."

Somehow, it didn't sound like the compliment she'd intended.

He still took it as one. "Why, thank you, Jane." His arm pressed closer around her.

Okay. What else had Curran told her to say? She racked her brain trying to think. Before she could pull it up, the next words out of her mouth came from Mary. "You are an enlightened gentleman, with opinions I confess I seek to hear."

Enlightened. Had she been *thinking* that or was Mary rooting around in her memory? If a reference to Byron looking phenomenal without his shirt came up, they were all in serious trouble.

"You flatter me," James said with a winning smile. He

leaned toward her to land a kiss on her forehead. He looked very pleased. Too pleased. He had words to say as well.

She made her tongue again follow her command. "And do you find me . . . ?" Really. She shouldn't have to fish for compliments. The guy didn't have that big a job to do.

For a second, he appeared startled, as though he had to jolt himself back into the moment. "Endlessly fascinating," he repeated.

"Thank you, sir. And . . . ?"

"Beautiful." To his credit, he dropped his tone on the word, saying it as though he truly meant it. "Fragile."

Mary took over again. "There are others far more worthy of such praise," Jane said with an embarrassed duck of her chin.

No there aren't, she wanted to snap back at Mary. She wasn't any too sure she would call the pairing of "beautiful" and "fragile" praise unless it was also combined with the "strong" and "fearless" Curran had used. Jane was a lot of things, but a china doll too beautiful to handle *absolutely* wasn't one of them.

Before she could figure out how best to respond, James was leaning toward her, his face to one side. Then he kissed her, in a slow, rolling way at first, before moving on to practically sucking the life force from her lips.

Hey. Victorians weren't supposed to behave like that.

When he pulled back, he held tightly to her as though concerned she would drop into a dead faint at his feet. As though the magnitude of his kiss would be too much for her. "Jane," he whispered, a smile on his face.

A woman would hope that the swagger, the satisfied self-confidence would at least have something backing it up. But oh, *no.* James was a lousy kisser.

What had she told Anne about that? She needed some of her own advice about now.

A rustle came from the side, some sort of noise that caught the attention of both of them. It was a servant, the one Jane had seen Benton Dempsey throw things at after she retreated from his room. "Sir! Please forgive me," the woman pleaded. She dropped both a curtsy and her gaze in deference. "It is a matter of urgency," she said to the ground.

He turned toward her. "Yes, uhh." He made a snapping motion with his fingers. "What is it?"

Jane was willing to lay odds the woman had worked at Afton House for years, but James couldn't think of her name. Given the reason Anne had offered up for Jane being the one to marry James, she'd have to assume he would take that bet. Only to lose.

"It's Mr. Dempsey, sir. Your father. Miss Dempsey says you need to come at once." The woman's eyes were saucers in the moonlight.

Benton Dempsey. He must be near death. Jane felt a stab of regret. Though grumpy and narrow-minded, he was straightforward and oddly likeable. And she knew he'd held out a hope he wouldn't voice, a hope that Mary would see fit to let him finish out the book alive.

James straightened into a commanding stance, his hand leaving Jane's back to tuck into his jacket, as befitted the heir to a vast estate, Jane supposed. "I see," he answered. "You may go now . . ." Still apparently unable to pull up her name, he waved a hand in dismissal.

"Yes, sir." Another hastily bobbed curtsy and the servant left.

"Jane," he said to her. "My father lies upon his deathbed. I must go to him."

"Yes, James. Please. Go." *Go, James. Really. Take your time.*

He dropped a kiss on her forehead. "I shall be back, my dear one."

God, she hoped not. "And I shall be waiting."

With that, he left her alone in the moonlight, where she imagined that Mary made her appear quite picturesque. A solitary figure on a stone bench, in the shadows and slivers of white light, just kissed soundly by the man she loved. Who would, he had as good as promised, return to do it again.

Jane, Anne and Mrs. Hathaway sat in a row in the drawing room, waiting for news. Anne fidgeted while Mrs. Hathaway made nervous sounds, sucking in air through her front teeth. Jane, in the middle of the two, was about to see if Mary would allow her to put a hand out to still both of them when her aunt volunteered, "We should call for the carriage. To carry us home at once. It is not seemly we be present at such a time. Whatever will the family think of us?" She pressed a handkerchief to her nose and blew loudly.

The woman would give up her marriage commission so easily? Unlikely. She had an ill husband to support. And a blossoming business, apparently. Anne and Jane exchanged looks. "We shall see, Aunt Hathaway," said Jane. "I am certain we are not considered ordinary guests."

The woman's gaze shot to Jane. "Has he asked you then?"

"He had very nearly done so when the servant arrived to summon James to his father's bed."

Disappointment creased Mrs. Hathaway's face. "I confess I cannot imagine why he simply does not do so. He has written to your father and most assuredly received a reply." The handkerchief fluttered in front of her. "Your father would not delay in this matter."

Jane itched to come back with something that would turn the woman's world upside down. Something like, *What makes you think I'll say yes?* But she couldn't do it.

HIS AND HERS253

That would only upset the frail storyline Mary had built and result in disaster for everyone. She sniffed. She could swear smoke still hung in the air.

Instead, she spoke the words written by Mary, "Perhaps there are arrangements yet to be made, Aunt Hathaway."

With a reluctant nod, the woman acknowledged this could be correct.

"And I do know James to be a most devoted and conscientious son," Jane said. "He is even now praying for his father's safe journey to Heaven."

"Yes, yes," agreed Mrs. Hathaway. "Such a son any father would be thankful for."

The door opened and James came into the room, followed by Violet. Both appeared solemn and serious. The three women seated on the stiff furniture straightened.

"It is done," James said. "His spirit is safely gone to Heaven, carried there by our farewells and most earnest prayers."

"Oh, James." Jane rose and went to him, laying a hand on his arm. "We shall leave at once."

He raked a hand through his hair. "No."

"No?" asked a surprised Violet, from behind him.

"Your presence comforts me, Jane. I need you here."

"But the arrangements that must be made . . ." murmured Violet.

"Jane is soon to be my wife. And I insist it be no other way than she, Anne and Mrs. Hathaway stay."

A collective gasp went through the room. Jane was surprised to find herself one of the gaspers. "Your wife?" she heard herself ask.

"Now, Jane, I suppose I have not yet asked you formally, but surely you know my intentions."

"I had hoped, sir . . ." She sounded about ten years old.

Mrs. Hathaway shoved herself up from her seat, bounding over to the three who stood. "This is wonderful!" she said, clapping her hands. Then she seemed to remember that the circumstances, overall, were not the most joyous and recovered herself, dropping her hands to her side.

"Yes," echoed Violet, with some uncertainty. "I am pleased you have found happiness, Brother." Stepping forward, she laid a kiss on Jane's cheek. "And I shall welcome you most fondly as my sister."

"Violet, you know that your home will always be here with us," James said. "There will simply be another mistress to relieve you of your more arduous tasks."

"Yes," Violet answered. She didn't look at all convinced. Jane felt sorry for her.

Mary must have been thinking the same thing. "Violet, I have always wanted another sister," she said, putting a hand out to grasp the other woman's. "And I am so pleased it is to be you."

Gracious *and* kind. Points for Mary.

Violet responded with a hesitant nod.

So all was well in this tight, or at least not unraveling at the moment, family. Wait a minute. Had James ever actually proposed?

The house quickly shifted into mourning, with all of the curtains drawn, the coffin given a place of honor in the dining room and a heavy sense of quiet descending over all inhabitants of the house. There were a multitude of funeral arrangements to be made, apparently, and all were determined and discussed in hushed tones, as though speaking too loud would indeed wake the dead.

Jane's family, when word was sent by Mrs. Hathaway, was appalled that the three would remain at such a time. That may have been mitigated somewhat by the apparently welcome news that Jane was to marry James Dempsey. The

Ellingson parents subsequently seemed inclined to defer to their soon-to-be son-in-law's decision in the matter.

Curran Dempsey had, for all intents and purposes, disappeared, causing an ache in Jane's heart that would not go away. She looked for Curran around every corner, in every hallway of the house and in every row of the gardens. She even ventured to the stables to try and find him, having to back away and flee before the grooms could ask what she was doing there. She wouldn't have known what to tell them.

James reported to Jane, with no small degree of relish, that he had not allowed Curran at the bedside of their father. "He will be seen now," James said to Jane, "for the imposter he is. He has no claim to the name of Dempsey and I shall insist he renounce it. And this place."

She had, as Mary penned, expressed her agreement and admiration for James, a man who could take such command at a sorrowful time. But in her heart, she longed for Curran and dreaded the day when Mary would have her marry James.

Of course, knowing James as she was now beginning to, the ceremony might be over before Jane realized it had happened. If the same could be said for the wedding night, she'd be ecstatic. Thank God she had the stone. She could use it to carry her back before the "I now pronounce you . . ." was finished.

When was Mary going to end this book? Jane had cooperated, had been a good little character. It was time now to be done. Conclude it once the church bells rang and the newlywed couple came down the steps. Jane would be released to live her life. Regretting the one person it didn't include.

Her chin began to lift and her shoulders straighten and she knew Mary was writing again. The author had been pouring all of her energy into the book lately, writing deep into the night, mostly about funeral arrangements that included mourning clothes, selecting guests, the number of horses, the gravediggers and letters to various relatives. Personally, Jane thought she was spending way too much time on all of it, but maybe that's what they did in this time and other people would find it interesting.

She didn't. She just found it inordinately sad that Benton Dempsey's oldest son hadn't been allowed to be at his deathbed for a farewell. And the constant ache in her heart at not seeing him herself would not subside.

She stepped into the drawing room. "Have you seen James?" she heard herself ask Violet.

"He has gone into the city," Violet replied, looking up from her embroidery. "He is expected to return tomorrow."

"I see."

With that, Mary switched to writing more about funeral arrangements, including the large, dark curtains hung from every window, and Jane was temporarily freed as the object of the writer's pen.

But James did not return that day, or the next. Curran did not appear, either.

Jane tried, on several occasions, to channel the author, to no avail. Not even the hint of a picture or thought. She'd even gone back to the painting a few times, talking directly to it in the hope that Mary would hear her.

Nothing.

In Mary's next scene, Jane found herself in the dining room, eating with Violet, Mrs. Hathaway and Anne, when a servant broke in, her face contorted with alarm. "It's the Misters Dempsey. You must come quick!"

All four women scrambled out of their chairs, to the door and then to the front hallway, where they saw the reason for the servant's concern. Curran supported what looked to be a barely coherent, unshaven James, his hair at all ends and reeking of booze.

"What has happened?" cried Violet.

"James!" echoed Jane. She turned to Curran. "Sir! Is he injured?"

"The injury is only to his pride," Curran replied, his gaze even and unruffled.

"I have lost it, Violet," James said, his eyes wild and unfocused. "Lost it all. Our father would not be—" He hiccupped. "Pleased."

She moved to him, hands on his arms. "What do you mean, James Dempsey?" she asked, shaking him. "Tell me at once."

James stumbled and nearly fell to the floor, stopped only by Curran lifting him back up. "I've lost it," he repeated.

Jane took a step toward him. "James, what have you lost? Do tell us. We are all quite concerned."

"The estate. Afton House." A drunken laugh rolled out of him. "To Curran, the bastard child."

"No!" the two women said together in horror. Behind them, Jane heard Mrs. Hathaway swoon.

"Is this true?" Violet demanded of Curran, her face twisted with rage.

He gave a small bow, while still managing to hang on to James. "I confess it is. Your brother professes to be adept at cards, but he is in fact no match for me." A tight smile followed his words.

Violet's face crumpled and she reached out to lean against the wall. "We are ruined," she said, voice breaking.

"Ruined," repeated James. Raising his fist, he tried to take a swing at Curran, who ducked easily. James spun and stumbled again. He would have fallen had Curran not caught him and set him on his feet.

This was a hero? Mary had a lot to learn about life and love, and men, in general.

Jane took another step forward. "Give him to me," she instructed Curran. "You, sir, are to leave this place. James will tell you so himself, as soon as he is able."

"That shall be difficult for him as I am now the owner of this place." His eyes met hers. They were hard and cold. A villain's eyes.

But she saw something else there, she was sure of it. Something Mary couldn't see. A look meant for Jane alone. And she understood it.

He'd done his part to help rescue the story. Made a move only a villain would be capable of. Now it was up to Mary.

She held his gaze, even as she heard herself say, "There is one rightful heir to this estate. James Dempsey. You will please take your leave before I call the servants to help you do so."

"Bold words for one not yet a member of the family," Curran said, thrusting the weak-kneed James upon her.

"I am so desperately sorry," James pleaded as she and Violet, between them, carried him up the stairs to his chambers. "The bastard tricked me."

Violet murmured something tearful that seemed to approach sympathy, but Jane remained mute. The words Mary wanted her to say hovered on her tongue, knocking around at the inside of her firmly closed mouth to be let out.

Not this time.

She couldn't go through with this, with marrying James. It would all be a lie, and a bad one at that. Jane could unwittingly be doing more damage to Mary's story by staying. She couldn't help James, not like the story had been set up to have her do.

Straightening out someone with a gambling addiction would take an enormous amount of patience and love. She had neither for James. She had only a certain sympathy for him and that wouldn't be anywhere close to enough.

Yes, she cared about all of the people in the story. About Anne, the sister she'd never had. Violet, who had accepted her circumstances in life with as much grace as possible and kept on plowing through, hoping for something better but knowing the chances of it happening were zero to none. Benton Dempsey, who had given his life for the sake of the plot. Mrs. Hathaway, who, despite her zeal to get Jane married off at all costs, had likely had a less-than-happy life herself. Even James, whose own self-absorption and Victorian mores prevented him from seeing that he had a pretty good family around him. He was, in a way, a victim of his times.

Most of all, Curran. The man she could be herself with. Who quickened her heartbeat as much as he did her confidence and sense of self. When she was with him, life was easier somehow. She didn't worry about what she might say, what she might do, what she might break . . . *Oh.* Right. With Curran, she didn't *have* accidents.

"Jane?" Violet stared at her. They were standing before James's door. A servant had been shooed away, after being told the women could take care of James by themselves.

Jane bit her bottom lip to keep from saying any of Mary's words. Ouch. Biting harder now.

She reached down to open the door and they went inside, where they laid James on the bed. He mumbled still, repeating Curran's name over and over.

Violet looked at her across the bed. Jane succeeded in forcing out her own words. "I cannot," she said.

"Jane?"

"I cannot," she repeated.

"Marry him?" Violet moved swiftly around the bed. "But you must. Don't you see? We shall *all* be ruined."

"No." Jane walked backward out of the room. "It is not . . ." She strained the muscles of her mouth hard, shoving the words out, "Best for him. Or best for me."

Then her shoulders sagged as Mary released her pen, no doubt as worn out by the struggle as Jane.

James's sister gripped Jane's arms. "You *must*." Her eyes were wild and filled with fear.

"I cannot."

From behind the closed door, she listened to Violet's long, lonely wail. And tears sprang to her eyes. It shouldn't have to be like this.

Chapter 20

Jane walked down the long, winding staircase, hand trailing along the carved banister, her mind a world away. It was only when she reached the landing that she realized she hadn't thought once about the possibility of falling headfirst and cracking open her skull. For some people, that would represent the overly dramatic. For Jane, it was entirely realistic.

Yet it hadn't occurred to her once *and* it hadn't happened. If she didn't have more important things to concentrate on, she'd spend time mulling that one over. She didn't get a chance. In the next minute, her shoulders and chin rose to the graceful Book Jane level. Mary was writing again.

She heard a pounding at the door and the footsteps of the servant who scurried to answer it, her shoes tip-tapping on the floor. A booming male voice asked for Mr. James Dempsey.

As the servant stuttered a reply, Jane came up behind her to say, "Mr. Dempsey cannot be disturbed at this moment, sir."

"It is a matter of utmost urgency," the man insisted. "He will wish to see me." Without waiting for a response, he tossed his overcoat to the servant. With a full brown beard, round stomach and double chin, he looked something like a bear in Victorian clothing. Jane could imagine him dropping to all four paws with a growl.

"Surely it can wait until tomorrow when Mr. Dempsey is—" Another commotion, this time behind the man, interrupted her. And then Curran bolted through the door.

He pulled up short. "Mitchell," he said. "You have no cause to be here."

The insistent visitor whirled around to face him. "Far more cause than you." His expression turned to a snarl. "I am here to right an injustice."

"You are nothing but a delusional fool," Curran shot back. "Be gone."

Instead, the bear man turned to shout up the stairs. "James Dempsey. I must speak with you, sir!"

Jane's eyes went from the man to Curran and back again in alarm.

"Can you not see that this is a house of mourning, sir?" Curran asked. "Pray lower your voice." The last was not a request.

Mitchell appeared caught off guard. "I had heard of the elder Mr. Dempsey's death," he growled. "May he journey well to Heaven."

Curran took a step toward him. "Leave, now."

"I have business here." The bear in him reared up to show his claws, only temporarily dissuaded by the Dempsey family's sorrowful situation.

"If you will not leave of your own volition, I shall be only too glad to help you do so," Curran thundered.

"Stand aside!" ordered Mitchell.

So Mary was going for high drama. That much was clear.

"Stop," moaned a voice from above. Jane looked up to see James at the top of the stairs, head in his hands.

"Mitchell. Why must you—What is the meaning of this?" A loud hiccup and he tried to straighten, with little success.

Mitchell took a step forward. "Sir, a travesty has occurred. I must speak with you."

James shook his head, the picture of drink-addled despair. "Can it not wait until morning?"

"No." The answer was firm.

"Very well." James began to descend the stairs, none too well.

Violet showed up behind him, her face pinched and her movements stilted, as though they caused her pain. She attempted to take his arm.

"Away with you, Violet. Surely I can—can walk." He motioned her away and then proved he couldn't walk by stumbling on a stair and descending four at once. He put his hands out to catch himself and then pulled himself back up.

Why would Mary write her hero this way? The illusions she must have had to sacrifice to now portray him diminished as a hero. Inwardly, Jane shook her head. It was a hard thing to accept about someone in real life. Might be just as tough to do it on paper.

Jane felt her legs move as she rushed forward and up the stairs. "James," she heard herself whisper. "Allow me to help you. Please."

He gave her an uneven, tousled smile. "As you wish, Jane. But I am perfectly fine—" Another stumble. It was a good thing she hadn't been drinking, too, or they both would have ended up at the bottom of the stairs headfirst. "Are you quite well?" he asked. "I thought you appeared somewhat—" A hiccup. "Fatigued today. It cannot be easy for you."

So the softer, more solicitous side of James existed, though it could be hidden well at times. "Yes, James," she whispered. "I am well. Do not worry about me."

When they finally did arrive at the bottom of the stairs, miraculously unscathed, two men stood before them— a glowering Curran and a defiant and still determined Mr. Mitchell.

"What is it, Mitchell?" James asked, the weariness of too much alcohol heavy in his voice.

"It is simply this," said the man. He paused dramatically before continuing with, "Curran Dempsey cheated you this night."

"Preposterous," Curran announced. He turned a furious gaze on James. "Have you put this man up to such an assertion?"

James stood a little taller, yanking at the edge of his jacket. "I did no such thing. Though it appears to me clear—It appears clearer to me what may have trans . . . pired here."

Curran made a disparaging sound and took a step away.

"I observed it with my own eyes," said Mitchell. "And had the proprietor of the establishment spirit away the cards this man held before he knew they were gone." He aimed an accusing finger at Curran.

Jane could feel her face registering shock. Inside, she could only think, *Curran left his cards on the table? Literally?* Didn't sound like something a very *smart* villain would do.

Mary, apparently more occupied with the men, allowed her to glance at Curran, whose face was turned away from the others. He looked back at her, anger contorting his face. But in his eyes, she saw something else. Something just for her that she could see him fighting to retain.

Even though she couldn't be sure what she read in his eyes, she could be sure that something had just passed between the two of them. A sense of understanding, of acceptance.

He had done his job. And done it well, within the confines of the author's imagination. To the side of her,

James was requesting, in a loud, injured voice, to see the cards. Mitchell was only too happy to supply them. Jane took a step toward Curran and next saw him give her the slightest . . . *yes*. Wink.

In that moment, she knew she would never meet another like him. A hero miscast as a villain, with heart and character big enough to put the story, the author and the other characters first. A man with a strong enough sense of self that he didn't have to be right or even understood by everyone.

He only wanted *her* to understand.

If Mary hadn't been holding her upright with grace and poise, Jane might have fallen right over at Curran's feet, begging him to take her. Take her now. On top of all the melt-your-heart qualities he had, those eyes turned her into a woman driven by an army of hard-charging hormones, straight into his bed. Talk about squishy insides. If he so much as touched her, she'd turn into Jell-O. Jell-O melting in the heat of a tropical island. The thought of his arms around her, his skin pressed against hers . . .

She was a mess. Of longing. And Mary didn't even seem to notice.

"I knew it," James proclaimed, his speech clearer. Who needed detox when you had a writer calling the shots? "Knew that you were only able to win under the most underhanded of circumstances." He held up the cards and then threw them at Curran, where they scattered and fell to the floor, landing at odd angles. One caught on Curran's jacket, where it remained lodged. The King of Hearts. Mary probably hadn't noticed. Jane did. "You, sir, are a cheat. And there is no one more despicable than a man who would cheat his brother."

Curran turned back to aim a withering stare at both James and Mitchell, but there was, Jane saw, also an amused glint in his eye, as though he silently applauded James for finally standing up in a heroic sort of a way.

"You will leave Afton House at once," James pronounced. "And never darken this door again." He stepped toward Jane, putting an arm around her. "Jane, who will shortly become my wife, and I shall never welcome you here. Our trust has been betrayed. Once betrayed, it can never be regained."

Point taken, James, she thought, her eyes on Curran. *Stop, already.*

He didn't. "You have been served the utmost of kindness and have chosen to repay it with deception—"

Curran broke in. "I shall take my leave of this place. You have seen the last of me."

But James apparently had a parting shot. "I alone am the master of Afton House. As it should be."

The door slammed behind the love of Jane's life. Her army of hormones fell back, disappointed, while her internal gymnast jumped straight off the trampoline to sprawl on the floor.

"How very brave of you, James," she heard herself say, laying a hand on his arm. "To think he might have stolen this place from its rightful owner." Of course, if James didn't have his little *problem* and hadn't been out gambling the place away, then none of it would have happened at all. Curran had managed to come up with a plan much better than the author's, one that seized on James's weakness and used it to a villain's advantage.

"He will never seek to threaten our happiness again, dear Jane," James replied. "I have ensured it."

That he had. By default, anyway. *End it, Mary. End it now.*

"And we shall be married, Jane. Without delay." He gripped her shoulders tighter.

"A wedding!" From behind them, Mrs. Hathaway clapped her hands.

When had she appeared? It figured the woman would be right here when the wedding came up. Probably adding up her commission at this very minute. Dashing off a letter to her husband to tell him that they could pay the doctor.

"I am so happy, James," Jane said to him. *If you count feeling emptier than you ever have in your entire life as happy, then, sure . . . Happy.*

"As am I, my dear." His grip on her tightened.

She felt her expression turn serious. "But no more wagers, James."

"Anything for you, Jane."

She knew he didn't mean it. *He* knew he didn't mean it.

A pause and her shoulders sagged once again, telling her that Mary had put down her pen. For now.

James dropped his arm from around her and turned to leave. The director had, for all intents and purposes, yelled, "Cut."

Jane didn't let him leave. She grabbed his arm. "Is that the end? What will she do now? What is she planning, do you know?" Desperation mixed with sadness to course through her voice, through her body. *What had Mary done with Curran?*

"Calm yourself," James said, but not unkindly. One eyebrow lifted. "She will, of course, move next to writing the funeral. And then the wedding." He dropped his voice so the others would not hear, an unnecessary move since they were already moving out of the room. "Poor Jane. You are feeling nervous, no doubt, about what comes after the wedding? There is no cause for worry."

Why? Was he planning on leaving her at the altar? Because that was about the only way she wasn't going to have to worry about the wedding night. Mary should be the one worrying. A lot. Jane wouldn't keep James out of trouble after the book finished. She'd only leave him. And that was if she could manage to first be *with* him.

Curran had done his part to guarantee a happy ending all around. Now Jane had to do hers. And do it now. Before Mary began writing again.

She had to make James see the flaws in the story's resolution. Or get Curran to intervene. Talk to Violet. She discarded each option almost as quickly as she thought of it, for different reasons. James would never go for something tougher than what was in front of him. Curran had already intervened and been rewritten for his trouble. And Violet, intent only on ensuring she continued to have a place to live, had little to no influence or impetus to change things.

She watched as James swaggered from the room, full of his own success as a hero. He was perfectly happy with a sucky ending. Wouldn't be thinking of anything different on his own, that much was for sure.

She could never, ever marry this man and pretend things were okay. Feelings that strong were bound to cut through the passive character Mary had created and wreak havoc.

Because Jane would, after all, be Jane.

The hallway was strangely quiet, with the gaslight casting eerie shadows, when Jane walked up to the portrait of Mary and stood before it. She placed her hands on either side of the frame, gripping it so the carved edges pressed hard against her fingertips, and gently lifted it up and then down so that she could stare directly into Mary's eyes.

The painting was heavy, and Jane, with her newly untoned body, could hold it up only for a couple of minutes. Gently, she set it on the floor, against the wall, and brought a chair over so that she could sit before it, again staring into Mary's eyes.

"Talk to me, Mary," she whispered. "I'm your heroine."
Nothing. *Come on, Mary.* "I know this can't be easy for
you. I'll help." Jane concentrated, as hard as she could,
staring deep into the artist's rendering of the author's
intelligent eyes. There was a sensitivity there that Jane realized she must have missed the first time. They possibly had something in common, the two of them. A fear
of being discovered for who they really were. And finding it to be lacking.

She locked her gaze on Mary's unseeing one. And
then, she caught a glimpse of something that was there
and gone, like a television screen that wavered and faded.
She leaned farther forward, until there was only an inch
or two between the painting and her nose. The picture
came back a few seconds later and this time, stayed.

A young woman at a plain wooden desk, her skirts covering most of the chair where she sat, with only the toe of
a shoe poking out from underneath. Before her, sheets
of paper, a small vase of flowers and a pen in an inkwell.

Mary stared at the paper and then at the pen, for what
seemed like several minutes. At last, she put her head
in her hands, the picture of despair. As Jane watched, a
tear splashed onto the papers. And then another.

Tears formed in Jane's own eyes as her heart ached for
the author. Not being able to get the character of James
right had to wrench at Mary's very soul. Wait. Who was
Jane kidding? Mary didn't have the heroine right, either.
Because of a wish and a stone that had managed to make
its way into the author's story, uninvited.

When Jane's tears began to roll down her face, the picture of Mary abruptly disappeared. Jane lifted a hunk of
her skirt to her eyes, dabbing at them. She'd wanted to
talk with the author, maybe see the images that James
and Curran did. She hadn't expected this.

If only Mary had picked a different heroine in the first

place, someone who would actually fall for James, would love him enough to insist he do what was good for him—

Hold on. If Mary had picked—That could be it.

A new heroine. If she worked this just right . . . Jane wiped the top of her hand furiously across each eye.

It wouldn't be easy, but maybe, just *maybe*. It could be done.

Jane's search for the right candidate began immediately. And of all places, it began at Benton Dempsey's funeral, as mourners began assembling inside the church. With quiet and, she hoped, reverent footsteps, Jane followed others into the long, narrow sanctuary.

Rows of candles burned on either side, providing sparks of flickering yellow in the otherwise dim light. Centuries of holiness mingled with damp and incense to make her feel very small under the high ceilings. Not the usual spot for matching up eligible people, but she figured no one should mind . . . too much . . . if she found James a new wife in here. Given what had happened to her already, God had to have a sense of humor.

Mary would begin writing at any time. Jane found an empty spot near the back and turned slowly on her heel, with a nonchalant air. She didn't know what James's type was, but she could do a pretty good job of guessing.

Her eyes roamed over the women she could see, dressed in black fabrics that did nothing to flatter anyone including herself. That one had a hard look to her face, that one huddled too close to her mother. That one. There. Hmmm. A possibility?

The young woman stood by herself, her eyes downcast, but darting from side to side. She looked to be a delicate beauty, with porcelain skin and a long, aristocratic nose that gave her an Uma Thurman sort of presence.

Wheat-blond hair was piled on her head in the style of the day, but on her it wasn't a bad look. Jane allowed herself a brief moment of envy before zeroing in on her target again.

An older woman came up to say something to the Uma lookalike, who gave a bob of her chin and a shy half smile in reply.

Perfect. If she gave a smile like that to James and really *meant* it, who knew what could happen? Jane began to move toward her, circling in from the side, doing what she could to look casual while scanning for a ring. If the woman would just move her hand a little to the right . . . *No, not that way. To the* . . . There. A clear shot at the finger and . . . *Yes,* nothing on it!

A little less casually now, Jane moved up from behind, gliding to a stop at the woman's side. "Hello," Jane said, keeping her voice pleasant and nonrushed, even though she knew there was no time to lose, that she had to find out very fast if this woman could be the one who could get Jane, and all of them, really, out of this mess—

"Hello," Uma Woman said, turning to Jane. "You're Miss Ellingson." Her voice was laden with refinement and sweetness.

"Yes, I am. And you are?"

"Mildred Watkins," she replied. "You are a guest at Afton House, Miss Ellingson?"

"Mildred Watkins," Jane repeated, tapping her chin with her finger. "Mildred." A beauty like this and she got saddled with a name like Mildred. Oh, Mary hadn't noticed her. Hadn't noticed her at all.

"Do you like being called Mildred?" Jane inquired as her finger tapped faster.

"I do not understand," Mildred said, her finely arched brows wrinkling in confusion. Exactly how did she accomplish that without tweezers and a template? Jane wondered.

"No, no. You wouldn't," Jane mused, watching her intently. Then she glanced over at James, who was standing next to his sister, talking with mourners and the minister. Back to Uma. "What would you think about being called Jane Ellingson, instead of Mildred Watkins?"

"One does not choose a different name than that which was given." The sweetness of her expression was replaced with the ladylike equivalent of *Are you an idiot?*

"Mary Bellingham is the one who gave your name to you. She can change it."

The nostrils in Mildred's finely sculpted nose flared as she raised her chin. "Perhaps you did not understand that I am called Mildred."

So . . . part Uma, part Paris Hilton.

"I'm not sure, but I *think* this could all be very simple." Jane flicked a finger in the direction of James, taking care not to look at him while she did it. "You're familiar with our hero, I presume?"

"Mr. Dempsey?" Mildred's eyes grew wide.

"Yes." Whoops. Better clarify, just to be sure. "Mr. *James* Dempsey."

A fervent nod.

"What do you think of him?"

"Oh, Miss Ellingson, I could not say."

Jane lowered her voice. "I'm not going to *tell* anyone. But he is handsome, isn't he?"

"Terribly handsome." It came out in one breathless whisper before Mildred clamped her mouth shut.

"Let me try something out here. I know you're called Mildred and you're probably very happy with that, but bear with me." Jane raised her voice to call, "James?"

He glanced over and excused himself from a group of

people to walk to Jane. Then he saw Mildred. "Hello."
He gave a half bow.

"Sir. It is a pleasure." Mildred cast her eyes down again,
the picture of a demure woman. "My family was well acquainted with your father."

"Indeed?" A smile curved at his lips and he bent his
head toward her.

Granted, a funeral wasn't the ideal place for James to be
hitting on women, but he *was* a self-proclaimed ladies'
man and Jane *was* trying to make this exact thing happen,
so . . . She bent her own head down, trying to see his eyes.
That would tell her if he was interested—

His head popped back up. "Oh. Jane."

"James." She glanced at Mildred and then back at
James. They stood looking at each other. "Mildred was
just telling me what high regard she has for your family.
Especially you, James. I can't imagine why you haven't
met before."

"I confess I cannot, either," James replied, his voice
taking on a new huskiness. "I would have remembered."

Mildred dipped her chin and let it roll toward her
shoulder in a display of shyness.

James reacted by straightening, putting one foot toward
her and puffing out his chest. The peacock spreading his
feathers.

Jane smiled brightly, having seen enough. "I think
your sister is looking for you, James."

"Uh, yes. Of course. I must go to her." He ran a hand
through his hair, eyes still on Mildred. "Violet is quite
distraught."

"Sir, I am most sorry to hear that," Mildred murmured.

"Yes. Well." He paused. "Your family name. I did not
ask it. How very foolish."

Mildred had just opened her mouth when Jane cut in,

"James! Violet really needs you." To emphasize the point, she gave him a little push.

He frowned at his arm and then at her. "Of course." He left, but with two backward glances at Mildred.

Jane crossed her arms in front of her, satisfied. Did she know how to pick 'em or what? Then she turned to Mildred. "How would you feel about playing a heroine?"

It took some convincing, because Mildred seemed certain she would go straight to literary Hell if she tried to take on another character's role, but Jane finally got the woman to agree that slipping into the role of Jane Ellingson, just for a minute or two, could be worth it.

"If it works," she entreated Mildred, "Mary will go with it. She'll think she got the eye color and some other things wrong earlier and she'll start writing Jane as you because you're a much better fit." A few more things than eye color, but it was all just physical description. Damn. She wouldn't mind having that nose. *Never mind.* "You'll be the heroine of the story, with a handsome guy, lots of money. Security."

The other woman's eyes lit up. "Everything I have longed for."

"See? It's perfect."

Mildred's expression changed to one of trepidation. "And if it does not work? I shall be written out." Her voice trembled.

"No." Jane shook her head. "I have this all figured out. *I* will be Mildred Watkins, here in the back. So your character is not gone. I'll be sort of holding your place."

"Mr. Dempsey is most handsome," Mildred breathed.

Well, that was one thing Mildred and James could agree upon immediately.

Mildred's hands grasped Jane's. "You are certain it is allowed?"

No. "Yes," she assured her. "Really. It will be fine."

A hesitation and then, "Forgive me, Miss Ellingson, but why would you wish for another to take your place?"

People were actively milling about now, their voices rising to echo in the cavernous stone hall. No time for anything but direct, blunt honesty. "I don't love him," Jane answered. "I've tried, but I just don't. He deserves better than that." She paused. "And so do I."

Forehead wrinkled, Mildred seemed to be trying hard to puzzle that one out, but was apparently too polite to question it. She was perfect.

"There's only one thing I ask," Jane said.

"Yes?"

"He has somewhat of a gambling problem. You need to help him stay away from that. Can you do that?"

A firm nod this time. "My father had the love of strong drink. My mother and I turned him from it."

How had Mary missed her? Talk about inattention to detail. "Okay. Let's go see James." She took hold of Mildred's arm. "Quick, before that pen starts going. Remember, once it does, you're Jane Ellingson, here with an aunt and sister, and I'm Mildred Watkins." They started making their way toward James. "Are you actually here with anyone?"

"My mother. She was feeling quite faint. She is seated there, in the corner."

The mother would have to be clued in so that she didn't make . . . *a scene.* Jane choked back a nervous giggle.

When they arrived at James's side, Jane reached behind her to pull forth Mildred. "James, I want you to meet the new Jane Ellingson."

Chapter 21

James's eyes lit up with interest when he saw Mildred at Jane's side. Then he seemed to hear what she had said. He shook his head. "Forgive me, but—?"

"*This* is your new heroine. Her name was Mildred, but now it's not. It's Jane."

"You cannot choose a new heroine. That is only for our author to determine." But his words were spoken slowly and while his eyes were fixed on Mildred.

Jane moved between them and into James's line of vision. He blinked and stepped back. "Why not?" she asked. "Mary made a mistake. This is who the real heroine should be."

"Our author does not simply discard characters."

Jane clasped her hands behind her and took a step away from them, looking around her. Was it her imagination or did it seem as though these people were shifting positions, becoming more organized in where and how they stood? Mary must be moving around her desk, getting ready to pick up the pen. "She won't be discarding a character, James. I will be Mildred. We're substituting someone who will work better for you and we're giving Mary a chance to see that."

He cleared his throat. "It is you I shall marry, Jane. And only you."

"Me?" She had to point to herself to be sure, since James's eyes were again on Mildred. If she were a person who took offense easily, she might do so right now because he seemed to be protesting this whole thing a little less vehemently than he could.

Actually, *any* woman, whether she took offense easily or not, would be a little miffed at the way James was getting ready to strut his stuff for a new heroine. His "only you, Jane," had lacked a little something known as sincerity.

On the other hand, this was what she had wanted and what she'd set up to happen. Mildred's eyes were already sparkling. She'd do. Just fine.

A hush began to descend on the room, starting at one end and rippling through to the other. "It's time!" Jane ran, as fast as she could, to the back wall of the church, where she'd first seen Mildred.

She hadn't quite made it there when she felt the familiar grip come over her, raising her chin and lifting her shoulders. She fought against Mary's hold with all of her might, trying to make it to the fringes of the action. It felt as though she were pushing against an invisible brick wall.

Then she heard James in a raised, clear voice, say, "Come, my dear."

Since she wasn't the dear on his arm, she suspected he'd decided to plunge in with both feet and go with this new heroine. It wouldn't take a person with a low threshold for taking offense to question the depth of his affection if he would so easily take up with someone else. And be just fine with it.

She could breathe again. Barely, but she could. She used that to get herself the rest of the way to the safety of the wall, where she tried to blend in with the other mourners.

An older woman glared up at her from a chair. "Who are you?" she asked in a fierce whisper.

"Ja—I mean, Mildred." She nodded her head, hoping to convince herself. "Mildred Watkins."

"My daughter?" asked the woman. She didn't sound pleased. "I believe you looked quite different not ten minutes ago."

Jane gave a nervous laugh and was immediately subjected to scowls from other mourners. Right. A funeral. But Mary's attention must be completely focused on the two in the center of the church to be allowing this side dialogue to happen unnoticed. To Mrs. Watkins, she said, "People put far too much emphasis on appearance. Do you not agree, Mother?"

The woman gave an audible *"Humph"* and turned her attention back to the Dempsey family and James's new heroine.

So far, no cry of "Imposter!" No repercussions from the heroine switch. Mary would, it appeared, go with the change and change the details of physical description later, Jane supposed. Too bad the author had nothing like a global search-and-replace function. It would save all that ink.

Curran wasn't here. He was missing his own father's funeral, the chance to say good-bye. And Jane was missing Curran, with a fierceness she'd never known existed inside her. The hole inside her heart, the sense of emptiness, grew until it seemed it would consume her entire being in one gigantic ache of loss. Maybe it was a good thing he wasn't here. Seeing him would only cause her heart to shatter into the two millionth piece.

It was time. She had to go. Back to her real life. To give Curran, James, Anne, Mildred, Violet . . . all of them, a chance at continuing on to that happy ending, she had to leave.

She let her eyes sweep over them one last time. James, standing stiffly upright. An okay guy, all things considered. But not someone she could make a happy-ever-after life with. Anne, with a spirit and budding sense of adventure this era desperately needed. Violet, a woman who'd been given a rough road in life and a backpack of bitterness to take with her on the journey. And even Mildred, who'd had the courage to go for something bigger than the role she'd been assigned.

There was another reason Jane had to leave this place. Until she came to terms with everything she'd left behind, she wouldn't be able to move ahead. She'd live every day wondering if she could have said something different, done something different, on her own, without someone else writing it, and had everything turn out okay. And those accidents she was so prone to. What if— and this was a very big what if, but it had only just popped into her head—What if they weren't accidents at all but rather things she did to sabotage others . . . and herself?

She let that one roll around in her mind for a minute, clunking and clanging against all the outraged reasons it wasn't true. But those reasons weren't out in full force, it turned out, because they became very quiet, very fast.

Ah-ha, you might say if you were a Dr. Phil type of person. *Might be onto something here.* No way to tell for sure, but she owed it to herself, and her beaten-down sense of self-esteem, to find out.

Jane reached into the secret pocket in her dress to pull out the stone. Her ticket back home. As soon as Mary had finished writing this scene, *maybe* even before, she would be gone, no longer a part of the story. Her fingers stabbed at the fabric, searching. Mildred's mother would have to find another daughter . . . She pulled at the pocket, growing more agitated with each passing second. What was this? The stone had been right—

It was gone. *Gone.* It couldn't be. She'd put it there earlier. For safekeeping. And in its place a—piece of paper?

This couldn't be happening. Her thoughts were bumping, crashing into each other, spinning out and diving off cliffs. Without that stone, she couldn't leave. And if she couldn't leave . . . She pulled out the piece of paper with trembling fingers and raised it to her eyes. Bold handwriting, in dashes of black ink. *"Come to me,"* it said. The message was signed with a single letter: *C.*

She had to go to him. Now.

The relative ease of her shoulder and chin movement told her she was flying under Mary's radar, allowing Jane to fall back behind the others and move slowly along the cold wall undetected, her heart pounding at the thought of seeing Curran. How had he managed to slip a note inside her pocket? To move his fingers so close to hers without her knowing and turning into a quivering bowl of mush at his feet. Oh God.

When at last she reached outside, she breathed in huge gulps of air, just to give herself some grounding in . . . what? Reality? A laugh that swirled and choked came out of her until she could imagine herself in a rocking chair, muttering with each forward and back motion about the life she'd almost had. And the love she'd almost—

He wasn't there. Anxiously, she scanned the landscape near and far, the village houses, the blacksmith's place, the tree horizon and gently rolling hills in the distance. He had to be. She couldn't stand it if he wasn't.

"Looking for someone?" she heard a voice ask from behind her.

She spun around. "Curran!" She stepped forward to fall into his arms in relief so great it rendered her limbs useless.

He caught and held her tight. The ache inside her faded,

one small piece at a time, until an unbelievable longing flooded through her. "You're here," she whispered.

"I did not leave," he whispered back.

"I was so worried."

He brushed a piece of hair from her forehead. "You must not worry, my love. It takes up areas of your heart best put to other use."

She pulled back, gripping his arms. "Are you going to be all right?"

His expression turned deadly serious, even as his eyes melted everything inside her that wasn't already lava. "With you at my side. Yes."

"I can't." She shook her head. "I'm not supposed to stay with you. I left a life that—that didn't work. I have to put it right before I can be with—be with anyone." What was she doing, saying? Was she out of her mind?

"I have horses waiting. Leave with me now. We shall ride far from here." His voice was low, urgent.

She could see them doing just that. She and Curran, riding far, far away. It was the stuff fairy tales were made of.

And she couldn't do it. No matter how much she wanted to. Even as she yearned to jump into his arms and run away with him, galloping into the sunset on a horse, she couldn't do it. She'd be offering him only half a person. The other half was in Seattle, waiting for a come-to-Jesus soul searching that might answer the questions that had plagued her for much of her life.

He deserved more than half a woman.

"Curran." She put her index fingers to his lips. "I cannot go with you. But as you leave, I want you to know that I will never, ever forget you." A lump the size of a tennis ball formed in her throat, making it difficult to swallow, to talk. She tried, anyway. "You are absolutely the hero of this story, whether you want to be, or not." Then she gave him a wobbly smile. "I've never met anyone quite like you. Which makes me think I've had a very big hole in my life. Until now."

He trailed his finger gently down her cheek. "And shall I, as I leave, take your love with me? Tucked safely in my heart?"

"Yes," she breathed. "You will." An explosion of tears hovered dangerously close by.

"You shall have mine, as if you did not know," he rumbled. His thumb moved across her cheek, with a touch both rough and soft. "My love shall occupy the part of your heart you had previously given over to worry. Leaving you quite without the ability to grieve as we part, but only to remember what we had for far too short a time."

She couldn't even answer that one. If she had tried, nothing would have come out. She wanted to say how desperately she would miss him, how much she loved their conversations, their kisses, the way he'd teased her, held her. She wanted to say how much she regretted that they'd never share a night together, making love over and over, until the sun streamed over their glistening bodies in the morning. How she would have liked to have had an entire lifetime of moonlit nights and sun-kissed days with him. Grown old together, strolling in a garden on afternoons when they both had white hair and wrinkled memories.

Somehow, it seemed as though he understood she couldn't talk, and instead he read it all in her eyes.

"Yes," he whispered. "We are of the same mind." Then he folded her into his arms, held her tight, and put his mouth on hers in a kiss that had her lifting not one, but both feet from the ground.

All conscious thought suspended, drowned out as it was by surging, rushing love, lust and lunacy. She *almost* abruptly changed course and told him she'd go with him. Instead, she sank back downward until her feet again touched the ground. When he released her, she concentrated on getting back her breath. It was the only thing she *could* concentrate on.

He held out the palm of his hand. "Could this be what you seek?"

She looked. The wishing stone sat squarely in the middle, glinting up at her. Her knees buckled and he caught her with his free hand. "Yes," she said. "That's my stone." She tried to smile, but it came out in something closer to a quiver. "You're a pickpocket."

"One of my many skills." He gave her a wink that devastated what little rational thought she had left. "I have known," he said slowly, "that this stone somehow claimed a part of you. I selfishly hoped I could claim that part for my own." Taking her hand, he put it in her palm, wrapping her fingers around it. "Farewell, Jane. I must leave before the funeral concludes."

Her throat hurt. So did every other part of her. "Farewell."

"Perhaps . . ." He looked away and then back at her. "We shall meet in another tale."

She nodded miserably. "Perhaps."

Then he put a hand under her chin, lifted it, and blew ever so softly on her nose. Just as he had with his horse. *Respect,* he'd said that conveyed, and so much more.

She hadn't before known what it meant to swoon. Now she did, finding that, after all, she'd rather not know.

Curran strode to a tree where two horses waited. In one powerful motion, he lifted himself up and onto his horse without his eyes ever leaving hers. Then he raised a hand, touched it to his lips and urged the animal to gallop away.

Out of her life. The part of her heart that he now occupied folded up tight and shut the door.

Gradually, she became aware of a stir beginning from

somewhere behind her. She glanced back at the entrance of the church, where she could see one person and then two, emerging from its door. Dully, she realized that she had to get out of here before Mary spotted her at the wrong spot in the scene. As such a minor character, she could be zapped into oblivion.

Her hand shook as she opened her palm. With her other hand, she began to rub the stone in a circular motion, repeating the words that jumped back into her mind. *"A posse ad esse."* Focusing all of her energy on the small stone, she whispered, "Please. Take me back home. Let me start again."

The commotion behind her became louder. *"A posse ad esse,"* she repeated. *"Ple-ee-ase."*

A loud boom on her right scared her as much as it sent relief shooting straight through her. She remembered that sound. It had delivered her here. Then came the rushing, deafening sound of air, whirling and spinning all around her. And the sense of being knocked off her feet and flung into darkness, where she tumbled head over heels until at last she landed.

She opened her eyes, slowly at first and then wider. She was sitting on the floor, in her apartment, which appeared to be just as she had left it. There was her jacket, on her favorite overstuffed chair. Her purse, open. The newspaper she hadn't picked up.

Nothing looked any different from when she had gone. Yet half a lifetime had passed. Hadn't it?

Reaching for her purse, she thrust her hand inside to pull out her cell and flip it open to look at the date. Wait. That couldn't be right.

The same day. Only five minutes past the time when she'd made the first wish. How was it even possible? She sank back to the floor. How was it feasible to launch yourself into the plot of a book? Maybe she'd actually only passed out for some reason and had been lying on the floor until she just now came out of it.

She put a hand to her head, checking for injuries. None that she could find. Her head felt fine. Carefully, she pushed up from the floor until she stood. Then she walked to the bathroom, almost afraid to look in the mirror, but badly needing to.

There she was, the same person who had come in the door, what . . . less than half an hour ago? Watching her reflection, she put her palm up in front of her face and gently blew, causing the breath to wash over her nose even as her eyes filled with tears. She would not forget Curran. Ever.

He occupied that piece of her heart that she had always given over to worrying.

Chapter 22

Jane finished putting on her makeup in the morning light, giving extra attention to the dark circles that had suddenly appeared under her eyes. Not that she should be surprised. She hadn't slept all night. The images of Curran that went through her head, the memory of his lips on hers, were nothing but torture. He was so close and yet so far away. Had he ever even existed or did she simply have an unbelievable imagination hiding out in head-injury land?

Maybe she'd never know. But whatever happened, she would keep him safely tucked inside her heart, while she faced up to all of her done-wrongs in present-day Seattle.

She decided not to get her customary frappuccino on the way to work. Too much chance for something to go wrong. She could come in through the door and dump the entire contents on the senator. Really not the start she was looking for in this era of a new Jane.

Once at her desk, she stowed her purse inside, brushed a microscopic piece of lint from her very best suit and, her heart pounding, walked to her boss's door. It was open.

She moved to just inside the doorway. "Excuse me. Chase?"

"Yes?" He spun his chair around until he faced her. "Jane. You're here."

"Is there—" She didn't quite know how to phrase this. "Anything I can do to help fix what happened yesterday?"

He gave a heavy sigh and pushed his bottom lip over his top. "So far we've dodged a bullet. The big fire down on the waterfront yesterday was a lucky break. The media's all caught up in reporting on that."

"Oh. Right." Probably the only place where you'd hear a big fire thought of as a lucky break. Unless you were in a business less than legal. But then, working in politics did seem to skirt close to the edge sometimes.

"And one other lucky break. It seems the fax machine jammed right before it sent the release to the *Times* and the *P.I.*"

Jane caught her breath. "Really?" The *Seattle Times* and *Post-Intelligencer:* the two biggest newspapers in the state. Now that *was* a lucky break.

"Really. So how'd you manage that?"

She shrugged, unable to keep the smile from her face. "Good karma?"

He gave her a look that said he doubted that. "As for the others, well, so far no one's been that fascinated by the bill for apple growers."

Relief washed through her. "That's great."

"Don't be too happy, yet," Chase warned, picking up a pencil to tap it against his desk. "Not going to last. Somebody's going to pick that thing up and read it."

"Yes." Jane nodded furiously. "I know. What can I do?"

"Nothing. I have it under control." He made a magnanimous gesture.

That's not why Jane had come in. It was a huge relief to find out the situation *might* not be as bad as she had thought—yet, anyway—but that wasn't good enough. She had to help make it right. "Chase, I need to learn from this. Please give me a chance to be involved in however we fix it." Then she held her breath, waiting for the "You're fired," the lecture about the audacity of a twentysomething coming into the office of an experienced political "operative," as he liked to call himself, and having the nerve to suggest she could do something to fix the problem she'd created.

She waited with her breath held for what felt like a lifetime, forcing herself to keep her eyes open instead of squeezing them shut and slinking backward out of the room. Chase remained sitting at his desk, looking either stunned or deep in thought. She couldn't tell which it was.

"All right," he said finally. "There's a meeting this morning at ten to go over the plan I've come up with. I think it may be time to address this thing head-on."

Jane began to breathe again. "You do?"

"The senator has held on to it too long. It was bound to come out sometime. If we work it right, I think she could come out of this okay. As long as we're ahead of the story. Grab on to it. Make it our own."

He needed to be chomping on a cigar while he said that, Jane decided. That would complete the look. In fact, she might get him one, just to celebrate. Her not being fired. The senator not hiding her past. Anything else that seemed right about the day. She couldn't stop the grin that took over her face. "Ten o'clock," she said. "I'll be there."

"Good." He thrust a stack of paper at her. "Take a look at this before the meeting. I worked on it all night."

"Thank you. Really. Thank you, Chase."

"Yeah, yeah." He dismissed her with his hand. "Don't make a habit out of doing that kind of thing."

"Of course not. I won't. Not again." She backed out

of the office, papers in hand. "I'll go over this before the meeting."

"Yup. See you then." He had already spun back around and started typing on his laptop.

Her job. She still had it. Which meant she still had a place to live, a way to eat, the means for supporting her frappuccino addiction.

Life was . . . well, if not *good,* at least somewhat sort of okay.

Jane picked up the phone to call her friend Holly, a rock the size of a baseball sitting squarely in the middle of her stomach. She started the conversation by begging Holly to let her get a replacement dress FedExed in from wherever. Then she'd offered to *drive* to wherever to pick up the replacement, if that would help.

Holly had been frazzled. The bride-to-be, the day before her wedding. Totally understandable. "It's okay, Jane," she'd said, while yelling in the background at her sister. "Molly, bring me that. You're not making the favors right! I told you to use the red ribbon. Weren't you listening?"

"Holly," Jane pleaded. "The dress."

"Oh. That." Again, Holly turned away from the phone. "Lolly! Get over there and help Molly, please."

Jane had never understood why her friend's parents had decided it would be a great idea to name their three daughters Holly, Molly and Lolly. Good thing they hadn't also had a boy. They wouldn't have had any choice but to call him Wally. Wasn't as though you could throw a Jason into that group.

Holly came back to the phone. "The stain is out. I told you not to worry about it."

Red wine? How?

"A miracle worker who masquerades as a dry cleaner. No one will ever know it was there."

Jane gave a shout of pure joy.

"Hey," said her friend cheerfully. "What are you trying to do, make me lose my hearing right before the wedding? How am I supposed to know when to say 'I do'?"

"I'm paying for the dry cleaner."

"Sure. If you want. I know I gave you a pretty bad time when it happened, but it was my wedding dress and I even thought you might have, you know," Holly paused. "Done it on purpose."

"On *purpose*?" Jane was horrified, but at the same time, the same suspicion niggled at her, taking the level of horror down a notch.

"Right before that, we'd been talking about that scum-sucking Byron. And then we started talking about Greg and how great he is and I guess I was doing some bragging about how he would never have done anything like that, and then we started going on about the wedding." Her friend's voice dwindled away.

"Oh, Holly." Jane could hardly breathe. It was all coming back to her. Those feelings she'd had, the jealousy and shame that had jabbed at her until she could barely see straight. Her hand that held the glass of wine had been shaking . . . "I'm so sorry. I may, you know . . . Omigod, have done it on purpose. Without even realizing it. I really—I don't even know what to say, I feel so bad."

"Don't worry about it. If it had been me instead of you, I might have done the same thing."

No, she wouldn't have, but it was nice of her to say. "What else can I do? Please. I have to try and make this up to you."

"You can come over here and keep me from killing my sisters. If I see one more favor made with pink ribbon, instead of red, I'm going to—Lolly! Use the *parchment* paper! Got it?"

"I'm on my way. Out the door now," Jane said, grabbing her purse and keys. "Leave it to me. I'll get the favors done right and keep you from killing your sisters, the cat, the neighbor's dog, your mother, anything else that crosses your path."

"Perfect," Holly said, trying to sound relaxed and not managing it at all. "I need you."

"I'll be there practically before we're off the phone."

"Oh, and Jane, one more thing?"

"What is it? Did you forget something or run out of ribbon? Do you need me to stop and pick more up for you?"

"No." She could hear Holly muffle a giggle. "There's red wine here. I want you to stay six feet away from it at all times."

Jane stopped. And grinned into the phone. "Where's the wedding dress?"

"Upstairs. In a bag. Safe from you."

"Like I said, I'm on my way."

Holly was a friend to keep for life.

Holly's big day had arrived. Jane did her best impression of a bridesmaid's walk down the aisle, taking care not to fall in the heels Holly had insisted she wear. If she crashed and burned here, she'd take out an entire row of wedding guests. The aisle seemed a lot longer today than it had at the rehearsal. In fact, it seemed endless.

The last time she'd been in a church . . . never mind.

She kept her hand on the arm of her assigned grooms-man, who was the nervous younger brother of Holly's fiancé, Greg. They weren't halfway down the aisle yet and already his face was covered with a sheen of sweat. In a stiletto fall, he'd probably take out the row on the opposite side.

One step at a time. Keep your mind off potential disaster. Glance around at the guests. Demurely.

To her left, she saw three women she and Holly knew from high school, sitting together as they always had in class, ready to verbally pounce on anyone who didn't fit their mold of the perfect high school student. Or who had a simple, perfectly understandable accident in chemistry lab. Why had Holly invited them? She was too nice. Although you only had to look as far as the red-wine incident to know that.

A couple of rows down, Jane saw a few more people she remembered from school. And some from the company where Greg worked. She'd met them at a party he'd had at his place. The party, in fact, where she'd met Byron, who worked two cubicles down from Greg.

No one else she knew. The rest all seemed to be well-wishing strangers. To her, anyway. Probably not to Holly and Greg.

More careful steps. They were halfway down the aisle. Holly's parents were up ahead, turning in their pew. Jane switched her gaze to the other side, where she could look beyond the sweating groomsman to see more people she didn't know. A little girl in pink, a woman in a shade of fuschia that shouldn't see the light of day. In the next aisle, a man in black. A very good-looking man who . . . *Byron.*

Why hadn't she thought about the fact he would be here? Of course he would. He and Greg were cube-buddies at work.

She and Greg's younger brother moved a few more steps down the aisle. He was blocking her view. Maybe she'd been wrong. It hadn't really been Byron. Or, if it was, maybe he wouldn't notice her. Okay. Not much chance of

that, since she was on bridesmaid parade and there was
nowhere *else* to look until Holly came down the aisle.

She modified her wedding walk just a little to slow her
step so the groomsman would move ahead and she
could duck her head around the back of him to make
sure that was Byron. Could have been some other guy.
No. It was Byron. And Greg's brother, in confusion, had
come to a halt. They were only three-quarters of the way
down the endless aisle and Holly's mother had a frown
on her face.

Jane smiled brightly at Greg's brother and gave his
arm a little tap with her hand. Then she took a step forward as if wondering why in the world they would have
stopped. Poor kid. He moved with all the agility of a
robot, and a drop of sweat actually clung to his chin. She
pulled her hand out a little early, so as not to catch that
droplet on her bare arm, and breezily went to take her
place standing with the other bridesmaids. No matter
what she did, she wasn't going to look at Byron.

Scum-sucking, Holly had called him. She could be
right. Or not. It was Jane, after all, who had made the
sudden proposal. Which, come to think of it, *might* have
had something to do with Holly's wedding and Jane's
own longing for a happy ending of her own.

Happy ending. Whoops. Delete. Can't think about
that now. She smiled brightly. What had happened to all
the people she had come to know and care about? She'd
tried to find Mary's book online, with no luck. She'd
have to do a search of bookstores that carried rare and
out-of-print books.

The flower girl made her uncertain entrance at the
back of the church, followed by a truly beautiful Holly.
Jane beamed at her friend. And then stared at Byron.
Her eyes went from Byron to Holly, back again and back,
until she felt like a tennis ball. Holly arrived at the altar,

kissing her father and taking the arm of her groom. The bridesmaids turned to face the priest, causing Jane to breathe a sigh of relief. All that back and forth was making her dizzy.

But, that was pretty much it. She wasn't having quite the reaction she would have thought. She'd been surprised and taken aback to see Byron but, oddly enough, that rush of humiliation about their last meeting wasn't there. Neither was a surge of excitement at the sight of him. Instead, there was a mild interest, without much to back it up.

So she'd said something she wished she hadn't. She wasn't the first one to do that and wouldn't be the last. And so Byron was a nice guy. He wasn't the first one and wouldn't be the last.

She sighed, earning a curious look from the bridesmaid standing next to her. Jane straightened and smiled brightly. Eyes forward. This was Holly's day.

The reception was held at a hotel on the water. Once the photos were over, Jane walked in behind Lolly and Molly, who were arguing over who had made better favors. She put her hands on the two pairs of shoulders. "I thought you both did a great job," she said. "Holly loved them."

"Thanks!" they gushed at once. Only ten months apart, they were often mistaken for twins.

Jane left them, wandering over to the ice sculptures and the tables piled high with food. She wasn't hungry but did accept a crystal glass of champagne from the waiter who offered. Then she watched as Holly and Greg made their grand entrance, her friend grinning from ear to ear in a wedding dress that blissfully showed no evidence of a wine crime.

As she lifted her glass to take a sip, she heard a low voice at her side. "Hi, Jane."

She answered without turning. "Hi, Byron."

Neither said anything for a minute. Then he said, "I didn't call."

She thought about flinging off a casual, *"I didn't notice"* but decided against it. He'd know she was lying. Instead, she answered, "I didn't call you, either."

"Things have been going—fast."

"Too fast for you." She was pleasantly surprised to realize it didn't hurt to say it. *That* much, anyway.

He didn't reply, but she glanced at him long enough to see his nod and then the hesitance as he tried to figure out whether or not he should be agreeing.

The DJ started the music. People around them raised their champagne glasses. Jane lifted hers. "It's fine. Really. We had a great time, but I think we're done now," she said lightly. A small, sad smile curved at her mouth, but not for the reason Byron would have thought.

She'd lived half a lifetime in that few minutes she'd been gone to Afton House. Byron had his good qualities. Handsome. Generous. Adept at sneaking out of a room undetected.

What he wasn't . . . was Curran.

Holly passed by several feet away. She looked at Byron, then back to Jane and mouthed, "Are you all right?"

Jane gave the smallest nod she could. "I'm sorry, Byron, but I need to go. Being a bridesmaid has its responsibilities and all that." She turned and gave him a quick peck on the cheek. "It was great seeing you."

"Jane." He put a hand on her arm. "Thanks for being so understanding."

She gave him a rueful smile, then a shake of her head. "It's not that I'm so understanding. It's just that . . ."

Trying to figure out how to say it, she finally settled for, "A lot of things have changed."

He cleared his throat. "Maybe—"

"I could enter the wild and wacky world of bridesmaiding? What a good idea." She smiled as a small knot of regret formed somewhere in the vicinity of her heart. She wished she could fall, and stay, in love with Byron like she had with Curran. If she thought things would still work between them, she would stay and fight for him. Instead, she gave him a gotta-go smile. "So I'd better go rescue Holly from her sisters. If she names her first daughter Polly, I'm never speaking to her again."

Byron lifted his hand.

Jane lifted her own hand, allowing a sense of sadness to curl her fingers.

Then she walked away. Knowing his eyes were on her, she kept her chin high and put an extra oomph into her hips, which were tightly encased in the sheath dress. Just because she could. She might be alone, a spinster-to-be, but she could do it with class.

As she put down her glass of champagne and prepared to do her round of hugs and congratulations, there was only one thought uppermost in her mind.

No matter what happened now, she was going to be okay. Better to have loved and . . . well, not exactly lost, but the same general idea . . . than never to have loved at all.

"Jane!" Holly's mother was folding her in an enthusiastic hug, no doubt fueled by relief that Jane held nothing in her hands.

"Mrs. Devon." Jane hugged back. "It was a beautiful wedding."

"Oh, I'm so glad it's over," Holly's mom breathed without conviction. She squealed, "Hi" in a few different directions over Jane's shoulder, fluttering her fingers. Mrs. Devon was English and even when she squealed "Hi," it came out sounding formal. She turned her attention back to Jane. "I was terribly worried when Kevin stopped all of a sudden. I could only hope that nothing had gone wrong."

"Nothing went wrong," Jane assured the woman. "It was just a really *long* aisle."

"Yes. Well. We were so lucky to get this church." Another high-pitched "Hi!" over Jane's shoulder.

"I'm just going to find Lolly and Molly and see if there's anything we can do to help," Jane said. It was the first excuse she could think of to leave Mrs. Devon in her element.

"Oh, that would be lovely." Then, as Jane began to turn away, Holly's mother grabbed her arm. "Wait. Could you do me a favor, dear?"

"Of course." Knowing Holly's family, a favor could range from putting an apron over the bridesmaid dress and pitching in to serve appetizers to taking over for the lead singer in the band. No musical ability required, only proximity to Mrs. Devon when she thought of the idea. Jane braced herself.

"My nephew is here. It's wonderful, really. He came over from England to represent the family. He doesn't know anyone but us and we all have so much to do. Could I introduce you, dear? Would you make sure he gets something to eat and has someone to talk to?"

Great. Man-sitting. She'd have to hope some traits didn't run in the family.

Something to the side of Jane caught Mrs. Devon's attention. "Oh, look, it's the Carltons," she said in delight. "Hello!" Behind her hand, she whispered to Jane, "My husband's boss. His wife's a stuffy old bag. But I must go over there." Then she grabbed Jane's hand. "Andrew's a bit quiet, but you won't have any trouble with that, will you, Jane?"

Quiet could be a welcome relief after the British freight train that was Holly's mother. Besides, Jane was still in the do-anything-to-make-up-for-the-dress mode.

"Andrew!"

A tall man with thick dark hair stood by the window. When he turned at the sound of his name, Jane caught her breath. His eyes. Those dark pools of mystery, confidence, vulnerability . . . that could melt her insides on sight. And did.

Curran's eyes.

Her knees buckled beneath her and she had to stumble to keep from falling.

Andrew reached out to steady her. Mrs. Devon, her eyes on another part of the room, didn't notice. "Jane, this is my nephew, Andrew. Andrew, this is Holly's friend Jane. They've known each other since they were children. I thought you might enjoy . . . Beth! Beth Carlton. How lovely you could come." And she was gone.

Jane was barely aware of the woman leaving since her stomach was performing somersaults so energetic she had to press her arm into her middle. How had this man, who looked so much like Curran, suddenly dropped into her life? "What did you say your name is?" she managed.

"Andrew." He put out a hand. "And you are Jane, childhood friend of the bride."

She watched her hand reach toward his as though it were detached from the rest of her. But when his skin met hers, there was nothing detached about it. His hand was strong and warm and his clasp on hers caused a symphony of violins inside her to begin a frenzied riot. Omigod. She hadn't thought that would ever happen again.

"I am—am." She stammered. "Sorry, I just—You look very much like someone I know—knew."

"Ah." He nodded his head. "I presume you must have

liked this person since you have not run screaming from me?"

"Very much." Her answer gushed out with heartfelt honesty.

He didn't seem to mind. "Then I am the fortunate one." With a grin, he released her hand, leaving her feeling suddenly bereft.

Time to regain her ability to function. If only he wouldn't look at her like that, with those eyes that turned her all squishy and unable to think. He even had a nose like Curran. A jawline . . . And his hair . . . "Have you ever read a book called *Afton House*?" she blurted.

He started, obviously taken aback. "How very odd that you should mention that book. I wasn't aware anyone in the States had ever heard of it."

So it had been completed. Written. He *knew* the book. "By Mary Bellingham?" She had to be sure they were talking about the same one. The book that had changed her life.

"Yes. Mary Bellingham." He nodded. "It was the only book, I believe, that she ever wrote."

"How do you—?" Jane straightened her traitorous knees, willing them to do their job and keep her upright. She put her hands on her hips, trying her level best to appear casual when she was anything but. "How do you know the book?"

He smiled, glancing away and then back at her. The effect of the smile buckled her knees so that she had to grab on to his arm or sprawl on the ground in her sheath dress.

"Are you all right, Jane?"

"Yes." *Nooooo.* "Just, you know, lost my balance for a minute." But she didn't let go.

He laid a hand over hers, helping her hold on and graciously ignoring the fact that she seemed unable to make her limbs work. "*Afton House.* It's been a book of some discussion in my family, for generations."

"Why?"

He lifted one eyebrow, which caused an utterly adorable wrinkle in his forehead. Goose bumps ran up and down Jane's arms.

"It is said that a character in the book was based on an ancestor of mine."

"It was!" Another reaction without thinking.

Andrew laughed, showing white, perfectly even teeth. "And you know this? Do you know my family?"

"Maybe." The one word was soft, barely audible.

He heard it. "Then you know that this ancestor was, in fact, the villain of the story."

"But he wasn't one. Not really."

"Really? I quite enjoyed the idea that he was. And it has been the stuff of family legend for some time, now. I would hate to think it not true." He motioned toward a waiter's passing tray of champagne. "May I offer you a glass?"

"Yes. *Please.*" God, yes.

His voice lowered. "I actually have long suspected he was not quite as villainous as made out to be in the book because he ended up giving a great deal of his family money to charity when he passed away. He never married, though, which might indicate something." He handed her the glass of champagne and took one himself.

Jane took a gulp. Then another. "He never married?"

Andrew shook his head. "Some sort of heartbreak early on. Lived to a grand old age, though. Curran, his name was. Curran Dempster."

"Dempster." Mary hadn't even tried hard to mask the name. Good thing there weren't libel suits in those days. This time, Jane's knees gave up entirely. She sank toward the floor, the glass of champagne going with her.

Andrew caught her before her bottom hit, holding

her up with strong arms and helping her to a chair in the corner. Taking the glass of champagne and setting it on the floor, he squatted down before her, balancing on the balls of his feet. "Jane, are you ill?"

Someone else had asked her that. Years and years and only days ago.

"I'm going to be fine," she answered truthfully. "Just fine." Taking his hand, she managed to stand up. "I think I need to get some air."

"It would be my pleasure to accompany you." His smile said he meant it.

Once they'd left the noise of the reception behind, they strolled the hotel's deck, finding a place to stand and look at the water. "Tell me about where you're from?" Jane asked.

He began to talk, telling her about the rolling hills of the countryside where he lived, the family connection with Mrs. Devon and what it was like to grow up in England. After a time that seemed way too short, he said, "Your turn. I want to hear about you."

She talked slowly at first, but then more easily, telling him about her own life and about knowing Holly. She even found herself telling him about the red wine and the wedding dress. Funny thing was, it didn't hurt quite so much in the retelling this time. In fact, once he laughed, she did, too. And then it turned into a bigger laugh.

It felt good, the sun in her face, the water sparkling before her eyes and Andrew Dempster's gently rumbling voice beside her.

And best of all, being able to laugh about Holly's dress.

"Are you going to tell me about this person I resemble?" he asked.

She looked into his dark eyes. Familiar, but different. "Someday. Maybe."

Epilogue

Two years later

The hills of the Dempster estate were indeed rolling and Jane loved strolling through them. She'd adapted pretty fast to life in England and had never felt the need to tell Andrew why it felt much like coming home.

There was a lot she didn't have to tell him. A lot that he seemed to just know somehow. Including the odd co-incidence of her name and the name of the heroine in *Afton House*. That character, though, Jane had pointed out, didn't look anything like her.

After a thorough search of bookstores, he'd located a rare copy of the book and presented it to her on their first wedding anniversary. Nostalgia had hit her in waves when she'd touched the cover, opened the fragile pages and read the words. She'd gently run her fingers along the paper, over Curran's name. And her own.

And then she'd closed the book. And that chapter in her life.

To start a new one.

GREAT BOOKS,
GREAT SAVINGS!

When You Visit Our Website:
www.kensingtonbooks.com

You Can Save Money Off The Retail Price
Of Any Book You Purchase!

- All Your Favorite Kensington Authors
- New Releases & Timeless Classics
- Overnight Shipping Available
- eBooks Available For Many Titles
- All Major Credit Cards Accepted

Visit Us Today To Start Saving!
www.kensingtonbooks.com

All Orders Are Subject To Availability.
Shipping and Handling Charges Apply.
Offers and Prices Subject To Change Without Notice.

Discover the Romances of
Hannah Howell

My Valiant Knight	0-8217-5186-7	**$5.50**US/**$7.00**CAN
Only for You	0-8217-5943-4	**$5.99**US/**$7.50**CAN
A Taste of Fire	0-8217-7133-7	**$5.99**US/**$7.50**CAN
A Stockingful of Joy	0-8217-6754-2	**$5.99**US/**$7.50**CAN
Highland Destiny	0-8217-5921-3	**$5.99**US/**$7.50**CAN
Highland Honor	0-8217-6095-5	**$5.99**US/**$7.50**CAN
Highland Promise	0-8217-6254-0	**$5.99**US/**$7.50**CAN
Highland Vow	0-8217-6614-7	**$5.99**US/**$7.50**CAN
Highland Knight	0-8217-6817-4	**$5.99**US/**$7.50**CAN
Highland Hearts	0-8217-6925-1	**$5.99**US/**$7.50**CAN
Highland Bride	0-8217-7397-6	**$6.50**US/**$8.99**CAN
Highland Angel	0-8217-7426-3	**$6.50**US/**$8.99**CAN
Highland Groom	0-8217-7427-1	**$6.50**US/**$8.99**CAN
Highland Warrior	0-8217-7428-X	**$6.50**US/**$8.99**CAN
Reckless	0-8217-6917-0	**$6.50**US/**$8.99**CAN

Available Wherever Books Are Sold!

Visit our website at **www.kensingtonbooks.com**